MW00906473

Dex

Sheri Lynn Fishbach

A middle school kid
with a lot on his plate.

ISBN: 978-1-943978-04-5

Printed in China

CPSIA Tracking Label Information:
Production Location: Guangdong, China
Production Date: 4/15/2016
Cohort: Batch 1

Library of Congress Cataloging-in-Publication Data available.

10 9 8 7 6 5 4 3 2 1

Cover designed by Arlen Schumer

Published by

Persnickety Press
120A North Salem Street
Apex, NC 27502

www.Persnickety-Press.com

This book is dedicated with love, gratitude, and thanks to:

Beverly Swerling, my mentor extraordinaire

Reese Schonfeld and Erica Shusas Racine for their guidance and encouragement

My son, Adam, for his boundless support and genius

My daughters, Brittany, Alana, and Hayli for believing in me

My Cindy, Ron, Casey, and Courtney Cortazzo for hanging in through thick and thin

My Wendi, Eli, Jacob, and Tye for listening, caring, and keeping it real

My mom, Gloria Fishbach, for being all things amazing

My Uncle Jack for lovingly stepping into several shoes

Arlen Schumer for his brilliant cover design and keen vision

Ellen Hornstein for her generous help and wisdom

Erika Callahan for her input and expert advice

Brian Sockin for his kindness, insight, and loyalty

All my incredibly wonderful family and friends for always being there

And my life-honey, Brad Langer, for just about everything

With special thanks to Daddy, Dad, Jeff, Lenny-mom, Cheryl,

and all my other shining stars in the sky-

Hope I'm doing you proud as you watch from above...

C.L.F.

Chapter 1

Dex woke up with his forehead covered in sweat and his legs kicking an imprint into his mattress. He looked over at the floor, where his navy blue sheets and comforter had landed. What kind of dream was that? Sarah. It was always about Sarah. This time he was edging toward a raging volcano filled with tomato sauce trying to save her as the sun began to cook the grass around him into a frenzied web of pasta al dente. As he tried to run, strands tangled themselves around him from head to toe and squeezed his bony arms and legs. Trapped, he struggled to free himself. Was it hopeless?

Dex pushed himself out of bed to make the feeling go away. He walked over to his TV, still on, where Julia Child was now wielding a mini-blowtorch over her Baked Alaska. Great. There was no escape. Even Julia was failing him. He shook thinking about how close he had come to falling into the bubbling volcano.

But it was just a dumb dream. Something had to distract him. He watched as Julia happily took her dessert out of the oven. How many times had he seen this episode of *The French Chef*? Thirty, forty, two hundred times? It was all because he was a poor sleeper, a condition he inherited from Poppy, his grandfather. After he spent most of kindergarten awake all night, Poppy recommended a healthy dose of old cooking show reruns on his favorite channel, the Eatz Network, to lull him to sleep. So even if it meant dreaming of balsamic glazes and dressing chickens, at least he occasionally woke up knowing how to poach eggs or wrap a cake in fondant.

It certainly made his cooking class easier and more about fun than about work. And then he remembered. Mrs. Baker, his *International Cooking* teacher was in his dream too. She was holding a giant fork in her hand, raking the meadow clean as huge parmesan cheese flakes fell from the sky. He had called out asking her where Sarah was.

"Over there," his teacher had said, pointing the fork toward an enormous food processor, "she's making a lovely marinara sauce with that hot, muscle-y guy on the wrestling team."

Stupid Hunter Clark was unfair competition. He was probably born with humongous biceps. Sarah had to know that most guys weren't super-human like that, even when she was hanging onto the lip of the tomato sauce volcano ready to become a sacrificial meatball. Even when she was calling for help and Dex couldn't break free from the twisted spaghetti. Even though Hunter had swooped her up into his arms. No, she didn't know guys weren't like that. Even in the dream, Sarah could count on Hunter.

Dex took a deep breath and ran over to his laptop. He brought up Facebook to check if Sarah had responded to his friend request. It had been almost a week since he sent it and every day of silence brought the same torture. Why didn't she want to be friends with him? She didn't know about his dream. Did he have gopher breath? Ear wax hangies? Or was it even worse--was he invisible to her?

Never mind. So what if Sarah didn't friend him back? He still had a business to run, after all. It was almost dawn already and he still had lettuce to wash, tomatoes to slice, and chutneys waiting to be blended. Eventually she'd have to notice him. Especially once he could finally afford the *Gymbuff.*

Dex glanced at the poster pinned to his closet door. A shirtless, muscular guy on a beach was lifting a barbell that looked as big as a mini refrigerator. One day, Dex promised himself, he would look like *that* guy. All it would take was time and money. A different dream to think about. He was working on it.

Dex went to his jellybean dispenser, a decade-long fixture on his desk, and he gave the crank a full twist with his double-jointed wrist. Like his Poppy, he could twist his hand almost entirely around. He reached down and picked out a handful of jelly beans. They were all green. Maybe lime, maybe sour apple, or pear, or watermelon. The thing was, every day could bring a new flavor. It was up to him to make the best of it. When Dex was little, Poppy would say, “When life hands you lemons, whip up a meringue!” Dex had learned all the flavor combinations of jellybeans possible by the fourth grade. Even his math teacher was impressed when he handed her four beans-- a vanilla, a toasted marshmallow, a cream soda, and a buttered-popcorn-- and she agreed that it really did taste like a Rice Krispie treat.

Dex popped the dark speckled one into his mouth. Pear, *blecchh*. He should have remembered. He sloshed his tongue around his mouth a few times to get the taste out, then crossed the room to flip on his light. He gave the picture of Poppy and Geema hanging on the wall a good morning tap. The picture was taken long before Dex was born, when they first opened Poppy’s Kitchen. Poppy always told him they had a line around the block that first day: half were there for matzo ball soup, the other half for minestrone. By the time dinner came around, he and Geema were so tired of working on opposite sides of the kitchen they threw both soups together. The best food always happened that way. Poppy’s Matzo Ball Minestrone became a local legend.

For the first time since he started his ‘Dex the Food Dude’ lunch stand at the beginning of the summer, Dex wondered about the future. Not the near future, like what cookie would go best with his artichoke tuna salad, but the distant future. Like, would he be the one in the picture someday, standing in front of his family's restaurant smiling? He took one more look at the photo and shook off his daydream, then headed to the shelf in his closet. He reached up and grabbed his profits. They were in his grandfather's ginormous tomato cans. When Dex was a little boy, Poppy had given them to him to use as a bank.

"Oh man," he exclaimed, shaking his head after counting the last dime. Some days his daily ritual of taking out the cans and counting his stash was enough to give him a small heart attack. Today was one of those days. He'd had to buy stuff to replenish his stock and now it looked like he'd never earn the six thousand dollars he needed to pay for the *Gymbuff.* Plus tax.

He tried to calm down. It would be okay. Geema always told him, "Dex, Rome wasn't built in a day. There's a lot to conquer before you can have an empire." He'd go with that. The good news was he was still managing to stay ahead and, unlike the kid in gym class who worked as his neighborhood's pooper-scooper to make money, he liked what he was doing. He looked at the totals he had jotted down in a small notebook. It wasn't that terrible. In a century he could probably afford to buy his own fitness club.

Before he got dressed he gave himself a critical once over in the full-length mirror behind the bathroom door. He wasn't sure what he liked the least, his long, lanky frame or the enormous zit that was battling his chin to take over his face. Didn't he have enough to deal with? Maybe he could get rid of it. He sprinkled some water on his face and caught the floating island between his two pointer fingers.

"Yuch," he cried as the zit popped its gooey grossness onto his clean mirror. "Great, now it looks like I'm wearing a candy apple on my chin."

There was no time left to feel bad for his sorry face. He slapped on a square of toilet paper to cover the still-oozing monstrosity, put on his clothes, and marched into the kitchen to make the day's lunches.

Looking at all the ingredients he had lined up for today's menu made Dex feel better. There was just no way to look at a ripe, red tomato without smiling. It was an example of nature's perfection and he knew how to show it the respect it deserved. He looked at the clock and grimaced, realizing he was running behind schedule.

"Dex?" asked a half-mumbled voice that sounded like it still belonged in bed. "Is that you?" the voice continued.

"Yes, Mom, it's me," Dex replied while chopping a cucumber into fine slices. "What are you doing up so early?"

Marla shook her head to imply she didn't have an answer and poured herself a cup of auto-brewed coffee. Dex thought she looked a little more tired than usual. She was only in her forties, but time wasn't being kind. Her hair was a mousy shade of blonde that flatly framed her roundish face, and since she had to give up the gym when his dad lost his business, her waist had gotten too thick for her jeans. It was weird, since in old family pictures she seemed like someone who would never look like a grown up. Dex wondered if she cared. Probably not. He took a tray of piping hot cookies out of the oven and Marla snatched one.

She sat down at the kitchen table, careful not to get in his way. There was a very big wheelbarrow in the middle of the kitchen, but Dex was used to working around it. He had no choice. It was his portable restaurant. The wheelbarrow didn't slow him down a bit. Marla was as unfazed by the wheelbarrow as was her son.

"A lot of orders today," Marla said, looking around the kitchen. "Is something special going on?" She didn't seem particularly interested. Most of her attention was being given to carefully rolling off her beauty gloves.

"Not really. I think people are telling people, that's all."

"That's the way any good business starts." Marla took a bite of her cookie. "It's word of mouth," she said as she took another bite, "And in a word-- outstanding!"

Dex looked at his mother appreciatively. Growing up in a restaurant had made her a tough critic. If something didn't taste right she wasn't shy about making her opinion known and whether he liked it or not, she was usually right. He took both jalapeno raisin cookies and wasabi tuna parmesan subs off his debut menu when she said they tasted like hot, smelly feet. Some combinations, he was learning, sounded better in theory than in practice.

Pickles. He needed pickles. Bottom cabinet. Nice. He couldn't open the jar no matter how hard he tried. Marla got up like she was on auto-pilot, grabbed the jar from him, and opened it effortlessly. Great. His mother was practically sleep-walking and she was still stronger than he was.

She must have noticed his dejection and quickly added, "You loosened it. Made it easy."

Another look at the clock told him he had less than an hour to get another round of sandwiches and two dozen cookies made.

"Dex honey, do you know where the cream is?" Marla asked through a sip of coffee.

Dex quickly opened the cabinet, pulled out the coffee creamer, and set it beside his mother's cup.

"No, no, sorry," Marla apologized. "I meant *my* cream."

"Ohh!" Dex opened a cabinet next to the spice rack and pulled out one of the many hand creams and lotions standing on the shelf.

"Thanks," she said, slathering on some minty goop. "Guess what--I have a commercial today! And Alicia is coming home! That's why I'm up. I have an early appointment at Minelli's to get my hair done." Marla got up and put her coffee mug in the dishwasher.

Dex looked confused. "Mom, I think you're going to look great, but your hands are the only thing they ever film."

"I know honey, but I still want to try to look good. Especially with Leeshie coming home. Maybe you haven't noticed, but I've been a little down since your dad lost the business," she said, picking up a rose-colored cream and rubbing it on her hands.

Dex wasn't about to tell her that he had noticed and was thrilled she was anxious to make changes, so he continued to build his sandwiches and let her talk.

"And when I'm down," she continued, "I eat too many carbs and don't pay enough attention to how I look."

Dex was silent for an uncomfortable moment, but when he felt his mother struggle to offer a better explanation he took her off the hook. "Mom, yesterday is history. Make today a reason to be happy."

Marla nodded, letting a couple of small tears pool in her eyes. "How'd you get so smart?" she asked, putting her gloves back on.

He had seen the quote on Facebook, but she didn't need to know that. "I have good teachers," he said, whipping together a coconut icing.

Marla gave him a tight, handless hug. As she turned to leave, she stopped and added, "Dex honey, please take the garbage out before you go. I don't want Geema to end up doing it." She started walking and stopped to turn to him again.

"And Dex..."

"Yeah, Mom?"

"Thanks," she said, softly waving goodbye with both gloved hands.

Dex scanned the kitchen, happy that he didn't have much of a mess to clean. After a late start, this morning had gone faster than he'd anticipated. He took out the last batch of cookies from the oven and set them on the cooling tray. They smelled more than good. He took out a black Sharpie and a piece of computer paper, then wrote:

New Item: *Caramel Sea Salt Crunch*

Then he taped the sign to an empty, lined fruit basket his family had once gotten for the holidays. It was just the right size for a few dozen cookies and fit comfortably in the giant wheelbarrow.

While the cookies were cooling, Dex tried to lift the two full garbage bags his mother had asked him to take out to the curb. What were they throwing out, boulders? As much as he tried, there was no way he could carry both bags at once. "*Gymbuff*'" he said in an audible whisper.

Cookies cooled, Dex began to set up for the morning rush. He had started his business during the summer when he realized that the only way he could make money was to figure out something he could do on his own. Babysitting meant dirty diapers and he didn't want to deal with those. Tutoring would mean more studying and that was a big "NO WAY." Mowing lawns was impossible with his grass allergies, and dog-walking was only okay if the dogs didn't weigh more than he did, which was usually not the case. It didn't take him long to figure out that the only thing he was really good at, that he really loved, was cooking.

Unlike the lemonade stand he had when he was seven, this time he needed legal approval to sell food. Luckily, one of his father's best former clients worked for the town and knew how to make Dex's business legit. It also didn't hurt that the guy couldn't go more than a day without another fix of Dex's fig and brie spread on a raisin bagel. Now, only a couple of months later, Dex had a legal business and a growing list of regular customers.

Maybe it was destiny. His mother told him that when he was born, his grandfather swore he had the hands of a master chef.

"Look at those fingers Marla," Poppy had said, "they were meant to roll meatballs and knead dough."

Then, according to his mother, Poppy held Dex very close, kissed each of his tiny fingers, and promised to teach him everything he could about food, family, and life. From as far back as his memory could reach, Dex remembered being in the kitchen with his grandfather. Poppy was the best teacher he ever had.

How many kids could say they learned how to crack and whisk eggs before they could speak in complete sentences?

Whether they were home or at the restaurant, it didn't matter, there was always something his grandfather wanted him to smell or taste. Usually he made a game of it; especially if it was something important. Like when he was five and Poppy taught him about herbs and spices by playing the blindfold game. Dex remembered hating the smell of mace, but loving the warm scent of cinnamon. His grandfather cautioned him, "Like using a certain color to paint a beautiful picture, Dex, there is always a special place for any ingredient to shine."

Why was he daydreaming so much today? Dex looked at the wheelbarrow and realized he was missing his change box. He went back to the house smiling as he heard the familiar sounds of everyone getting ready to start the day. Routines made him feel comfortable, like life wasn't just one big 'what's next.' He got the change box and went outside to greet his customers.

A pretty African-American woman in her fifties pulled up in a big school bus and parked in front of the yard. She clopped down the bus steps and onto the lawn.

"Hey Rhonda. What'll it be today?" Dex asked politely, already knowing what she wanted.

"Hey sweetpea, how you doin' this fine morning?"

"I'm good," he said, already getting her order together.

"Good is good," she said, taking seven dollars out of a small change purse. "Now let me see, can I get that pistachio-crusted tilapia burger you made me yesterday? Mmm, that tasted even better than my Aunt Elodia's catfish cakes, and they won a blue ribbon at the Smyrna County Fair!"

"Thanks Rhonda, I'm glad you liked it. Here you go," Dex said, handing her the sandwich, "With a little extra mayo, the way you like it. And, don't forget your cookie."

"Oh I won't," she said, perusing the choices and settling on an oatmeal toffee crunch bar. "You are one smart businessman, Dex," she said, trying to stuff everything into her too-small lunchbox. "I told all my friends about you."

"This is a new recipe," he said, handing her a salted caramel cookie. "Try it and tell me what you think. It's on the house."

She thanked him, took the wrapped cookie and looked for a place to put it. There was no room left in her lunchbox or her pockets.

"Guess this is gonna be breakfast. Lucky me," she said unwrapping it, as she walked away.

By the time she got to the bus, the cookie was gone and she turned to give a "thumb up" to Dex.

Dex liked Rhonda. She smiled like she meant it, which wasn't the case with a lot of adults. She had been his first customer. His house was on her route, and she had seen the signs he had put up around town announcing his grand opening. From that time on she never missed a day. She always seemed so appreciative. And even better, she didn't treat him like he was some kid who didn't know what he was doing. Dex found himself making new things for her to try.

Poppy taught him to find inspiration in everything, "especially the last place you'd think to look," he would say pointing his finger in the air like it could be anywhere. So, while some kids could recite the numbers and batting averages of their favorite baseball players, Dex could rattle off the menu items at each stadium food stand. As a tribute to his favorite team, he even created a dish he called Yankee Pot Pie, with hotdogs and baked beans in a hash brown crust topped with onion rings. Poppy loved it so much that during the World Series, he put it on the menu at the restaurant. A few weeks later, Poppy had his heart attack and passed away. The dish became a sad memory, and Dex could never bring himself to make it again.

It made sense to be thinking about Poppy. It was almost two years now and Dex still couldn't believe he was gone. This would've made him happy, Dex thought as he bent down to adjust his *DEX THE FOOD DUDE* sign. He was securing the sign's base in the ground when his friend and assistant, Kyle, surprised him with a tap on the shoulder that nearly knocked him over.

"Sorry, I didn't mean to scare yoooooooou," Kyle said, letting out a huge burp.

Kyle didn't bother to excuse himself. His burping was a condition he'd had since he was a toddler and anyone who knew him for more than ten minutes had no choice but to get used to it.

"Is everything okay?" he asked, laying a few wrapped sandwiches out for display.

"Everything's fine. I was just thinking about stuff."

"Dex, man, you have to stop thinking and start doing," Kyle insisted. "It's almost 7:30 and you're not ready yet!" The line would often form in seconds and Kyle wanted to be prepared.

"I'm not?" Dex asked confidently.

“Where are the apples?” Kyle asked, now arranging the cookies in a neat pattern.

Dex was ready to yell at Kyle. Who did he think he was, his mother? But then he looked down at the wheelbarrow and sure enough he had forgotten the fruit. Rhonda was allergic to most fruit so he hadn’t noticed his mistake. Great, Kyle could run his business better than he could. He was annoyed at his absent-mindedness. How could he have forgotten something that basic?

“Oh man, I left them on the kitchen table. Can you get them? Ron and the construction guys should be here any minute and their order is always complicated.”

“No proooooob,” Kyle burped and headed to the house.

As if on cue, a construction truck pulled up in front of the stand, followed by a taxi, a minivan, and a motorcycle. The drivers of each filed out and onto the lawn in a small line. A short article in a local paper introducing Dex brought in an influx of people from the community to “watch the little Food Dude serve up some of the most innovative cuisine under the sun.” That article gave Dex the publicity he needed to attract attention.

Kyle came out with the apples just in time to help. In moments, there was a small crowd of regulars in a long line on Dex’s front lawn. In front was Ron, the builder putting up the condos near Poppy’s Kitchen, who usually brought at least two hungry guys from his crew with him. Next was the cab driver, Kaleel, who promised to buy Dex a *kadai* (Indian wok) for Christmas. Then there was a newer regular, Wilma, a caregiver at the senior center who rode a Harley and bought a dozen cookies a week to bring back for her clients. And from the Odyssey minivan was Herb, Rhonda’s friend, a semi-retired radiologist who loved sweet pickles and babysat for his grandchildren twice a week.

Seconds after everyone left, Dex could see his own school bus coming. He ran into the house to put the money in the emptiest soup can and got lucky that the bus had to stop for a light before turning onto his block. Kyle gave him a high five but all Dex could think about was how close he had cut it. He hoped the stress hadn't made his massive pimple any angrier than it had been a couple of short hours ago.

Chapter 2

Just before the bus came to a full stop, Dex quickly handed Kyle a sandwich.

"Hurry. Put it in your book bag," he said. "It was the only one left."

Kyle gave the offering a quick look. "Turkey Stuffing Surprise?"

Dex nodded. He knew this sandwich, filled with sliced turkey, whole cranberry sauce, homemade crouton stuffing, topped with crushed sweet potato chips, was Kyle's favorite.

"This too," he said, handing him a wrapped cookie.

"Yes!" Kyle exclaimed. "Thanks!"

The bus screeched to a halt. Dex got on the bus first and sat in an empty seat toward the middle. Kyle followed and sat down next to him. Without any warning Kyle let out a long burp. A few kids giggled but neither Dex nor Kyle acknowledged them.

"We were so busy I didn't even get to ask you how your doctor's appointment went," Dex said, a little guilty.

"It was lame. He thinks it's emotional," said Kyle, staring out the window opposite his seat. "He said there's nothing wrong with meeeeeh," Kyle said, burping even more forcefully.

A girl in the back shouted, "Ugh, Kyle!?! You ate a granola bar for breakfast again, didn't you?"

Both boys ignored her.

"Emotional?" Dex shook his head. "You're not crying, you're burping."

“I know,” Kyle nodded. “It sucks.”

Kyle let out a small burp and changed the subject.

“Did Sarah friend you back yet?”

Dex winced, remembering what a helpless weakling he’d been in his dream.

“Nah, not yet,” he answered indifferently.

Dex looked out the window and saw his nemesis, Hunter, and another muscular kid riding on Speed Fit exercise scooters. Having one of those definitely raised your coolness level. They were like treadmills on wheels so that the faster you’d run, the faster they would go. Only the rich jocks had them, and seeing Hunter whiz by made Dex even more determined to get the money he needed for the *Gymbuff.*

“Girls are impossible,” Kyle offered. “Tracey Waters hasn’t friended me back yet either and it’s been *days*. I think you have a better chance with Sarah.”

Make him stop, Dex thought. The only thing worse than talking about Kyle’s burping problems was talking about how much of a loser Dex was for not getting anywhere with Sarah.

The bus stopped and in walked Liza, a light-skinned African-American girl Dex referred to as the “coolest person he’d ever be friends with.” They met in a baby gym class when they were four months old, and grew up together. Their parents were friends too, which was important since Liza’s home life wasn’t typical in their town.

Not everyone in their area was as *liberal* as Dex’s family, but Dex’s mom Marla said her parents taught her to *make sauce not war,* and that intolerance caused more pollution than the toxic waste destroying the ozone layer. It was a message that made a lasting impression on her and resulted in her having more friends from different cultures than most people. By the time Dex was born she had gone to weddings and baby-namings in India, China, Uruguay, Israel, Scotland, and Vietnam.

Like his family, Dex didn't focus on differences. He didn't care that Liza's situation was considered unique. She had a great family and it bothered him that there were times she had to defend that. Big deal. She had two dads. Two gay dads. One was her biological father, but it was anyone's guess which one because looking at them you could never tell. Her birth mother was a friend of her dads, but she lived in Kenya and rarely visited. Liza didn't talk about her much and didn't seem to miss having her around.

Liza's dads owned *Minelli's,* the salon Marla swore made ordinary women look like divas. Dex used to love going there when he was little. He and Liza would play rocket ship on the swivel chairs until they were ready to puke. Now the only time he felt ready to puke was when he thought about Sarah. He was officially weird.

Speaking of weird, who was that guy standing next to Liza? A pale, white kid dressed in big baggy jeans and a du-rag covering a mop of corn rows had followed her onto the bus.

"Hey Dex. Hey Kyle. This is my cousin, Jordan," she said hesitantly. "He just moved here."

"I told you, it's Jordy, shorty," he said in an accent Dex couldn't place.

"Right," Liza agreed, clearly avoiding an argument.

"Look Kyle, I got you these."

She reached into her backpack and pulled out an economy sized bottle of *Tums.* A few kids turned to look at her and applauded.

"Hold up, this must be the dude wit da mad frog fog." Jordy laughed. "Uhhhhhhh!" He imitated a burp.

Liza smacked him. "Shut up! Jor-DAN! He's my friend."

Kyle thanked Liza as if she'd given him Super Bowl tickets and took the bottle. Jordy seemed annoyed and started walking toward the back of the bus. Before he got to a seat, his huge pants suddenly fell down around his ankles, revealing giant black boxers that resembled a *Hefty* bag more than underwear. One girl's eyes bugged out of her head and she stared at him with her mouth wide open.

"Wut!" he said, pulling up his jeans like nothing had happened. He went to the back of the bus and sat down in a seat away from everyone.

"What's with him?" Dex asked Liza, pointing his chin toward Jordy.

Liza pursed her lips. "He's going to take a lot of getting used to. His mom, my aunt, got a new job and that boy did not want to leave Florida."

"I've been to Disney World and nobody talked like that," said Kyle.

"Yeah, really," Dex added, "he just sounds weird."

"What can I tell you. He's my cousin and he and my aunt are living in my house 'til they find their own place. I think he acts all ghetto to be like his dad. He misses him. Jordy's actually fun when you get to know him."

"What happened to his dad?" Kyle asked.

"He left to become a rapper. Went to L.A. a few years ago and that was that. Never heard from him again.

"Wow, his dad is black? Jordy looks whiter than me," said Kyle, puzzled.

"Who said he's black?" Liza said.

"A white rapper?" Kyle asked, "Like Eminem?"

Liza laughed, "He wishes! He sounds more like an old Justin Bieber. That man's never going to be famous."

Liza turned to look at Jordy who was listening to his iPod with his eyes closed.

"I feel bad for Jordy," Liza said, turning back around. "He's going to need friends who can deal with him," she hesitated, then added, "I was hoping you guys would, you know, be nice to him—please."

"Liza, of course we'll be friends with him," Dex said, without a moment's thought. "He's your cousin."

Kyle nodded then suddenly banged his open palm to his head. He whisked out a piece of paper from his book bag.

"Crap. I forgot. I have a quiz in math. I gotta study."

He turned away from the conversation to review his notes.

"Oh, before I forget, tonight's our last dinner at Poppy's

Kitchen for a while. Geema says we're closing to renovate," Dex explained.

"That's cool," said Liza. "Maybe now you could get a gelato machine. Gelato's mad good."

"Yeah," Dex agreed. "Do you guys want to come for dessert?"

Kyle nodded without turning back.

"Doesn't your sister get back today?" Liza asked.

"Yeah."

"So what are you making?" Liza looked back to see Jordy still in the same position.

"Alicia's favorite. Triple Chocolate Ganache cake with Oreo Buttercream frosting."

Kyle, still engrossed in his notes, let out an approving sigh. Dex noticed that Liza looked uncomfortable.

"And, of course, your cousin is invited," he offered.

"Thanks Dex," Liza said relieved.

"Oh man. I forgot to tell Geema where to find the welcome back sign."

He pulled out his phone and started a text.

#

Golda Marino gave her short, reddish hair a little lift from the back as she sat uncomfortably in the seat opposite Nan May, her bank representative. Nan was in her fifties, round-figured, platinum blonde, wore heavy eye shadow, and looked chronically confused. Especially now, as she stared at her computer trying to locate Golda's restaurant accounts. Golda felt tense from the start of their meeting and Nan's persistent blinking tic was both annoying and hypnotizing. Blink, blink, blink. Golda, a petite woman, thought if she stared at Nan any longer she would get seasick from the fluttering blue waves of her eyelids.

Why do women paint themselves like that, Golda pondered, as she questioned whether her own cheeks could use more blush. But then she thought about why she was there and decided that looking pale might best serve her purpose. Golda needed a financial miracle, not a trip to a cosmetic counter. Besides, she hadn't even looked at another man since she lost her beautiful Ralphie.

"I can't seem to locate that account," Nan said with a mesmerizing succession of blinks. "But I'm sure it's here somewhere."

"OH!" Golda jumped as if she'd been poked by a cattle prod. She dug deep into a handbag that looked bigger than her to find the source. Vince, her son-in-law, mentioned her cell phone would vibrate if she got a call or a message, but she wasn't expecting to get knocked off her chair.

"Ah," she said retrieving her still-buzzing, pink, sparkly phone, "I have a text message. Looks like it's from my grandson."

Nan smiled obligatorily and continued blinking into the computer. Golda interrupted her.

"Excuse me, but I'm having trouble reading this. Can you please do me a favor?" Golda handed her the phone.

"Oh sure," Nan said in her squeaky voice taking the phone. She plastered on a smile as if she were performing a monologue for an audience.

"The welcome back sign's in the desk drawer under the file for Mom's hand jobs?"

Nan raised her eyebrows, but Golda was too busy looking for an envelope to notice.

"Oh--okay. I know where they are," she said, finally seeing Nan's expression.

"My daughter's a hand model," Golda exclaimed.

"Uh-huh," said Nan, nodding.

"Really. Anyway, I also got this in the mail today. Sorry I forgot to give it to you before. I'm a little preoccupied. My granddaughter is coming home from an internship she had over the summer and we're having a little party at my restaurant to welcome her home."

Golda was definitely nervous. She rarely shared personal business with anyone, especially strangers. And few people were stranger than Nan May.

"I hope you can help me," she pleaded in almost a whisper.

Nan pasted on another smile. "Let's see what we have here."

As she read, her blinking was uncontrollable. Golda imagined Nan flying around the bank propelled by her lashes and decided this was a woman who must live alone. Finally, the pattern stopped when Nan looked back at the computer.

"Well Mrs. Marino, this is the account I was looking for and it appears that you have been unable to keep up with the payments for, uh, *Poopy's Kitchen*."

"It's *Poppy's Kitchen*, sweetheart. That's a typo."

"Oh, sorry," Nan said flatly. "So, are you here to satisfy the debt today?"

"Well I suppose that would depend on how much you'd be satisfied with," Golda chuckled.

Nan responded by laughing loudly and snorting multiple times.

"Of course," she resumed, "Let me jot down that amount for you."

Nan handed Golda a slip of paper.

"Here is the current balance.

Golda looked at the paper and sighed heavily.

"Oh dear," she said, "I don't think you're going to be satisfied at all."

Golda slumped back in her chair.

"You know," Golda defended, "my late husband was a wonderful man, but he didn't know much about managing a business. He managed a little league team, and we didn't even have a son. He managed most of our shopping, and all our family reunions. He even managed to drive me crazy for almost fifty years. But he could never seem to manage our money."

Nan moistened her lips and took a sip of coffee from a large white mug sporting a pair of open pink lips with a green dollar sign painted over them that read, 'Money Talks.'

"Ralph never wanted to worry me," Golda continued, "I didn't even know things had gotten so bad until he was gone and I started getting bills from all kinds of creditors." Golda wiped a stray tear from the corner of her eye.

"I am truly sorry for your difficulty, Mrs. Marino," Nan said, back to blinking. "But without payment, the bank will be forced to repossess the property. Perhaps you should consider selling."

"Sell? I can't do that to my family," Golda cried getting up to leave, "I told them I was closing to renovate."

"Well Mrs. Marino, I suppose our little meeting is over." Nan rose and gave her a weak handshake. "Should you require further assistance I'm here Monday through Friday, nine to five."

Golda left the bank so deep in thought she didn't even feel the morning drizzle sprinkling on her uncovered head. She looked up at the gray sky and sighed, "anything else you haven't mentioned dear husband?"

Chapter 3
Poppy's Kitchen: 1985

"Okay, this is the power switch and this red one must be to record. So many buttons." Poppy looks away from the video camera he has set so carefully on the shelf above the kitchen counter. He shrugs his strong shoulders and reties his sage green apron, the one he swears is his magical tool for making his secret pesto come to life. He shoots a quick look at the camera. Then he mutters, "Ugh, it's still too low."

Poppy looks around for a moment, spies a giant-sized tomato can on a nearby shelf and, groaning with effort, he hoists it and lumbers toward the camera, continuing to regard it with great suspicion.

"I hope this can help, but I don't want to see it too well or I'll get stage fright. *Mamma mia*, the things I do for the people I care about."

Poppy wedges the camera strategically between two cartons of pasta.

"Ah, this looks good. Like I would spend twenty dollars on a tripod when I have my tomato cans. Hah!"

After moving the camera into place, he shuffles along the white tiled kitchen floor to a counter brimming with ingredients.

He smiles and takes his oversized stirring spoon off its hook, taking care not to disturb his array of whisks, slotted spoons, spatulas, pizza slicers, giant forks, and pasta rollers. Each of these precious tools hangs on the wall in two neat rows, surrounded by a cherry wood frame. Poppy and his wife Golda put up the frame together earlier that year. It was an anniversary gift from their friends, Ruthie and Stuie, who knew Poppy treated his tools like treasured friends and thought they deserved a royal portrait. But right now, his pesto sauce was about to become king, the framed friends and ingredients its loyal subjects. Poppy runs his thick, stubby fingers through his salt and peppery hair and starts his proclamation:

"Alright, here goes. This is my going-away gift to you, because after all these years of pestering me, I'm finally giving in. This is Poppy's Pesto."

He puts a finger over his mouth and lowers his voice.

"Shhh. Remember...It's a secret."

He crosses over to the camera to see if it's working, then cheers with satisfaction when he sees all the right buttons are lit.

"To truly create food worth eating, you have to prepare it with passion," he says, holding a bunch of parsley to his nose and inhaling deeply.

"The sauce," he continues, "is like a person. To get the most from it you have to treat it with respect and love it with all your heart."

Poppy puts his fingers to his lips and gives them a kiss.

"If you don't, you'll end up with a bitter tasting mess and people politely telling you they had a big lunch and can't eat another thing. Believe me, if it's good, they'll find room."

"Let's begin," he says as he lightly salts a cutting board.

"First, fresh basil. Nothing wilted or slimy."

He raises his knife in the air like a scepter and chops the herb into a fine chiffonade in seconds.

"Pignoli nuts."

He grabs a big handful and sets them in a small frying pan on top of the range.

"Lightly toasted," he explains, "to bring out the richness of the flavor."

"Extra virgin olive oil," he continues and hugs the gallon-sized container like a baby.

"Canned bean liquid," Poppy says in a hush, almost afraid to disclose the importance of this key, untraditional ingredient. "I know, I know, sounds crazy, but, one day when I was low on oil and heavy on the lunch crowd, I had to think of something that could add creaminess without overpowering the delicate balance of flavor."

"It was when I was stirring the beans into my pot of minestrone soup that the idea hit me. I could hear the leftover, starchy liquid singing to me from the cans. Everyone raved and better still, no one has ever been able to figure out the method to my madness. The name of this pesto could be called accidental magic, but Poppy's Pesto has a better ring to it. You know, I'm going to write all this down while I do it, so there's no confusion later on!"

He goes into a small drawer and pulls out a pad and a pen.

As Poppy finishes writing down the last ingredient, the phone rings from outside the kitchen. He quickly tops the sauce with a final sprinkle of cannellini bean liquid, and then tastes it. His face lights up and he lets out a satisfied 'Humph!' He notices a drop of sauce on the recipe, gives it a quick wipe, then leaves to answer the still clamoring phone.

Chapter 4

"What time tonight?" Liza asked while getting off the bus.

"Um...," said Dex, preoccupied. Did his grandmother even get his text? "Like 7:30?" he said, unsure how the evening would go.

"Okay. Sounds good," Liza said, walking through the double doors of the school.

"Yeah, I wouldn't miss that cake for anything," Kyle said from behind her, and then added, "Well maybe not anything, but, you know, most things."

He waved goodbye with his math notes and disappeared into the sea of students rushing to class.

Liza and Dex continued to walk down the wide hall. The popular kids were hanging out by the vending machine next to the cafeteria and Dex still couldn't figure out what made spring water and *Skittles* so appealing.

"Should I bring anything?" Liza mumbled, applying a thick layer of coconut *Chap Stick*.

"Nah, I'm good," Dex assured, "Geema's picking me up after school and we're going shopping for everything I need."

Dex was grateful he had Liza in the same homeroom so they could walk there together in the morning. She made him feel less alone in the big, unfamiliar middle school building he was still trying to get used to. When school first started, Dex could tell some kids thought he and Liza were a couple. They would nod, smile, or 'high five' their approval at them. Liza thought it was funny and would occasionally put her arm around Dex just to promote the comments and gossip. She insisted it made them cooler if people were talking about them.

They had a good laugh for a couple of weeks, but decided to give it a rest when Kyle had asked them if they were going out and keeping it a secret from him. Even though he'd said he hadn't thought the rumors were true, he'd sounded relieved when they told him it had all been for show. "In middle school," Kyle had said, "you can't be too sure about anything unless you hear it straight from the source. And unfortunately, even that isn't always reliable."

What was reliable was the massive attack of butterflies that would invade Dex's stomach whenever he'd see Sarah. It was unavoidable and it was happening now. She was standing at her locker, brushing her long, dark hair into a ponytail. Dex let out a little nervous cough to take the edge off hoping Liza wouldn't pick up on anything. It was too embarrassing to have a thing for a girl who—Dex watched as Hunter came up behind Sarah and put his hands over her eyes--liked someone else.

#

It made sense that Dex's favorite class was *International Cooking*. It was an elective and the only other choice that would have fit into his schedule was ballroom dancing. Admittedly, he could have used some instruction in how to do more than rock and kick someone's ankles, but there was no way he'd allow himself to look that lame in public. No, he belonged exactly where he was, especially now, since Sarah had just walked into his class with a new schedule, having switched from another *International Cooking* class. She was directed to a seat a few away from his where he could stare at her striking profile as much as he wanted.

"We're going to continue our unit on International Breads," said Mrs. Baker, looking a little less attractive to Dex since praising Hunter in his dream. "Today we're ready to knock back our *halla* dough for the second kneading."

Dex saw Sarah cringe and raise her hand.

"Excuse me Mrs. Baker."

"Yes, Sarah?"

"It's *CH-allah,*" Sarah said, correcting her. "From the back of your throat."

"Oh, okay. Thank you for bringing that to our attention," answered Mrs. Baker with a scowl that Dex wasn't sure anyone else detected. "Anyway, that should get all the air out and make it easy to shape. If you work quickly, I think we may have time to get them in the oven by the end of the period.

Some of his classmates looked puzzled, but he was sure that was because Sarah was Chinese and they couldn't understand how she would know anything about the Jewish bread called *challah.*

Mrs. Baker demonstrated how to handle the dough and added that since the class was small they would work in assigned pairs. Dex began to pray Mrs. Baker would make him and Sarah partners. It would only be fair. After the dream, she did kind of owe him.

"Dex, why don't you work with Sarah," Mrs. Baker said as the butterflies in Dex's stomach mounted in a quivering frenzy.

Dex breathed deeply as he and Sarah walked over to their table. *Don't puke, don't puke,* became his silent prayer, because if he did, she would never have anything to do with him. He offered her a nervous smile and said he would be happy to get whatever they needed from the prep kitchen. She shrugged an 'okay' and took out a small mirror from her pocketbook.

Dex tried to look nimble and athletic as he juggled the oil they needed to grease the baking sheets, the eggs for the egg wash to glaze the *challah,* and the large baking trays to set the breads on. He thought of Rachael Ray, one of his favorite celebrity chefs who always challenged herself to get everything to her work area in one shot. She usually did and he was glad that this time he had too.

"So we have eggs, oil and baking sheets," Dex said, trying to impress her with how much he had been able to carry.

Sarah shrugged again and wiped something from under her shiny bottom lip. Unsure of what to say, Dex started making the dough while Sarah scanned the room offering mini waves of her hand to a few people she knew. He tried to figure out something to say that would get her attention, but he didn't have to.

"Sarah," Mrs. Baker said, nearing their table, "two people, two *challahs,*" she said, making an effort to pronounce the word as Sarah had suggested was correct. "Get to work."

Great, Dex thought, now Sarah was forced to acknowledge him and he still didn't have anything intelligent to say. He divided the ball of dough in half and placed a mound in front of her. She gave him a look that said 'thanks...I guess' and began kneading the dough as if she knew exactly what she was doing.

Dex was in awe of her method, but more importantly, he finally had something to say to her. "That's a really nice ring," he said, looking down at her finger.

"I know," she answered, lifting the dough with her fist, "I picked it out. Early bat-mitzvah present."

She continued to work the dough in silence.

Dex thought about asking her where she got it, just to keep the conversation going, but decided that would have sounded too desperate, even for him. He was taking out his frustration on the dough when Mrs. Baker announced that class would be ending shortly.

Sarah looked at the clock and deftly began braiding the dough.

"You're really good at that," Dex heard himself say without having thought about it. He was beating an egg to brush over the top of his bread.

"I should be. I help my Bubbe finish making *challah* every Friday when I get home from school," she shared.

"My grandmother makes it too. But she can also make *foccacia*. I'm a pizza bagel, actually. Italian and Jewish."

He let out a little chuckle. Sarah didn't respond. They continued working until Sarah let out a small gasp.

"Hey!"

"Yeah?" Dex asked, excited.

"Have you seen my ring?" Sarah was frantically searching the table.

Dex searched with her for a moment then grabbed a toothpick from the counter. He delicately poked into her loaf of braided dough. It was tricky. All the raising and resting was about getting the yeast to make air bubbles in the dough. Poking at it before it was baked could make the *challah* collapse like a pricked balloon. After a few seconds, he extracted the ring. Sarah's braided miracle still stood proudly on the sheet pan, ready for its final rise.

Dex handed the ring to Sarah, waiting for her thanks and praise.

"Thank God," she said, quickly snatching the ring from him just as the bell rang.

#

The cafeteria was getting more crowded as kids who had gone on a morning field trip returned in time for lunch. Dex, Kyle, Liza, and now Jordy, were sitting at a half-empty table of their own, having agreed weeks ago that it was better than sitting with a bunch of perfect-looking people or obvious losers. Dex wasn't sure they really felt that way, or if they said they did to make themselves feel better. They were good-looking too, though. Weren't they?

"A toothpick?" exclaimed Liza.

"It was all I could find!" Dex defended.

"It's not like he used his-- fiiiiiiiger!" Kyle burped, scarfing down the last of his sandwich, and taking out a butterscotch pudding cup.

"You didn't have no dental berries on that pick-stick did'ya?" Jordy asked, with a smirk.

"Gross. No!" Dex was annoyed, but proud of himself for figuring out what Jordy meant. "You guys weren't there. You should've seen how great she braided the dough."

"And you just loved playing her doughboy, didn't you?" Liza teased, and gave Dex's cheeks a little pinch.

She and Kyle laughed.

"Shut up!" Dex's face was getting red. "Both of you."

"Yeah. Leave da sucka alone. Bad 'nuff he all love-thumped wit a who-dat," Jordy noted, leaving everyone perplexed.

After a few silent moments Kyle finally asked, "I give. What's a 'who-dat?'"

Jordy eyed the group, sure someone would understand, but the silence remained. "Duh, it's a chick dat don't even know you breathin'! You know," he said, raising his voice to a squeaky screech and imitating a girl, "Who-dat?"

And with that Jordy got up and stretched, holding onto one side of his pants to be sure they didn't fall down again.

"Sarah knows I breathe," Dex mumbled.

"No, she don't," Jordy cackled.

"Sorry Dex, but I think Jordy's right," Liza admitted, playing with the cap from her water bottle. "Sarah is all about Sarah. She was in my dads' salon yesterday getting tips and scheduling her bat-mitzvah tans. That girl is really into 'Fake and Bake.'"

"A butt-what? What she tanning her butt for?" asked Jordy.

"Not butt, *baht*! Bat-mitzvah," Dex corrected. "It's this thing when a Jewish girl turns twelve or thirteen. She says some blessings in temple and usually there's a big party to celebrate her becoming a woman."

"I've seen Sarah. She don't look like no woman to me."

Jordy's scanned the room, his eyes landing on a girl with a sizable chest. "Now that girl," he pointed with his chin, "is ready for a bat-mitzvah."

Kyle nodded in agreement.

"It's a symbolic thing," explained Dex.

"Do guys get one too?"

"Yeah. That's called a bar-mitzvah."

"Cool. What you get to drink?"

"It's not that kind of bar," Dex sighed.

"You become an adult and you don't get to drink. Damn."

"We don't become real adults. It's not like we start paying taxes or anything."

"No, but Sarah got to buy some awesome make-up," Liza grumbled.

"Who caaaaares anyway," Kyle broke in as he relieved himself of another burp. "It's not like we're invited."

"That's cause you a who-dat. Laytah gaytahs, gotta go slit a worm." Jordy shuffled out of the cafeteria.

Before they had the chance to start talking again, an extremely awkward kid, Jerry, from Dex's math class, timidly approached their table just as Dex noticed Sarah walk into the cafeteria holding hands with Hunter. Dex's eyes were squarely on Sarah who stood with her back towards him as she and Hunter talked to another 'popular' couple.

"Hi," Jerry muttered, as Dex ignored him. "I'm sorry, I don't really know you. But my mom wanted me to ask you something."

Dex was confused, and too busy hating Hunter to say anything. But, Jerry remained a man on a mission.

"Uh, okay," he said, taking out a slip of paper from his front shirt pocket.

Jerry began to read:

"Could you make her a grilled A-high tuna sandwich with orange and cranberry relish on a bree-o-chee? For tomorrow?"

"Make a what for who?" Dex suddenly realized this was a business transaction.

Jerry handed him the note.

"Oh, Ahi tuna on a brioche. Sure." Dex typed a reminder on his phone, too engrossed to notice Sarah watching the conversation. "Your mom is Susanne. Tell her I say 'hi.' She's great."

Jerry blushed, nodded, and left as quickly as his legs would allow. Dex was typing another note on his phone when Sarah appeared.

"You make stuff like that?" she asked.

Dex jumped not expecting Sarah to be right there. He turned toward her and stared for a moment speechless.

"That's nothing," Kyle boasted, hoping to help ease the awkwardness of the moment. "Dex makes the beeeeh-st white chocolate chip cookies on the planet!"

"True. But my favorite is still his chocolate peanut butter brownies." Liza sighed and licked her lips.

Dex sat there listening to his praises but was once again too love struck to speak.

“Aren’t you in my International Cooking class?” Sarah asked.

“Uh-Yeah.” Dex tried not to sound insulted. “We just made *challah* together. Remember?”

“Oh right. That was *you*. We’re for sure getting an ‘A’ on those *challahs*. I got a ‘D’ on my apple tart in Ms. Hofpoodle’s class. That’s kind of why I transferred out.”

“I think it’s Hofnagel,” Dex said, immediately sorry he corrected her.

“Whatev. We should so be partners again.” Sarah turned and started walking away.

“Yeah definitely,” Dex said, loudly enough to make sure she heard him.

Okay, so she was kind of indifferent, some might even say a little mean. But Dex was hoping that with a little encouragement he wouldn’t be a ‘who-dat’ for very long.

Chapter 5

Dex stood in front of the school kicking a rock oddly wedged between two squares of the sidewalk. His grandmother was supposed to pick him up so they could grocery shop for tonight, but she had texted that she was running a little late. It was okay, he was glad to have a few minutes to himself, considering how frustrating the day had been. What if Jordy and Liza were right? What if Sarah would always forget that she and Dex were cooking partners? The thought made him cringe. It wasn't in his nature to give up without trying, but like the dumb rock stuck deep in the sidewalk, no matter how hard he could kick it, some things weren't worth the effort.

Geema's car, an aging, blue Honda Accord, pulled up as Dex was about to take another crack at the rock. Just as well, he thought. It probably would have done nothing but ripped my sneaker.

Geema smiled at him through the window.

"School alright?" she asked as he took the passenger's seat.

"Yeah. Got an A on my Italian test."

There was no way he was going to tell his grandmother that he was a loser who had a crush on someone else's girlfriend.

"Molto bene, ragazzo. Poppy would be so proud!"

For a Jew, Geema could do a surprisingly believable Italian accent.

"Is Alicia home yet?" Dex asked, anxiously.

"No. Your mom is picking her up before the commercial shoot."

“I’m glad she’s back.” Dex started going through tonight’s menu in his head.

“Yeah, we all are. Three months is a long time to be away.” Geema patted his hand like she was glad he wasn’t going anywhere.

“I can’t believe she got to bring Bobby Flay a latte!”

#

Entrée, the upscale neighborhood supermarket, was less crowded than usual. Dex and Geema breezed through the aisles, consulting the flyer not to miss any specials.

“Ooo-there’s a sale on fresh pickled herring in the appetizing department!” Geema exclaimed as Dex put his finger in his mouth to gag.

“Fine. I’ll go get it,” she said, walking away. “You get the bread.”

Dex agreed but couldn’t resist a quick trip to the ‘taste-testing counter,’ the launching pad for new products the store was adding to their inventory. Sometimes there were only a couple of things to try out, but other times it was possible to make a meal of the choices. Last time he was there he found a French herb goat cheese that he knew would pair beautifully with his baked vegetable loaf, and now the new ‘ParisianVeggie’ panini was on its way to becoming a best seller.

Dex’s thoughts shifted to the time Poppy received a larger shipment of ground lamb than he was expecting. Dex just assumed he would make sausages, a staple at the restaurant, but Poppy suggested they make ground lamb meatballs in a minty béchamel sauce. Without even thinking, Dex had let out a BLECCHH that made Poppy chuckle. There was no way that combination could work. But Poppy insisted that all the flavors would come together over a subtle rice pilaf. "Intuition plus inspiration," Poppy had told him. "That's what takes a morsel and makes it a meal." Of course, as usual, Poppy was right. He had a way of making the impossible delicious.

Dex was getting hungry and wondered what kinds of samples he would find today, but there was nothing but a 'back next week' sign on the counter. Great. Dex felt a jolt of panic. It would suck if that's the way the evening would go. He wanted Alicia's welcome home party to make her feel happy to be home. Three months was a long time and Dex had missed her more than he had anticipated. It might have been different if they had to share a bathroom, but since they didn't, he was anxious to have her back where she belonged, helping him make sense out of middle school. A blast from a speaker overhead brought him back.

"Good afternoon shoppers! Our fresh-out-of-the-oven garlic and onion boards are now on sale in the bakery department."

And suddenly he remembered he had forgotten about the bread.

The bakery counter wasn't that busy, but the stocky man with blonde spiky hair behind the counter was. He was sorting rolls in big boxes and transferring several at a time into large plastic bags.

"Hey, can I get some service here!" Dex bellowed.

Vince Rossi turned around grinning and tossed Dex a roll.

"And how can I help you, young man?"

“Very funny Dad. I’m here to pick up the bread,” Dex said, taking an approving bite.

“I know. Geema called me.” Vince grabbed a large bag from the corner. “I threw in a couple of boards. Maybe make a nice babaganoush or tapenade to go with ‘em?”

Vince wasn’t a chef but he enjoyed food and usually had creative ideas.

Dex took the bag and was immediately weighed down on one side. He was glad his father didn’t seem to notice.

A lady who looked like a giant pear walked up to the counter.

“I got to get back to work,” Vince said. “Listen, have fun cooking.”

Dex went down a few aisles looking for his grandmother. He found her in the soups, gravies, and sauces aisle and was happy to see room in the wagon for the bread. A jar of PRESTO’S PESTO caught Dex’s eye.

“Geema, we should try this stuff. Preston LeTray is an awesome chef.”

Golda looked at the jar, let out a small sigh, and put the jar back on the shelf. “I think he’s doing fine without our business.”

#

“Where’s Preston?” the director shouted as he nervously paced the floors of the Eatz Network studio. “There’s no time for games. I was just told Paula Deen is on Kosher Cooking with Cassie tonight. We have to shoot this commercial and get out of here.”

“I know,” said one of the cameramen, “Preston should be here by now.”

There were some mumbled complaints from the crew as they mulled about the big studio space making sure everything for the commercial was in place. Marla stood near the end of the large granite counter checking the controls on the microwave as one of the food stylists was prepping a plate of spaghetti. If it weren’t for all the cameras, wires and people, the kitchen, with its white wood cabinets, dark granite counters, and hardwood flooring, looked like it belonged in a house instead of a huge office building.

Alicia pulled a small compact out of her back-pack to check her make-up. Marla had picked her up at the airport over two hours ago and she was sure her blush had faded along with her lip gloss. Not bad, Alicia thought as her magnified image revealed more color than she had anticipated. It had been a while since she had been to the Eatz studio on a shoot with her mother, and even though she didn’t remember a soul, she still wanted to look good. In L.A., there hadn’t been one girl her age who didn’t carry make-up, perfume, and a hair-straightener at all times. She threw her bag over her shoulder and took a seat away from the action. The last thing she wanted to do was distract her mother, especially since Marla confided that it had been months since she had been on an assignment.

“He’s here,” the sound engineer announced.

Preston LeTray strolled in as if he owned the network and the building. His nose was pointed toward the ceiling and his face was scrunched like he was sniffing sour milk. A production assistant tried to get his attention, but he went unnoticed. Preston’s eyes focused on Marla who was busy setting up the dishes, but as he walked past he disregarded her and gave the director a strong tap on the shoulder.

"Where's Amber?" Preston demanded.

"Amber's home with her new puppy. He's teething," the director said, stacking the last dish. "Marla, I need you over here."

"And whhhhyyyy does this concern us?" Preston squawked.

"The dumb dog used Amber's finger as a chew toy. Luckily, we found Marla." He checked on the mics. "Listen Preston, we don't have all night. Just get your juice box or whatever junk you're drinking and get ready to roll."

Preston ignored the statement and grabbed a script lying on the counter.

"Nice to see you too, Preston," Marla said dryly.

"It *is* nice to see you." Preston's eyes barely peered out from behind the pages. "I just wasn't expecting to." He walked away quickly.

Alicia couldn't hear what was said from where she was sitting, but for the brief moment her face wasn't in her iPhone she caught Preston scowling at her mother. "Creep," she said to herself. Marla was one of the easiest people in the world to get along with. If he had a problem with her, it had to be his fault. Alicia was about to investigate further when the director called for everyone to take their places.

Marla was the first one ready neatly tucked behind the counter, the cameras only as high as her waist. It bothered Alicia that her mother never got to have the real spotlight.

Every shot in every commercial was always the same; Marla's beautiful, expressive hands displaying a product. Alicia couldn't understand how her mother could find satisfaction in a career that focused on having snipped cuticles and freshly polished fingernails. But Marla had reminded her numerous times that she was content with her freelance career and that being a wife and mother was more important to her than any job could ever be.

Marla didn't like being the center of attention. She enjoyed meeting people on shoots and going places without being recognized. Alicia hadn't thought about it much, but maybe she wasn't really that different from her mother that way. She liked the idea of being a film maker, the one behind the camera, choosing what was important. When she was in L.A., Alicia saw on a daily basis how shallow people could be, overly concerned about how they looked instead of passionate about how they felt. At nineteen, she didn't necessarily want everyone to know it, but she was glad to be home.

Preston paraded back into the studio carrying the script under his left arm and two large bottles of water. He took a long swig from one of the bottles, and put everything on a prop table near the set. Seizing a moment the director was consulting with one of the sound engineers, Preston quickly mopped his sweaty brow with a cloth he retrieved from his pants pocket and took his spot.

The director shouted for silence. "And, action!"

Marla's hands displayed the "Spaghetti", "Linguini", "Bowtie", and "Elbow" varieties of the product in steam-bag packages as Preston began to narrate.

My grandmother, Nonna Teresa, didn't just make pasta.

She made magic. Now, I'm bringing my family's special secret recipe to your dinner table. For the first time, you can have Presto's Pesto, any time, any place, with Presto's Pesto Dinners, in convenient, microwavable packages.

The whole time Preston spoke Marla's hands, and only her hands, were busy demonstrating how to prepare his product. First, putting a package in the microwave. Then, closing the oven door and pushing the settings. After, emptying the contents into a bowl and rubbing her satisfied stomach as Preston concluded:

So remember, on your next trip to the market plan your next trip to Italy with Presto's Pesto Dinners. It's even better than your Nonna's!

Chapter 6

"Geema, what time did Mom say she and Alicia would be here?" Dex checked the clock on the wall as he methodically sprinkled crushed Oreos over his large impressive cake.

"Dexy, you've asked me the same question every fifteen minutes. They'll be here soon." Golda bathed the roast in pan juices and tossed in a few handfuls of sliced portabella mushrooms. "A few more minutes and this baby will be done."

She looked over at Dex working at the counter. "The cake looks beautiful. Let it be."

Dex stood back and like any artist assessed his work with a critical eye. "Are you sure there aren't too many crumbs on the right side?"

"There aren't too many anythings," Golda assured him. "Why don't you get out of this kitchen already and help your dad put up the rest of the decorations. He can't do it all himself."

Dex skulked away from the cake like a parent leaving a kindergartener on the first day of school. A quick look around the dining room and Dex realized Geema was right. Vince had done a great job on the balloons and streamers, but there was no way he could hang the banner alone.

Golda came out of the kitchen to set the table. She walked over to the antique wooden breakfront at the front of the room and ran her hand over the curves in the wood. It was a beautifully handcrafted piece that she remembered being in her grandmother's dining room used to showcase the most elegant of her family's prized possessions. From the time she was a little girl she was told that someday it would be hers.

When that day came, years later, it was too big to fit in her house. She and Poppy had decided to use it in the restaurant to store the better crystal, silver, and china for extra special occasions. It had a stately yet warm presence and gave Poppy's Kitchen that extra dash of hominess that made guests feel like family. Golda shuddered to think about the restaurant being sold and the breakfront being used to help pay her insurmountable debt. Luckily, her focus shifted when she turned around and saw Dex sitting awkwardly on Vince's shoulders hanging a homemade giant cloth banner spelled out in neon pinks and purples.

WELCOME BACK ALICIA!

Just as Dex pinned the last tack, Golda glanced out the window and saw Marla's car pulling into the parking lot. "They're here!"

Vince and Dex scrambled over to the entrance while Golda quickly smoothed over the rippling corners of the lace tablecloth. Marla casually strolled in with a finger covering her lips to keep everyone quiet as Alicia trailed behind.

"Leesh," Marla said over her shoulder, "I'll be just a minute. Geema needs the big soup pot."

Alicia waited for a moment as Marla walked in.

"Oh Alicia, it's heavier than I thought. Could you come in? I don't want to strain my fingers."

Alicia smirked and walked in, confused to find everything pitch black.

"SURPRISE!!!" the group shouted as Dex switched on the dining room lights.

#

"I forgot how great the food is here," Alicia said, taking another slice of the roast while still chewing what was in her mouth. "Everything in California is a smoothie." She took another helping of potatoes. "I mean I like smoothies, but blueberry yogurt and kale have no business being married in a blender."

Everyone laughed which gave Dex a chance to give Alicia a quick once-over before she could notice. She was still thin. Her hair was still long and reddish-brown, but did she look older or something? She had only been gone three months but something about her face and the way she laughed made her seem different.

"I made a smoothie last week," Dex recalled. "Oreo mocha. I thought of you."

"That sounds awesome. You'll have to make me one." Alicia took a final bite of meat and pushed her plate away.

"I'd like to make a toast to our Alicia," Vince said, raising a glass of wine. I'm so happy that you got home safe, and that I didn't lose you to Johnny Depp." Everyone laughed knowing Alicia had developed a huge crush on the actor after seeing him in *Chocolat*. She was even more into him now since they'd worked together for a couple of days.

"Anyway, I hope you enjoy every minute of making movies as much as I'll enjoy every minute of watching them." He took a sip of champagne. "To Alicia."

"Thanks Daddy," Alicia said, giving him a hug.

A brief silence followed that made Dex feel a little uncomfortable. Was it possible to get used to your own sister being away? It's not like he'd enjoyed Alicia being gone, but now that she was back did they still have anything in common besides family? Maybe California changed her too much. She may have looked the same but she did say *awesome* like she was on *The Hills* or something. Dex didn't want to think about it, and jumped to his feet when Geema suggested they clear the table and set up for dessert.

Alicia looked like she was about to say something when her phone rang. Whoever called made her eyes light up and she dashed to the other side of the dining room to talk.

Before Dex could move, Marla stopped him with her gloved hand. "You alright honey? You look sad."

"Sad?" Uh-oh, were his feelings that transparent? Not cool. "No, of course I'm not sad," he said as if his mother had lost her mind. "I just hope Alicia likes the cake. That's all." Dex decided that wasn't exactly a lie. It certainly sounded better than *I hope I still like Alicia.*

A knock at the back door in the kitchen gave Dex a way out of the conversation. "Liza and Kyle are here. They missed Alicia too so I invited them for dessert." And before his mother could think of anything more to say, Dex went to answer the door before Geema had the chance.

"Hey! Hope we're not too late," Liza walked in ahead of Kyle.

"Nope. You're right on time," Dex assured her, crossing over to the drawer to get the sparklers to put in his Oreo and ganache masterpiece. He took out four, figuring that any more would make it look less like a cake and more like it was ready for take-off.

"Jordy couldn't mmmm-ake it," Kyle burped.

"He *got big bizzle on da page*," Liza said, mimicking her cousin.

"He has what?" Geema looked perplexed as she took the sugar bowl out of the cabinet.

"Lots of homework," Dex explained, surprising himself. It had only been a day, but he was already nearly fluent in 'Jordese.'

"Really? If you say so," Geema rolled her eyes, watching as Liza and Kyle lit the sparklers. Dex told them to bring in the cake to add to the surprise. Geema walked over to the main switches and turned off the lights again until nothing but the glow of the sparklers lit the path into the dining room.

"What's going on?" Alicia asked through the darkness. In moments Liza and Kyle burst into the dining room carrying the sparkling cake.

"Surprise!" they shouted in unison. Liza placed the cake on the table in front of Alicia.

"Whoa! It's not even my birthday!" Alicia exclaimed.

"True, but it *is* your welcome back party!" Liza cried.

Alicia went over to hug them leaving the cake to sparkle on the table. Dex noticed a few tiny embers escape and float up towards the ceiling, vanishing in the cool air. When Alicia returned to the table, she methodically took the sparklers out of the cake and held them until they went out. Everyone applauded and Geema turned the lights back on.

"That cake looks fabulous!" Alicia drooled.

"Yeah, but why does it smell like laundry?" Kyle sniffed.

“Burning laundry.” Marla sniffed too.

Dex looked up and saw the giant banner in flames just as the fire alarm went off. For a moment he panicked and couldn’t move at all. Was the fire his fault? He saw the embers, but they seemed to disappear.

Vince ran to get the fire extinguisher. That seemed like a smart idea. Marla clutched a menu and began to fan the banner frantically. That seemed like a good idea too. But Dex couldn’t think of anything to do. He looked at the table and saw a piece of the banner heading for his cake. Without a moment’s hesitation, he scooped up the platter and ran to the other side of the room. If nothing else, he had made the decision to save something.

“Ow!”Marla cried, looking down to find her glove burning at the tip. “Oh God! I burned my pinky!”

Dex watched as Liza got a glass of water for Marla’s pinky and Geema told Kyle where to find the first aid kit. There was no reason for Dex to feel purposeless; he was holding the cake, an important job. This whole party was about welcoming Alicia back with her favorite cake. Still, something was making him feel useless.

Vince finally set up the fire extinguisher and began hosing down the flames. Marla’s finger was soaking in a glass of water and Geema was snapping the cloth napkins from the table to keep them from becoming additional victims.

Alicia went over to Dex and patted his head. “You know, you’re my hero in all this.” She swiped a finger full of frosting and licked her lips. “You saved my cake. Clearly the best part of this whole party.”

Dex sighed in relief. Alicia wasn't gone after all. She was still his sister, the only person who really understood him the way he needed to be understood.

Chapter 7

Alicia woke up with a start. She looked around confused, not seeing anything familiar. Then she remembered--she was home and even though she was happy to be back, it was going to take some time to readjust. She scanned her room and was amazed she still had two huge duffel bags to unpack. She got out of bed, unzipped the first bag and started pulling out one item at a time. Where had she had room for everything in the first place?

She yawned and looked at the clock. It was already eight. As an assistant producer some mornings she had to be in by five. That's when she learned to live on lattes. She yawned again. If she were still in L.A. she would have been reviewing the prop list for the day's shoot at the studio. It wasn't the most exciting or glamorous job, but as she was often reminded, it was important.

Alicia, the director can't orchestrate a proper breakfast-in-bed scene without a serving tray and a glass mug of steaming cappuccino. Preferably hazelnut, sweetheart, since we'll have to smell it most of the day.

Her supervisors had certainly been a demanding bunch to please, but Alicia was smart and charming and had quickly learned how to make the situation work. After a few short weeks, she was the only intern who had been given the opportunity to direct a small scene in an independent feature film. That experience alone convinced her that she really wanted to be in the film industry and was pursuing the right career.

Getting a scholarship to attend the A.A. Neal School of Film and Fine Arts was just the opportunity Alicia had been hoping for. The fact that it was an easy car ride from home was a welcome benefit. There was no denying that she had enjoyed her time in L.A., but she was an east coast girl at heart and was glad to be back in time to see the leaves change colors and the snow paint the trees a glistening white.

The familiar sound of tapping fingernails at her bedroom door interrupted Alicia's train of thought. "That you, Geema?" she said, trying to fit a photo of her standing on set with Johnny Depp into a frame. She put it down frustrated that each time the photo was upright it would shift from the center to the bottom of the border.

Geema walked in carrying a small black case. "How did you know it was me?"

"No one else knocks with their fingernails."

"Oh Leeshie, I've missed you." Geema watched as Alicia fought to keep the photo centered in the frame. "Hand me some junk mail, Leesh."

"Junk mail?"

"It's a trick Poppy used. It'll fix exactly what you need."

Alicia handed her grandmother an envelope filled with expired coupons.

"You put this on top of the cardboard that comes with the frame to keep the picture set. Now when you put the back on, it won't slide anywhere." Geema set up the frame and left it on the desk.

"Thanks, Geema. And thanks Poppy. That worked!" She hung the photo up on her wall.

"I'm so sorry your welcome back party didn't go quite how we'd hoped," Geema sighed.

"Are you kidding? It was great. *Boss*, they'd say back in LA. Especially the part when the firemen came and finished Dex's cake.

"You're boss, Leeshie," Geema said handing the case to her. "I know you start classes soon. This is something Poppy would have wanted you to have."

Alicia unfastened the gold hinges and pulled out an old video camera. "It's still in great shape," she marveled. "Geema, this is amazing. I might be too young to say it, but they don't make cameras the way they used to."

Geema laughed. "You're right. They don't. But I'm sure it could use a new battery." She glanced wistfully as Alicia examined the camera.

"Your Poppy loved being behind the camera, just like you." She paused in thought for a moment.

"*Unlike* you," Geema continued, "he may have chopped off a head or two now and then, but you could still tell who was who."

Alicia gave her grandmother a kiss on the cheek.

"Leesh, I'm sure there are a ton of his movies in the attic. There were never enough hours in the day to watch all the hours he could film in a day. I'm not even sure what's up there. Probably a bunch of you and Dex as babies." She started walking out of the room and paused. "I think there are some blank tapes too. But I can never find anything up there."

"I'll go look," Alicia offered and held up a t-shirt she had gotten for Dex at a novelty store on the Sunset Strip. "What do you think Geema?" It was a chef at home plate wielding a whisk instead of a bat that read:

STEP UP TO THE PLATE.

#

It was way too early for gym class. Dex rubbed his eyes trying to keep them open as the coach explained their next unit.

"Has anyone here ever heard of boot camp?" Coach Logan looked around for volunteers to answer.

"Yeah," called out a wispy blonde without raising her hand. "That's where Gucci tries out their summer line."

A few kids laughed, but Dex just rolled his eyes. She probably wasn't even kidding.

"Not even close, Janessa," barked the coach. "Any other takers?"

Kyle raised his hand. "It's where guys in the army go to get buuuuuff," Kyle burped. There were a few snickers from his classmates, but not enough to stop him from finishing. "So they can fight all the enemies."

"Close enough. You okay Kyle?"

"Yeah," Kyle sighed as he pulled out the bottle of Tums from his pocket.

Coach Logan didn't miss a beat. "Alright, we're going to start off our 'Boot Camp' unit today. Let me show you the ropes."

Within minutes Dex found himself about to climb the rope next to Sarah's. If it had been anywhere but gym class he would have been thrilled to be paired with her, but this was just torture. The large, soft mat beneath them offered little comfort as Dex positioned himself to appear agile and confident.

"And...go!" directed the coach with a click of his stopwatch.

Sarah was almost halfway up the rope when Dex felt his shorts coming down. Each stretch made it worse. The choice was giving her a bigger lead or letting his shorts fall to his ankles. Dex stopped and adjusted his waistband with one hand. Sarah looked down at him with a little grin. Dex met the challenge and hustled to be even with her.

"Hey, how did you like Josh and Kayden's risotto in Baker's class?" Dex asked her eye to eye.

"Risotto?" Sarah chuckled. "I thought it was rice pudding!"

"Don't worry," Dex assured her, "Our couscous will be much better."

Dex was feeling pretty good once class was over. He had conquered the rope and Sarah had seen his success firsthand. He went into the locker room ready for work. Gym class was one of his busiest times of the day. Everyone was starving and wanted cookies.

The line in front of his locker was longer than usual. Some of the guys hadn't even gotten dressed yet. Dex understood. He was hungry too. He and Kyle were selling cookies as fast as they could. Between handing the cookies out and exchanging the money, it looked like they were running some kind of gambling ring.

Dex was just about to retrieve another box of cookies when Coach Logan's door swung open. Everyone ran in different directions. Kyle stashed a box of cookies in his locker and motioned to Dex that he had to leave.

Dex quickly threw the cookies he had out into a bag in his locker, hiding them like they were a carton of cigarettes. He was selling cookies, but he still felt like a criminal.

"Dex. I'd like a word with you," Coach Logan didn't look happy. "I know what you've got going on, and I'm sure you're well aware it's against school policy."

He pointed at Dex's locker and pulled a pink slip out of his t-shirt pocket. Dex's head fell forward as the coach began to write.

Busted. Dex was mortified.

Coach Logan handed Dex the slip. "So just fill my order and this," he made a circle with his pointer finger, "will stay our secret."

Chapter 8

Preston LeTray stood admiring himself in one of the many mirrors he had lining the walls of his spacious office. At a glance one would think he had the ideal look of someone successful: Strong, angular chin, clear, steel-gray eyes, and every hair on his head neatly glued into place. His suits were handmade to accentuate his broad shoulders as his lean frame had little else to showcase. Every detail of his look and a visit to his websites and fan pages told you he was the most popular, celebrated chef on the Eatz Network.

But upon closer look, the real Preston LeTray could not shine. The ever-present scowl on his face made him appear cold and uncomfortable, as if ice were flowing through his veins. He lived by his own motto: He who hurts first, hurts least. It was safe to assume that crossing Preston LeTray would result in getting kicked in the butt by his fancy Italian leather shoes. He enjoyed fighting. The only time he ever seemed to smile sincerely was when he could exact revenge on an enemy.

Despite this, Preston LeTray was a celebrity with a handsome face whom most women found attractive. It was a fortunate attribute and he had learned how to use it to his advantage long ago. His assistant, Yvette Bidet, was just the kind of woman to help him secure and further his position with the network. She had a quick, devious mind and luckily for Preston, she could not help but do whatever he asked of her. At present, this meant she was out getting breakfast for this meeting.

Preston had been working for weeks to establish his own development team to create new products and marketing plans. His latest idea came to him when he received a memo that a fellow chef was launching a new clothing line called *Tea-Shirts*. The shirts were to be constructed like flow-through tea bags, with a space for the head and slits down the sides to be fastened by laces. The designs were inspired by different teas and the whole project was being lauded as the most original product ever to be endorsed by the Eatz Network.

Preston's competitive nature would not allow him to be happy for his associate. Even though he already had a full line of prepared foods on the market and was hoping to come out with a new line of cookware, Preston felt he needed something spectacular and different to turn the network back to his direction.

He found Buford Beaumont, a scent specialist from Dallas, Texas, on Google. After a brief phone conversation, Preston sized Buford up as a big, smart oaf, who would work long and hard without asking for much in return except their agreed upon fee. Something for nothing was Preston's favorite arrangement.

Preston had no problem admitting that money guided his life. In fact, he was proud of it. There was no finer way to prove one's value than to be financially successful. "People with money and celebrity," he would often say, "have the world at their feet." People with empty wallets had creditors at their heels. He knew which one he wanted to be.

Buford was set to arrive at any moment. The meeting was scheduled to take place before sunrise to ensure that no one but the janitors would be in the building. He'd pressed a few dollars into their hands and asked them to kindly keep their mouths shut. Preston wasn't going to answer to anyone about his plans, and he certainly wouldn't give anyone the opportunity to steal his idea. Trust, he believed, was the food of fools, a useless ingredient that always resulted in a bitter dish.

Preston was still idolizing his reflection when there was a series of knocks at the door. He answered it peeking down the halls to make sure they were alone.

"A pleasure to meet you Mr. Lee-Tray," said a deep voice with a thick Southern drawl.

Preston cringed at the mispronunciation of his name, knowing full well that it would be pointless to even try to correct this behemoth.

The tall Texan wore a brown suede cowboy hat and shiny alligator boots that clopped as he walked into Preston's office. "I'm Buford Beaumont," he offered shaking Preston's hand hard enough to make him seasick, "but my friends call me Butie."

"Nice to meet you as well, Mr. Beaumont," Preston said, coldly letting the Texan know they were not, nor ever would be, friends.

Buford shrugged his shoulders and glanced around the bland, beige, meticulous room. He caught a glimpse of himself in one of the mirrors and dusted some lint off the shoulders of his jacket before he took a seat.

"You sure do know lots of famous folks," Buford said, looking at the wall of framed photos of Preston with various celebrities.

"Yes, it helps when you're one of them," Preston said affirming his clout. "Shall we get down to business Mr. Beaumont? I certainly have no time to waste as I'm sure you understand."

"Of course," Buford agreed and pulled out a large wad of cardboard squares from what seemed a very deep pocket.

“Whaddaya think of this one, Mr. Lee-Tray?” Buford handed Preston a square.

Preston held it near his nose and sniffed. He looked perplexed.

“First ya gotta take off the sticky strip. That’s protecting the scent.”

Preston fought to get the strip off without ruining his well-groomed nails. After several attempts, he heaved a sigh of triumph.

“Good,” Buford said genuinely, but the condescending tone made Preston sneer.

“Then you kinda gotta put it right up to your nose to get the whole effect.” Buford retrieved another square from his pocket to demonstrate. “If I were you, I’d put it up to jes’ one nostril, and close the other one, like this.” Buford’s moves were effortless. “And then switch it.”

Sensing that Preston wanted privacy, Buford tossed a bunch of samples on a chair and walked over to the wall behind the door to look at more photos.

Preston held the square up to his nose and took a deep breath. Although he tried to control it, he let out a huge sneeze.

During his second sneeze, Yvette entered the room carrying a tray of coffee cups and a box of donuts. Buford, who had been staring at a photo of Preston with Emeril LaGasse, swiftly turned his attention to the full-figured beauty dressed like a supermodel who had just joined them. She set the food down on the desk and pulled a tissue out of her purse.

"Here you go, Sugar. Sorry I'm late." She was about to offer an explanation when she realized they weren't alone.

"Yvette, this is Buford Beaumont, the head of my development team."

"Of course, of course." Yvette extended her hand for the introduction. "Charmed," she said, her voice smoky.

"Pleasure's all mine, darling.'" Buford kissed her hand.

Preston winced and adjusted his tie. "Yvette's been heading up our Presto Weight Loss Plan for the past three months."

"That's true." She slid off her coat dramatically. "I've lost two dress sizes eating nothing but Presto's Pesto meals." She took a seat. "I just finished breakfast on my way over. Pesto pancakes." Her stomach gurgled.

"Well you look lovely. I reckon I've never seen you before, but from my view I wouldn't mind seeing you again." Buford looked at Yvette with puppy dog eyes.

"Yvette, come smell this," Preston demanded ignoring Buford's declaration.

"Pardon me?" Yvette was confused.

"It's our new scent, little lady, *Pesto Breezes*." Buford handed her a sample. "We're aiming to use it for candles, air fresheners, maybe even on the boxes for the prepared foods."

Yvette sniffed it and smiled. "I'd know that smell anywhere." Yvette took another whiff.

"What do you think?" Preston asked gazing into her eyes. He had to do something to get her attention away from Buford and back where it belonged, on him.

“Delicious,” she said letting the ‘el’ lick her top lip. “The boss said you have to bring up your ratings Mr. LeTray, and this should do it.”

Her stomach gurgled again. She continued to sniff the sample as she sat down, unaware of the several other freshener samples she was now sitting on.

“Wonderful,” Preston sniffed deeply. “Is this the only kind we have?”

“Ha-ha,” Buford chuckled a little too enthusiastically. “Don’t you worry about variety, Mr. Lee-Tray. There’s plenty more to sniff where that came from.”

The three of them laughed so hard that Yvette accidentally let go a stream of gas from her behind. No one seemed to notice and she stood up to leave.

“Well, I’ll leave you gentleman to your business,” she said, clutching her stomach. “I’ve got some of my own to tend to.” She walked out the door and quickly headed to the ladies’ room.

“So what else have you got for me?” Preston liked where this meeting was headed and was finally enjoying himself.

Buford scanned the room for a moment, as he forgot where he had put the samples. He soon found them on the chair where Yvette had been sitting moments earlier.

“Mr. Lee-Tray, you ain’t smelled nothin’ ‘til you’ve tried out this one. *Sticky Buns.*”

Preston picked up the sample and put it right up to his nose. He sucked in as much air as he could to get the full experience, but as he did so, an enormously foul smell overwhelmed him. His knees buckled and his face scrunched in disgust as his eyes rolled back and he passed out.

Buford picked up the offending square from between Preston's fingertips and gave a cautious sniff.

"Hot dang!" he shouted. "Smells like a horse's behind!" He scratched his head baffled by what had gone wrong back in the testing room.

Chapter 9

Alicia sat by the window in the third seat from the front. It was a strategic move since she didn't want to be right on top of the professor, who still hadn't arrived, but she also didn't want to appear disinterested. This seat was the best compromise and since she was the first one there, she got to have her choice. She looked out the window and watched a couple of squirrels chase each other up and down a big oak tree. One was a diva and seemed ticked off about an acorn. She laughed to herself, imagining how she might shoot a scene like that. Part of her wished she could be running around outside like them instead of sitting in a chair trying not to be nervous.

There was no logical reason for her to be anxious, but it had been months since she had been in school and she wasn't sure she could sit through a three hour class without losing her mind. She took out a mint from the front pocket of her book-bag and watched as the rest of the class streamed into the room.

The last student to walk through the door made Alicia's heart flutter. He was tall with dark, wavy hair, a straight upturned nose, and the bluest eyes she had ever seen in her life. He smiled at some girl who waved to him and Alicia could see two deep dimples set on both sides of his perfect face. This guy wasn't just good-looking; he was gorgeous.

The professor didn't look anything like Alicia had imagined. She was young and attractive, even without make-up, and was dressed like a hippie in a long denim skirt, a purple top with a peace sign in the center, and a beaded band around her head. Why had she expected an older woman in a dull business suit? This was a film class. People were supposed to look creative and unconventional. Weren't they?

Alicia's thoughts about fashion statements came to an abrupt halt when Professor Jillian Stephens started class by singing 'Fame' a cappella. Midway through the song a few people were clapping and many had gotten up to dance. Alicia stayed in her seat. It wasn't that she was shy, but there was something about the scene that made her want to watch rather than participate. She turned her head toward the opposite side of the room and noticed that the gorgeous guy was sitting too.

By the end of the song, Jillian, as she asked to be called, was standing on her desk belting out the final lyric, '*Remember, Remember, Remember.*' Everyone applauded and those who were standing returned to their seats.

"Thank you, thank you," Jillian said, a little breathy. "Bet you never began a school year like that." She took a sip of water from the bottle on her desk.

"Why do you think I did it?" Jillian waited for answers.

"Element of surprise," called out a girl with beet red hair and a pierced eyebrow.

"Okay. Anyone else?"

"Well, you were singing about fame," said a short Hispanic guy. "I think the people in this class can relate to that. I think we all want that."

"Okay," said Jillian. "Show of hands. How many of you didn't clap or dance? How many of you just watched?"

Alicia raised her hand somewhat reluctantly. Had she made some kind of mistake without knowing it? A guy and a girl in matching sweatshirts sitting next to each other and Gorgeous Guy raised their hands.

“You two, in the back,” Jillian pointed at the sweatshirt couple with her chin. “Why didn’t you participate?”

“Um...” The guy turned a bright shade of crimson. “Um... she’s my girlfriend. And we were, um, kinda, um, making out.”

Everyone laughed including Jillian. “Glad I could be of service, but please don’t make that a habit in my classroom.” Jillian looked at Alicia. “How about you?”

Alicia cleared her throat. “I was feeling entertained. I didn’t want to change that.”

“And you?” Jillian asked Gorgeous Guy.

“Actually, pretty much what she just said,” he smiled at Alicia.

As if perfection weren’t already his, Gorgeous Guy also had a killer Australian accent. Alicia smiled back at him and wondered what their children might look like.

“There is no right or wrong answer,” Jillian chuckled. “I like to get a feel for my students. See how they react to the unusual.” She sat on her desk. “A film is an interpretation. As a filmmaker you create based on what you see, feel, hear, and experience. Then you decide what you will ultimately share with your audience.”

Alicia felt her nervous knots disappear. It was like Jillian knew exactly what to say to make her feel calm and excited all at once. This was where Alicia wanted to be. She was psyched to learn as much as she could.

“The focus of this class,” Jillian continued, “will be one project; to produce a short documentary that you will script, direct, and shoot. All finished work will be entered into this year's Apex Film Festival, where the winning project will be produced by Screenluvr Studios in Los Angeles. This year's theme is "A Work in Progress."

Suddenly, Alicia heard Gorgeous Guy's Auss-ome voice from the back. "Excuse me Professor,--"

"Please, call me Jillian," she insisted and pointed to the board, where only her first name was underlined. "And your name?"

"Ah right, Jillian," he nodded. "My name is Jazz. Jazz Kent."

Alicia's heart fluttered again. *Jazz.* What a cool name. Alicia and Jazz. It had a nice ring to it. *Stop being an insane person* she told herself. But it didn't matter. So what that she met him an hour ago. Some things you just know.

"Okay Jazz, what's on your mind?"

"This might sound a bit ignorant, but what exactly do you mean by a work in progress?" Jazz moved forward in his seat. "Like my mate's restoring an old car from the fifties that's been in a garage for years. Now you're saying I could film him rebuilding it and getting it to run...?"

Without hesitation Alicia supplied an answer. "If you document his thought process, like how he's going about rebuilding it and why this project is important to him, and then you followed that up with actual footage of the work being done, that would follow the theme." Alicia looked at Jillian for approval. "Wouldn't it?"

Alicia felt like an idiot. What would make her answer

like that? Did she want Jazz to think she was some kind of know-it-all dork?

“You’re right on target young lady. As long as you keep in mind that I’m looking for a documentary, not *Back to the Future*. Keep it real.” Jillian wrote that last phrase on the board. “And your name is--?” Jillian asked.

“Alicia,” she said faintly hoping to do some damage control.

“It’s refreshing to have confident people in class like Jazz and Alicia. I like when students are willing to speak their minds so freely.” Jillian sat back down on her desk.

Alicia tried not to blush. She loved the way Jillian said Jazz and Alicia like they were already together.

“But seriously guys.” Jillian checked her watch. “Jazz and Alicia have the right idea about this project. Feel free to help each other out. Take tonight and let me know your topic by tomorrow.

Jazz glanced at Alicia who offered a brief grin that implied she had barely noticed him.

Chapter 10

Another morning gone by and Sarah still hadn't confirmed Dex's friend request on Facebook. He was taking out his frustration mixing an innocent batch of chocolate cherry chip cookie dough when Alicia bounced into the room too awake for the hour. Dex thought she looked about ten years old. She was in bunny pajamas and her hair was in a messy ponytail on top of her head.

"It's really early," Alicia yawned. "What are you up to?"

"The usual. Making lunches. I sell them every day before I get on the bus."

"You do? Why?" Alicia asked.

"Uh...'cause I need money." Dex got a small bottle of vegetable oil from the pantry.

"Can't you just ask Dad?"

"I need more than that."

"For what?"

"Nothing. I'm just saving up." Couldn't she just shut up and leave him alone? Suddenly he missed having mornings all to himself. He began greasing and flouring cookie sheets hoping she would figure out he was too busy to talk.

"You're not going to tell me?" Alicia went to the refrigerator and nearly tripped over the wheelbarrow. "What's this thing in here for?"

"I just told you. I make lunches. That's how I get them outside."

“Okay, I guess. I’m not usually up this early.” She kicked the wheelbarrow out of her way with a light tap. “So I’ll ask you again, why do you need all this money? Why is it such a big secret?”

Alicia slammed the juice on the counter. “Oh my God! Dex, are you doing drugs?” She was near tears. “Because if that’s why you need money, I’ll kill you way before they will.”

“Leesh, did you leave your brain in L.A.?” Dex handed her a juice glass. “No. The closest I’ve come to doing drugs is sitting with Kyle when he’s popping Tums, which he says taste like moldy chalk. But thanks for thinking I’m that dumb.”

“I’m sorry. Of course you wouldn’t be that stupid.” She poured herself a glass of juice. “I’ve got it. You’re finally getting that ice cream machine you always wanted for your bedroom.”

“That’s not it either.” Dex was rolling the dough he prepared into small round balls about the size of a walnut and was placing each on the pans.

“When I was your age,” Alicia recalled, “I was babysitting for a nose job.”

“Must’ve been a scary-looking baby.”

“For my face, genius.”

“Guess you didn’t find enough kids to watch.” Dex laughed earning what he thought was the upper hand in this match.

“Shut up, Dex-lax.”

“Go away,” Dex finally said, “you’re making me late.” He put two pans in the oven.

"I don't get it. I thought you could tell me anything," Alicia sighed.

"Oh fine, just don't tell anyone or I'll post videos of you snoring on YouTube." Dex took a deep breath. "You know those infomercials for the *Gymbuff* 2000?"

"Uh huh. The guy looks like 'The Terminator' on steroids."

"Right--"

"What- you think you're too skinny or something?"

"Well, look at me." Dex turned around in a slow circle.

"Dex, you're twelve. You look fine. I'd even say you're cute."

"Thanks, but I don't want to look fine or cute. I want to look like the guy everyone chooses first in gym. I'm sick of people feeling like they have to hold me down when it gets windy."

"Dex, I've seen guys smaller than you."

"Maybe, but yesterday when I was climbing the ropes, I almost lost my shorts. The girl next to me was practically talking to my butt. And she'll never like me." Dex kicked the garbage pail. "Because her boyfriend is a wrestler. And I can never be a wrestler because no matter how hard I try, I can't make weight." He shoveled down a huge cookie letting chunks overflow from his mouth.

"I'm a loser," Dex moped. "Most of the time no one even notices me because they don't see me there." He checked the oven. "But that's gonna change. I'm getting the *Gymbuff* even if it costs as much as a car. I have to."

Alicia gave Dex a small but consoling hug. "I had no clue. I'm sorry. Can I help?"

"Not really, but you can spread some *aioli* on that *ciabatta.*"

"So...what are we making?" Alicia took an approving lick of the spread.

"Sandwiches for my regulars. But, I'm always trying out new stuff, like this." He pointed to an interesting pile of meat, cheese, and grilled vegetables on a platter.

"That looks great."

"Thanks, it's a work in progress."

Those words buzzed in Alicia's head and she suddenly jumped up and rushed out of the room.

"Where are you going?" Dex was now talking to the air.

Moments later Alicia returned with Poppy's movie camera and began filming Dex's preparations.

"Dex, you really are a genius. Don't pay any attention to me. Just keep working. Like I'm not here." Alicia toyed with the camera's control panel.

"But you *are* here."

"I know! You're my documentary." Alicia was filming him at every angle.

"I am? Okay. I guess that's kinda cool."

Unsure of how to work the camera, Alicia caught Dex in an extreme close-up. She accidentally zoomed into his ears, his nostrils, and his mouth while he was taste-testing his spinach dip. By the time Alicia figured out how to use the buttons, Dex w as hauling the wheelbarrow onto the lawn to set up for the morning shift.

"Damn! The battery's dead. Good thing I just saw a new one in the attic. Don't move."

Dex froze in place playfully for a few seconds as Alicia dashed into the house. He was setting up sandwiches when someone unfamiliar approached him.

"How ya doin' mate?" said an Australian accent. "I'm not even sure if I'm in the right place." He looked at a hand-scribbled note. "I'm looking for a store called 'Dex-something?' My uncle sent me...to pick up a sandwich?"

"Who's your uncle?"

"Clive Kent. He works in construction."

"You have the right address," Dex nodded. "Clive gets the sliced ham and cheddar with minced apricot and mustard glaze on a Kaiser roll." Dex prepared his order.

"Tell your uncle today's cookie is chocolate cherry chip. It'll make his day."

Jazz walked off to the side, took out his cell phone and texted the message. He was facing away from the house when Alicia came back ready to work. She had just begun to film when her camera caught another face in the frame.

"Hey there!" Jazz's eyes widened.

"Whoa! Hi!" Alicia yelped in shock and quickly turned off the camera. "I totally wasn't expecting to see you here."

“Ditto,” Jazz chuckled. “So, why are you here?”

Dex gave Alicia a quick wink the moment he saw her blush. He started helping customers as a small line formed and was hoping Kyle would show up before the crowd got too busy for him to handle on his own.

Alicia couldn’t contain her embarrassment. “Here?” she giggled nervously and pointed to Dex. “He’s my brother. And, and usually, I’m Dex’s sister with my hair down loose and wavy, wearing jeans, and—and-- really cool eyeliner.”

“Oh, well no worries.” He looked her over. “You’re quite lovely.”

“Thank you,” Alicia gushed.

“Your camera-”

“I know. It’s old. It was my grandfather’s.”

“I was going to say it’s amazing. My Uncle Clive gave me one that looks just like it.” He went to take the camera from her. “May I?” He examined it and gave it back to her. “They sure don’t make them like they used to.”

“You’re so right.”

“Since you’re filming, my guess is you’ve found your idea for class.”

Dex finished serving the last customer a lot sooner than he had anticipated. He walked over to see what his sister was doing and wasn’t very surprised to see her still talking to the guy.

“Dex, I was just about to tell Jazz that you’re my project.”

“Yup. That’s me,” Dex sighed. “A project.”

“A superior one.” Alicia said proudly. “I’m going to film my brother building his gourmet foods empire.”

“Yeah, like Caesar, but with better dressing,” Dex quipped. “Why would he care?”

Alicia gave him a look that warned *shut up* just in case he was going to take his questions too far.

“Jazz is in my class.” She couldn’t contain her smile.

“Okay,” Dex said, “this is starting to make sense.”

“Well it sounds like you have a fine subject in order, Alicia.” Jazz offered. “And lucky you, you’ll never have to worry about ordering lunch.”

Alicia was floating. Jazz remembered her name.

Dex put an extra cookie into Jazz’s bag and handed him the order. “Thanks for waiting.”

“The pleasure was mine.” Jazz was gazing at Alicia as he paid Dex.

If Dex had wanted, he could have easily kept the change and Jazz would have never noticed. But, he wasn’t that kind of businessman.

Chapter 11

The cafeteria was even more crowded than usual when Dex finally showed up to eat lunch. It was hard to imagine there were any students in actual classrooms. He would have been there earlier, but when class ended his Italian teacher asked him for tips on how to keep her stuffed shells from getting mushy. He didn't mind staying after, but the idea of sitting at some table by himself and scarfing down his sandwich was not very appealing.

He gazed through a sea of people standing on line at the vending machines and was relieved when he saw Liza and Jordy wave at him from their usual table.

"What up wit you, Flour Child?" asked Jordy, chewing a wad of gum.

"Yeah. You're late today," Liza chimed in.

"Forgot my lab notes in my locker," Dex explained and sat down. "Anything exciting happening?"

Liza and Jordy both nodded toward a table of geeky kids.

"Oswald asked his parents if he could get his tongue pierced and now they're sending him to military school." Liza took a bite of an orange segment.

Jordy popped a bubble with his gum and added, "Those folkers be jokers givin'the boy that go-by."

"Yeah, at least I was named after a diva," Liza boasted.

"We know, we know, Miss Liza Minelli," Jordy sighed. "Your daddy Chris's cousin like eighty times removed." He popped another piece of gum in his mouth. "And don't be singing that nasty *New York, New York* song again or I'm'a spit gum beebees at you."

“Oh hush, you don’t know good music,” Liza defended.

“I sure know bad music,” Jordy confirmed. “And don’t rap a word about my dad, Liza. I mean it.” He blew a huge bubble.

“Now kids,” Dex interrupted, pulling a bagel out of a small paper bag, “Play nice.”

Liza’s eyes widened and her jaw dropped when she saw Dex’s lunch.

“A bagel?” Jordy smirked.

“Sometimes it’s nice to keep things light and simple.” Dex took a guarded bite. “Just ask poor Oswald.”

Kyle came over to the table eating a corndog. “What’d I miss?”

“Kyle, are you crazy?” Liza scolded, pointing to the greasy dog. “That thing would make my granny burp like a frat boy! Why don’t you just jump off a bridge?!” She grabbed the corndog from Kyle just as he was about to take another bite and tossed it toward a trash can a few feet away. It ricocheted off the rim of the pail and hit Tracey Waters, the most popular girl in school, right in the center of her forehead. Everyone at her table, including Sarah, gasped as the corndog found its intended goal and sunk into the pail.

Tracey stood up, screamed a few words that surely would have gotten her detention, and scanned the room in search of the offending dog pitcher. Sarah left the group and went to speak to her gym teacher who was posted at the door on hall duty. Enlisting the rest of her entourage, Tracey stopped at each table asking for leads like she was an agent on CSI.

"Uh-oh! Dat sweetbeast on da hunt!" Jordy grabbed Liza by the arm, "C'mon, slick ya heels." He ushered her out of the cafeteria just before they could be questioned.

Sarah walked back into the cafeteria to get a soda and watched as Tracey and company continued to walk around in search of clues. No one seemed to have noticed the event and if they had, no one was talking. Kyle and Dex remained calm as Tracey reached their table.

"Did one of you freaks hit me with that disgusting corndog?"

"No. Why would we want to do that?" Dex asked smugly.

"Death wish," Tracey glowered.

"No. We like life," Kyle affirmed with several nods.

Tracey rolled her eyes like she'd been wasting her time. "Losers," she jabbed, giving Dex and Kyle one more disapproving sneer before turning back to her crew for supportive hugs. The love-fest ended and then, as if on cue, they all spun around in the same dramatic way and walked out.

"Well this was fun." Kyle zipped his book bag. "I gotta go. Spanish test." He left making sure to head in the opposite direction of Tracey.

Then, almost out of nowhere, Sarah was sitting down next to Dex. He was peeling a banana and her presence made him feel awkward. Her silence was even worse.

"So...you excited about your bat-mitzvah?" It was the only thing Dex could think of that would make her talk long enough for him to finish eating.

"Yeah, it's going to be amazing," Sarah exclaimed. "But, I have a little problem."

So much for that strategy. Dex looked at his banana and sighed. "What's wrong?"

"I need a favor. And I can't think of anyone better to ask than you." Sarah sounded worried.

"Me?"

"It's about my uncle, Yan Yan."

"Yan Yan? Gourmet Chinese straight from your grocer's freezer?"

"Yes, that's him."

"He's your uncle?!" Dex grinned. "Wow. That's awesome!"

"Nice man. Anyway, his daughter in Hong Kong went and had twins last night, a month early."

"Congratulations!"

"Thanks," Sarah answered, clearly underwhelmed. "But now my uncle can't come to my bat-mitzvah."

"Sorry."

"Me too. He was supposed to run the stir-fry station during my cocktail hour."

"That sounds so cool!"

"So, you'll do it?" Sarah asked, perking up.

"Do what?"

"Run the stir-fry station at my bat-mitzvah."

"Me?"

"Well you always look like you know what you're doing in class. You get 'A's on everything you make. And my parents said they can't find anyone on such short notice. The catering place only has guys that slice meat, serve pasta. Stuff like that."

"I guess." Dex couldn't imagine disappointing her.

"Great!" Sarah got up to leave. "My parents will call you later to go over the details."

"Sure," Dex said, tossing his banana into the trash.

#

Everyone was in the family room watching TV, except Dex who sat at the kitchen table eating a croissant. Between homework, corndogs, and Sarah's bat-mitzvah, he couldn't focus on any one thing. He was still amazed at how cool his parents had been when he asked if he could work the stir-fry station. Not only did they agree, but Marla said she would go with him in case he needed help. He didn't think that was necessary, but Marla loved catered parties and this one promised to be exceptional.

Alicia came into the kitchen just as Dex answered the phone.

"Hello?" he paused, "Mr. Rosenbaum?" He paused again. "Yes, this *is* Dex."

Alicia got a bowl from the cabinet and then went to browse through the pantry for a snack. She was taking her time about it and Dex figured she was listening to his conversation.

“Sarah told me about everything,” Dex relayed, wondering what she had said to her father about him.

“No,” Dex assured, “it’s not a problem at all.” He jotted a few notes on a piece of paper. “Yes, my parents signed the forms and my mom is coming with me.”

Dex was surprised when the conversation continued. “A videographer? Your videographer broke his arm? Oh wow. Uh, no I don’t really know anyone--”

“Yes you do!” Alicia beamed.

Chapter 12

"The last time I was at a bat-mitzvah it was yours," Dex said to Alicia, looking up as the sun filtered through the colorful stained-glass windows that bathed the synagogue in a soft glow. "Everyone said I was cute and I wasn't in charge of cooking anything."

Dex was staring down at the busy pattern on the carpet when a little boy in a blue suit burst through a side entrance running down the center aisle screaming 'Shazam!' He sideswiped Dex who nearly fell on Alicia. She quickly turned on her camera to record the commotion.

The boy's father apologized on the run as he chased after his son waving a big cookie with sprinkles in his hand. People stopped their conversations to watch the unfolding saga.

The boy ignored his father and continued to run, all the while making noises as if he were an exploding bomb.

"Ivan!" his father bellowed, offering his son another shot at the cookie if he would please behave.

Alicia followed the boy's path as he continued to run freely around the synagogue and out through another exit.

"Well, at least *you're* still cute," Alicia assured Dex, turning off the camera. "Not sure what the future holds in store for that little guy."

"Thanks," he chuckled as he gazed around the synagogue wondering why he hadn't seen Sarah yet. Was she taking pictures or talking to relatives who hadn't seen her since she started walking? Naturally, that was the moment Hunter walked in. Dex tapped Alicia's arm.

"That's Sarah's boyfriend," he whispered.

"Really?" she said, giving him the once-over. "Nothing special. You're way cuter."

"You're just saying that, right?"

"No Dex, I would never go out of my way to suck up to you." Alicia scanned the room and raised her eyebrows when she found the right spot to place the tripod.

"Come," she said, handing Dex a camera to hold as they walked to the back of the room.

"You look tense," Alicia said, as she set up the tripod near a case lined with prayer books. "How do you feel?"

"Okay, I guess."

"You guess? So you're nervous, huh?"

"No sugar Sherlock. I don't know. A lot of these people look uncomfortable."

"Really?" She was adjusting a knob. "I hadn't noticed."

"Well you should. It's your job," Dex snapped, but she was too busy setting up to respond. "Leesh, look at these guys. They're going to have to spend the next few hours stuck in the same suits and ties they have to wear for work."

"So? Big deal. The women have it worse."

Dex watched a group of women congregate in the back near the ladies' room. Some of them resembled mummies wrapped in dresses so tight Dex wasn't sure how they could breathe much less go to the bathroom.

"Wow. You're right," Dex mused. "And why do they have so much crud on their faces? Is the circus in town?"

Alicia giggled but didn't answer him.

One woman with fat, shiny red lips walked slowly past Dex. She was wearing glittery heels so high she could've joined Cirque du Soleil. Dex couldn't understand why people celebrated an occasion they wanted to enjoy by dressing in clothes and shoes that made it impossible.

Dex scanned the room and saw his mother talking to one of the guests. He was glad she seemed happy. She had lost weight and didn't need to wear a dress that forced her stomach in. He took note of her feet. Normal shoes. He was proud of her. Sometimes the little things mattered.

#

The rabbi chanted a few blessings and then called Sarah to the pulpit. Dex realized he had never noticed how long her hair was. Maybe because she wore it up a lot for school. Stupid butterflies in his stomach were making him feel sick. He wondered if this was how Kyle felt all the time. That would royally suck.

With all eyes on her, Sarah began to sing her portion of the service. As soon as the first note came out of her mouth, Dex was glad she was pretty. He saw a few people wince at times as she squawked her way through to the end. By the time she was done, Dex couldn't help but wonder if the applause was for her performance or because it was over.

Sarah was still at the pulpit when the rabbi called her parents to the stage to join her. If anyone thought Liza's family was different because she was black and had two gay, white dads, they didn't know Sarah. Sarah's dad was a Chinese Jew. His father had fought in Korea, met a Chinese nurse, and fallen in love. According to Sarah, it was her grandmother's decision to convert to Judaism. They were married and, soon after, Sarah's father was born.

As a graduate student, Sarah's father went to study international politics in Korea. While there, he met an American English teacher, a Jewish woman who was scheduled to return to the states the same time he was. They got engaged and stayed together throughout their time in Korea. When they came back, they got married at Temple Emanu-El in Manhattan, the largest, and often considered most beautiful, synagogue in the world.

The funny thing was, some of Sarah's relatives were very Chinese and some of her relatives were very Jewish. And some of them, like her family, existed somewhere in between. Her bat-mitzvah was the first time the two families and cultures were together since her parents' wedding.

The rabbi said a few words and Sarah's parents sat down, but she stayed at the pulpit. For some, this next part was more nerve-wracking than having to chant blessings in Hebrew. The bat-mitzvah girl was expected to make a speech sharing something important and meaningful to her. Sarah spent the next several minutes discussing her diverse, interesting background and went on to explain how each person in the room played an important part in shaping her life.

It wasn't surprising that there was thunderous applause when she concluded by saying, "As I look around the room, I see my wonderful parents, and all the people who care the most about me. Here we are together, Chinese, American, Jewish, not Jewish, and we're all family. Or, as my Bubbe would say, one big happy *mishpocha*."

The moment Sarah was done speaking, a group of guests and congregants started singing and, as customary, hurling soft, wrapped candies at her to make her introduction into womanhood as sweet as possible. She almost lost her footing laughing so hard as fruit gels and chocolate kisses fell at her feet. She managed to calm down long enough to steady herself against the pulpit, but that was no match for Ivan, the little boy in the blue suit, who shouted a triumphant 'Shazam,' as he tackled Sarah to get to the sweets.

Without thinking, Dex dashed to the rescue and lifted Sarah to her feet before anyone else had the chance. She looked a little pale, and Dex wiped away a stray tear that trickled down her cheek. For an instant, Dex felt like a superhero, and could see a better version of himself in her eyes. But then Hunter stepped in between them along with Sarah's parents and most of the guests, and the connection was lost.

Dex surveyed the room and noticed that Alicia and the tripod were gone and the large folding wall that separated the sanctuary from the reception area was still closed. She was probably on the other side setting up for the cocktail hour, something he still needed to do. He went out to the hallway hoping to find anyone who might be able to help him get started. All he found was Alicia near the cloak room filming Ivan's father carrying the brat out of the building upside down by his ankles.

#

Game time. Dex had been pacing up and down the lobby outside the reception area so many times the carpet had lingering impressions of his footprints. By now, he had a firm idea of how he would approach each dish and handle the crowd, but he was afraid he'd forget everything if he didn't get to work soon. He was surprised he hadn't been sent to speak to anyone, but he had never done this before and had no clue about proper procedure. Maybe everyone was expected to do their own thing without instructions. Seemed weird, but this wasn't Mrs. Baker's International Cooking class and anything was possible. At least he had his mom and sister. Marla and Alicia would be moral support even if he didn't need them for anything else.

A woman in a tuxedo vest suddenly came up behind Dex. Rather than talk to him though, she began prompting guests exiting the sanctuary to enjoy the cheese and fruit table that had just been rolled into the waiting area. Before he had the chance to get her attention, the woman left. Dex panicked. At the rate this crowd was eating, there would be no time for him to prepare. Just then a short, wiry man tapped him on the shoulder. He had a ridiculously thin moustache, was dressed in a too-big tuxedo, and wore a gold name tag identifying him as Enrique. "This *eesn't* even my *yob*, but they tell me bring you here. Come now please!"

Enrique was snippy, and Dex realized he must be the go-to guy whenever the hall was short-staffed. He felt sorry for the overworked man, who was swimming in his supplied tuxedo as he walked.

Enrique led Dex on a brief tour of the cocktail area, a dimly lit space studded with small tables and set apart from the larger reception room by yet another folding wall. Dex laughed to himself as Enrique ushered him past different tables that featured such dishes as: *WONTON MATZOH BALL SOUP, ORI-YENTL LENTIL, JEW GOO GAI PAN, SALAMI EGG FOO YOUNG,* and *BOK CHOY KUGEL.* There were dozens of bottles of *OY SAUCE*, forks, and chopsticks on every table. Aside from a 'Kids Only' *HAPPY HAMBURGER* table, each station echoed Sarah's Chinese-Jewish theme.

By the time they reached Dex's stir-fry station, Enrique was nearing a meltdown. Some "*idiota*," he seethed, had forgotten to put the pagoda napkin holders on the tables, and now the culprit had to "lose his head" for the mistake. *A bit much,* Dex thought as he shifted his attention to his new work space. A knot in an extension cord lying across the floor caught his eye. He knelt down to fix it and when he got up Enrique was across the room on his way out the door.

This was the real deal. Dex was on his own. Luckily, everything seemed pretty self-explanatory. In seconds he had the woks seasoned and with a few clicks and turns he found out the burners were easy to control. There were pre-prepared heaping bowls of chopped vegetables and sliced meats. The oils and sauces were neatly marked and in convenient squeeze containers that Dex decided he'd put on his 'to buy' list on his iPhone later on. All he had to do was put everything together and make it taste good.

Dex took a deep breath. It was all going to work out, and after this, Sarah would never forget that she was his partner in International Cooking. He tied the apron around his waist a little tighter and let his eyes wander around the room. Marla was chatting with Sarah's mother and Alicia was setting up her camera on a tripod near the dance floor. Dex was impressed at how relaxed Alicia seemed.

Relax, he said to himself loud enough to hear. It was a good word. He took another deep breath. A couple came over and asked for beef and broccoli. In moments, Dex was tossing ingredients and wielding his long chopsticks like he could run a stir-fry station in his sleep. After spending hours helping Jimmy, the owner, at Golden Chow, his family's favorite take-out place, prepare everything from wonton soup to deep-friend kumquats in plum glaze, Dex didn't expect anything less from himself.

A crowd started to gather around to watch him, and Marla proudly positioned herself to get a clear view. Alicia was now roaming with a portable camera and found a spot to make sure she didn't miss Dex's performance.

"That boy can really cook!" Mr. Rosenbaum said, savoring a bite of Hunan chicken.

"Yes, he certainly can and he's a natural in front of the camera," Alicia noted, then captured Dex in an isolated still shot.

Dex was tossing *lo mein* when he noticed Preston LeTray coming out of one of the kitchen doors carrying two trays, one of raw vegetables and another of *moo shu* pancakes. Dex was shocked. Why was a celebrity chef working at Sarah's bat-mitzvah?

Preston walked toward Dex's station with his head held high in the air, completely ignoring the chopstick house a few little kids had just made. With one less-than graceful step, Preston tripped over the house, sending the vegetables flying into the air one way, the pancakes another, and landing him flat on his face right behind the crowd of people at Dex's station.

Everyone was enthralled by Dex's performance and didn't notice. Everyone but Marla, whose eyes widened as the vegetables from Preston's tray fell perfectly into Dex's wok. The audience applauded with delight, thinking this was part of the show.

Dex shouted, "Thanks, Mr. LeTray!" too engaged to realize it had been an accident. He continued to cook and talk, all the while dazzling his audience.

"Preston. Are you okay?" asked Marla, crouching down to the floor.

“Fantastic Marla. Flipping fantastic.” Preston wiped a few pepper seeds off his face and stood up.

“Well it worked out great,” Marla grinned. “You couldn’t have planned it better!” She pointed to Dex, who was still busy serving up plates of food to amazed guests.

Preston grimaced, brushed off his clothes and walked out.

#

“See, Dex,” said a little, freckled-face blonde, “I’m like you,” she insisted, sprinkling salt and pepper into glasses of ice water. Without an assigned seat, Dex was stuck at a table in the ballroom with a group of little kids. He watched miserably as Sarah danced with Hunter. His blaze of glory during the cocktail hour seemed to wane as quickly as it had come.

Alicia saw him and walked over. “Why are you sitting here?”

“No choice,” he sighed. “I wasn’t really invited. There’s no room anywhere else.”

“Where’s Mom?”

“She had to pick up Dad and Geema. They’re going to that that new place with every imaginable pancake.” He took a cookie from a plate on the table and popped it in his mouth. “Chocolate Berry Bomb—that’s the best one. Liza’s dads took us.”

“Right. Mom promised Geema. Half-price for seniors on Saturdays.”

“Please tell me you’re ready to go,” Dex pleaded.

"Who's the guy in the gray suit?" Alicia said, ignoring him. "He keeps pointing over here."

"I don't know. Maybe he has a crush on you. Doesn't everyone?"

"Cute, Dexpert, cute. I'm serious," she directed Dex's gaze. "Him."

"I don't know. Someone said he's Sarah's uncle, some kind of TV producer. I made him a plate before, I think."

They sat for a little while watching people dance. One old couple, according to Alicia, made every song a waltz, while another found a reason to twirl and dip every few seconds. A short, chubby guy was moving like a professional until he dipped his tall wife so low that she nearly hit her head on the marble floor. He pulled her up as fast as he could, but she yelled something at him and marched away before he could coax her back.

Alicia was putting in a new tape when she noticed the mysterious gazer engage Sarah's father in what appeared to be a deep conversation. She jabbed Dex's arm. "Look at them. What do you think they're talking about?"

"Global warming?" Dex quipped. "The price of tea in China?" He made himself chuckle. "How should I know?" He threw his hands up in the air. "I want to go."

Alicia shook her head, "Aren't you the least bit interested in what they're talking about over there?" she asked, tilting her head.

"Yes, the least bit." Dex grabbed Alicia's hand and looked at the time. "See," he said, pushing her watch under her nose, "It's been hours. I'm tired."

"Stop being a child," she scolded, tugging free from his grasp.

"I *am* a child. Come on Leesh. We can go, can't we?" he whined.

"Soon," she snapped. "The party's almost over."

"So then can we leave?"

Alicia started to answer, but Sarah came over to them before she had the chance.

"Dex, can you please stay with me?" Sarah said her eyes glazed over with tears. "My parents will drive you home."

Dex glanced at Alicia sheepishly.

"Sure. I can stay with you. Right, Leesh?"

"No problem." Alicia smirked and rolled her eyes. "I'm going to get footage of guests leaving and then I'm heading home." She slung her camera case over her shoulder. "Happy bat-mitzvah, Sarah. See you later, Dex," she added as she walked away.

Dex turned to Sarah who looked more distraught than ever.

"What's going on?" Dex asked.

"You're so not going to believe this," Sarah announced. "Hunter broke up with me!"

#

Dex got out of the Rosenbaums' car and thanked them for the ride home. He flew into the house so quickly he didn't even feel his feet hit the pavement. He had to talk to Alicia. She was a girl, she would understand what he was supposed to feel and, more importantly, she would be able to tell him what to do.

"Leesh?" he called from the family room. He thought for sure she'd be watching *General Hospital*. It seemed like she had a way to set it on the DVR for 'all-the-time.'

"Hello?" Nothing.

He went upstairs to change and noticed Alicia's light on through the crack at the bottom of her door.

"Leesh?" Dex called, opening her door very slowly. His friend Dean had once told him about a time he accidentally walked in on his sister making out with her boyfriend, and she got so angry at him she threw his math homework in the litter box. Even though Dex's family didn't have a cat, he sucked at algebra and he didn't want to take any chances.

"Leesh," he said again as a warning signal, but there wasn't a sound. He opened the door and was relieved to find her alone, but why was she crying into her pillow.

"What's wrong?" He waited for some kind of response, but there was none. "Is this about that Jazz guy?"

"No! It has nothing to do with him," she retorted, handing Dex a typewritten letter. "It's this."

"This is a final notice to inform you that...," Dex's voice trailed off and he read the rest of the letter silently.

Alicia broke in. "Bottom line, Dex. We're losing the restaurant."

"How is that possible?" he argued. "Geema said we're just closed for renovations."

"Obviously she's been lying. Dad just lost his business, Mom does a commercial like every three months, and we're in school full time. I'm sure she didn't want us to worry."

"You're probably right," Dex mused.

"What now?"

"How'd you get this letter anyway?"

"I had just gotten home from the bat-mitzvah when the doorbell rang. A couple on Brook Hollow stopped by and dropped it off." Brook Hollow was the street behind theirs. Dex nodded.

"Somehow," Alicia continued, "it was delivered to them."

"New mailman," Dex said. "He likes my asparagus tarts, but he makes a lot of mistakes."

"Well, that couple made one too. They opened the letter before they saw it wasn't addressed to them." Alicia wiped her smeared make-up with the back of her hand. "Dex, what are we going to do?"

"Well, it says we have 'til New Year's." Dex scanned the page.

"It could say we have until pigs fly."

"Leesh, at least *try* to be optimistic."

"Okay. Fine." Alicia got up and looked out the window. "So what's up with Sarah? Must have been important if she had her parents take you home."

"Hunter broke up with her."

“At her bat-mitzvah. Wow! What an ass.”

“I know, but she said she likes this other guy.”

“You know him?”

“She wouldn’t tell me who it is.”

“It’s probably you.”

“I don’t think so.” Dex picked up the letter from the bed to read it again.

“Okay. So, what do you think we should do?”

“I say, we get the restaurant back.”

“You’re dreaming.” Alicia snatched the paper from Dex and tucked it away in her desk drawer.

“No, I’m working. And failure is not an option.”

“That’s a cute thought, but even all the money from your sandwich stand for the next twenty years wouldn’t be enough. Besides, isn’t that money supposed to pay for your *Gymbuff*?”

Dex inhaled deeply, and then let out a sigh.

“Plans change.”

Chapter 13

Dex shifted restlessly in his seat. The earbuds of his iPod landed on the glass conference table in front of him. He glanced around nervously. He was listening to Jordy's favorite song, 'Gangnam Style,' by PSY. That wasn't so terrible. But had anyone else heard the rocket take off in the pit of his stomach? Too bad, it wasn't his fault. It was already after five and he hadn't eaten anything since the tuna and ginger slaw wrap he made for lunch. Had he known he would be waiting forever to meet this Ezra guy, he never would have let Liza have his extra oatmeal cookie.

He thought about wandering through the halls in search of a vending machine, but the Eatz Network building wasn't the kind of place to find a Snickers bar. He wasn't even sure why they'd bothered to wade through afternoon traffic across town to get here. All his parents told him when they picked him up from school was that Ezra Langer, Sarah's uncle, and the president of the network, wanted to meet with them at his office to 'talk.' It seemed cool at first, but so far Ezra was, as his receptionist put it, 'regretfully detained in a meeting' and a few of his associates were doing all the talking. And only with his parents.

Since they'd arrived and been seated, Marla and Vince had been engaged in conversation with a round-bellied guy in a cream suit and a stocky woman in a chocolate-brown dress. Together they reminded Dex of a brownie a la mode which only made him feel hungrier. Vince was now explaining to the Brownie Woman how smart it would be for Eatz to team up with Entrée, the gourmet food market, to create and sell all kinds of products.

"Marketing and merchandising, that's where all the big money possibilities are," Vince asserted, stroking his newly grown goatee. "Just takes money to make money."

The Ice Cream Guy nodded and got up to take a phone call. Then two other people came into the room, a younger guy in jeans and Nikes, and a tall guy in a navy blue suit who looked almost as bored as Dex. They sat down and the conversation continued as if there had been no interruption.

Dex picked up his book bag and took out his homework. Maybe the distraction would help his hunger subside. But after finishing two social studies worksheets about the Potato Famine in Ireland, he was even more famished. It felt like at least an hour since they had arrived and Dex could swear the clock wasn't moving. He could feel his stomach twisting.

Dex couldn't wait. Since Marla had been dieting he knew there was no chance for M&Ms, but she would at least have one of those chocolate covered, cardboard bars she insisted were brimming with nutrition somewhere in her enormous pocketbook.

He gave his mother a nudge with his knee that made her jump.

"Ow," Marla exclaimed, furrowing her brow at him.

Dex didn't care. "I'm starving," he whined.

Marla's face softened as she dug into her bag, searching through every nook and cranny. At first she frowned like he was out of luck, but one more plunge and she was smiling.

"Here you go, Honey," she beamed as she proudly handed Dex a breath mint. Before he had the chance to protest, her back was in his face and she was agreeing with something Vince had just said about kids and food being a popular combination in today's demanding market.

Dex wasn't interested. He was a kid demanding food and

getting nowhere. Brownie Woman got up to refill her coffee cup, and Dex's stomach rumbled louder than a lawnmower firing up for a war on weeds. He got up from his chair and started to walk toward the door. Who would miss him? Judging from the past hour, he didn't even need to be there. Rather than bother his parents he offered them one quick wave he was sure they didn't notice and grabbed the sleek metal door handle. Ezra Langer nearly toppled over Dex as the two met face to face more closely than either had intended.

"Well, thank you young man, much obliged," said Ezra, assuming Dex had politely opened the door for him.

Dex just stood there like he had rocks in his socks. If he was supposed to make any kind of good first impression on this man, it was definitely time to go home.

"Why don't you come join us," Ezra said as he took his powerful seat at the head of the oblong table.

Dex heard him, but he still wasn't moving. Not only was he hungry, now he was nervous too. This was all too weird. Waiting was one thing, but everyone in the room stopped talking as soon as Ezra walked in. Why was this guy so important? And what could he possibly want from Dex?

"Dex, come sit down." Marla tapped the empty seat next to her.

Dex stared at his mother blankly, but found himself following her voice to the chair.

"First, I'd like to apologize for being late," Ezra said, acknowledging the clock on the wall. "Budget meetings can be relentless."

There were a few groans of agreement and then silence.

"I imagine you're wondering why I called you in." Ezra was now addressing Dex and his parents. "I'm a firm believer in the saying, 'If you snooze, you lose,' and frankly, after what I saw at my niece Sarah's bat-mitzvah, we simply cannot afford to lose Dex."

"Why? What did I do?!" Dex blurted out.

"One of the most difficult things on this great planet; you kept a crowd of people happily eating off their plates and out of your hands." Ezra turned to Marla and Vince. "That takes talent. The kind of talent that makes money."

"I'm not sure what you're getting at," Vince said.

"You want Dex to help one of your chefs, or something like that?" Marla asked.

"No, Dex isn't a side dish; he's an entrée," Ezra said, his arms outstretched. "You don't take caviar and treat it like tuna fish. You have to honor it."

Ezra stood up and walked over to the window. "I've discussed this decision with some of my associates, but for others this will be news as well." He took a moment at the tallest window in the conference room to watch a flock of birds pass.

Vince and Marla gave each other a quizzical shrug.

Ezra went over and put his hands on Dex's shoulders. "So Dex, how would you like to have your own cooking show?"

"What??? Me??? On TV??? Cooking?!?!?" Dex shrieked.

Brownie Woman's eyes nearly popped out of her head,

which let Dex know she was included in those who hadn't been told. The Ice Cream Guy was pretty shocked too, but the one in the jeans just swigged his Red Bull like he had known all along.

"Wow!" Marla was nearly speechless.

"Is this for real?" Vince asked, worried they were being set up. He and Marla had seen their share of reality TV, making caution his first instinct. That and a peek around the room for a hidden camera.

"Yes, it most certainly is," Ezra assured. "You, Dex, will be the youngest Eatz Network chef in history."

"This can't possibly be," Marla protested. "You don't even know our son."

"I know what I saw," Ezra defended. "Genius. I don't pass on genius."

Ezra turned his attention back to Dex.

"Like all our stars, you'll have a live show, cooking in front of an audience. But, please understand, this idea of mine is coming out of nowhere. The budget's already been set, so now I'm taking on a huge risk. I also have to consider advertising and marketing costs. Basically, I can't offer you much of a salary 'til we see where this goes. But, if I'm right, and luckily I usually am, I think you'll have more than a comfortable future to look forward to."

Ezra turned back to Vince and Marla. "What do you think?"

"I'm not sure I can think right now," Marla admitted. "What about school? Dex is only twelve."

"Almost thirteen," Dex argued.

"Absolutely," Vince said, ignoring Dex. "We can't neglect Dex's education."

"Understood," Ezra continued. "We'll only need him a couple of days a week after school. He'll rehearse one day and we'll tape live another."

Suddenly the conference room door flew open and in walked Preston LeTray, who sauntered in as though he owned the place. He seemed oblivious to the meeting going on and Dex noticed that he ignored everyone except for a slight nod to Marla. Preston stood over Ezra like a bully about to steal his lunch money and grimaced, annoyed that he couldn't have the room to himself.

Ezra scowled back as he excused himself to deal with his star chef. Their conversation didn't last very long, but Ezra seemed exhausted even after Preston left. He walked back to Dex and his parents and a big smile grew on his face. Dex appreciated the effort even though he could tell it was forced.

"So, what do you think?" Ezra asked again.

#

Preston LeTray huffed and puffed his way back to his office holding a new package from Buford when something stopped him in his tracks. He was extremely aware of scents, especially since meeting with Buford, and this one brought to mind a handful of vanilla beans. He sniffed a few more times enjoying the way it made him feel. Then he remembered. He was smelling Marla. He followed his nose and was unsurprised when he saw her by the elevator replacing a bottle of perfume in her bag.

"Congratulations, Marla," Preston offered, softly coming up behind her.

Marla whirled around to face him.

"I heard about your son's offer. You must be so proud."

"Thank you, Preston," Marla said, then took a deep breath. "Vince and I *are* very proud of him."

"You have every reason to be," Preston said as he hit the down button for the lobby. "You know I've thought about you since the shoot. You still look beautiful, the same as you did the night I hid your engagement ring in one of Poppy's garlic knots."

"That was a very long time ago," Marla answered, looking down at her wedding ring.

"Yes, it was. And for you, one big mistake ago. How is Vince, by the way?" Preston's upper lip began to twitch.

"We're fine, Preston. Just fine. I have to go," Marla insisted and quickly opted for the stairs, leaving Preston at the elevator alone.

It was hard for Preston to think about that night. He'd made such big plans for his future.

#

It was early summer, 1985, right after President Reagan's speech challenging Gorbachev to tear down the Berlin Wall. Preston had been listening to the radio on his way back from a wine-tasting when a commercial convinced him he desperately needed a pint of *Cherry Garcia*, the newest Ben & Jerry's flavor he had yet to try.

He pulled into the parking lot at *Pathmark*, the only supermarket in his neighborhood that stayed open late, and practically leaped out of the car. But when he got to the freezer case, they were all out of stock. Some nerve. He admonished the manager and stomped out of the store, letting his heels hit the floor with a continuous thud.

Preston got into his aging Datsun and slammed the rusting door shut. He clenched the steering wheel tightly. He wasn't just hungry, he was angry. What would make him feel better and satisfy his eager palate? Not pancakes, too soft. Not sorbet, too fruity. There had to be something. And then it hit him-- a big, fat *cannoli* from Poppy's Kitchen. He licked his lips and put the car in drive.

He knew it was past serving time when he arrived at the restaurant, but in a few months he would be family and the place would practically be his. The door was locked, but he could see a couple of employees cleaning up through the window. He knocked and knocked until a busboy finally opened the door.

"Sorry, we're closed." The kid had removed his black vest, but he was still wearing his white shirt.

"Not to me you're not," chided Preston. "Don't you know who I am?" Preston's eyes widened to monstrous proportions.

"Yeah, some wacked dude who's keeping me from getting the dishes done," the kid shot back, starting to close the door.

Preston stuck his leg through and forced the door back open. "I'm going to have you fired, you little twerp!" he spewed as he walked through the door.

Preston hadn't heard Marla tell the kid it was okay to let him in. She had been standing behind the partition between the kitchen and the dining room where she was hidden from view.

The kid rolled his eyes and walked away. Marla came out

taking Preston by surprise.

“Oh, good you’re here!” Preston exclaimed. “I wanted to tell you that I found just the right wine to pair with the *Croque-Madame* for the after-wedding brunch. Very fruity. You’ll love it.” Preston took off his coat and flung it over a chair. “Why don’t you get me a *cannoli* and come have a seat.”

“Preston, we have to talk,” Marla said, quietly.

“Well of course we do. We’re getting married in a few weeks.”

“Preston-”

“Marla,” he interrupted, “just go get me the *cannoli* and then we’ll talk.”

She sighed and left him sitting at the table. Preston surveyed the dining room. There were so many changes he would make once they were married. He’d start by getting rid of the insolent busboy and then move on to the dark wood tables and their over-bearing matching chairs. The lace tablecloths and the faded carpeting had to go too. The whole place was mediocre, and he decided he’d change everything except the address.

Marla came out with a *cannoli* and placed it dutifully in front of Preston.

“Come sit,” he said, as one might command a cocker-spaniel.

“I’m sorry Preston. I just can’t.”

“Of course you can. I don’t need you to get me anything else. This looks delicious,” he piled a forkful of the pastry into his mouth. “Well, a glass of milk would be nice.”

Marla went to the kitchen and returned with a glass of milk.

"Good girl," Preston beamed.

"This isn't going to work," Marla blurted.

"Oh, I know. I see how much I'm going to have to change this place," he noted and gazed around the room again. "But, don't worry. I'm up to the task."

"I'm afraid I'm not."

"You don't have to be. You just have to look as pretty as you always do." He took her hand and kissed the engagement ring he'd given her. "And, of course, be there when I need you."

"Preston, you're not getting it." Marla took the ring off her finger and handed it to him. "I don't love you. I can't marry you." She walked away without turning back.

"Love? Love is not what marriage is about--" Preston said into the air.

#

Poppy was in the kitchen prepping for the next day when Preston burst in and pounded his fist on the counter.

"Hey, hey!" Poppy exclaimed, "What's going on?"

"Your daughter has lost her mind," Preston roared. "She broke our engagement!"

Poppy walked over to Preston and put his arm around his shoulder. "I'm sorry kid. That's a tough break," he comforted, giving him a pat on the back before he went back to chopping vegetables. "These things happen. Sometimes life starts one way and ends up another."

The phone in the dining room rang.

"But, in the end, everything always works out for the best." Poppy excused himself to take the call.

Preston looked around the busy kitchen. Much to his dismay, every pot had its place and each herb was fresh and fragrant. Poppy was running this place like a well-oiled machine, and his obvious skills had led to the kind of success that made Preston seethe with envy. Marla had ruined everything.

Preston was sure he'd done everything right. He'd told her the things women want to hear, took her to the finest restaurants, bought her stupid little cards and gifts, and promised he would always take care of her. What more could she have wanted? So, he did what he had to do. That was her fault, not his. No one was going to push him away from his dreams without paying up.

A piece of paper was sitting on the counter near the stove. 'Poppy's Pesto.' It was a recipe. *The* recipe. The one that had critics clamoring and diners driving for miles. This piece of paper was the dream, his dream.

"You're right Poppy," Preston said to himself. "Everything is going to turn out for the best after all," he concluded in a whisper.

Preston whipped out a pen from his shirt pocket and searched for paper. He couldn't even find a gum wrapper. He snatched a piece of paper towel from the holder on the wall and without moving the recipe a single hair, frantically copied it in its entirety before he could be discovered. When he was done he stuffed the towel into his pants pocket and took off like popcorn in a microwave.

Chapter 14

"I can't believe it! Our Dex is going to be an Eatz Network chef!" Vince exclaimed, making a turn onto the highway.

"I'm sure Poppy's up there celebrating with a great big *cannoli*," Marla said, eyeing Dex in the mirror of the passenger visor.

"Yeah," Dex muttered. He was in his own world. He had woken up worrying about cooking class and not having enough time to soak the raisins for his spice cookies. Now he was ending the day worrying about having time for classes and his own TV show. His fingers hurt from texting back and forth with Kyle and Liza who sounded almost more excited than he did. The good news was that he might not have to wait forever to buy the *Gymbuff* and could get Sarah to go out with him by spring break.

Vince pulled into their neighborhood. The Eatz Studio was an easy ride from their house, only fifteen minutes if there was no traffic or construction. Dex noticed a school bus driving by and saw Rhonda at the wheel. They waved to each other as if she hadn't just bought a Canadian bacon and egg *panini* from him earlier that day. It was always more exciting to see someone unexpectedly.

"Who was that?" Marla asked, rubbing on some vanilla-scented lotion she'd pulled out of the glove compartment.

"Rhonda. She's one of my customers." Dex watched the bus disappear around the corner and suddenly became worried. "What's going to happen to my business? What am I going to do about my lunch stand?"

"You'll still have plenty of time before school to stay 'King of the Gourmet Lunch,'" Vince assured as he pulled into their driveway. "If that's still what you want."

“Yeah. I guess,” was all Dex could muster as he got out of the car, his head spinning so fast it was hard to move.

“Go on in the house,” Vince called out the window as he now pulled back out of the driveway. “Your mom and I have a few errands to run. We’ll be back soon. Hey, how about I pick up that kitchen sink pizza you like from Cortazzo’s?”

“Sounds great!” Dex yelled, with renewed energy.

The thought of the gooey cheese, mixed with the fried eggplant and the salty anchovies, got Dex moving again. Although now he had to tell Geema to save whatever she was making for another night.

“Geema?” Dex shouted as he ran into the house through the back door.

He popped his head into the kitchen, but no one was there. This was probably the only day Geema wasn’t preparing something at this hour. He checked the family room, but it was dark. Great. When he had nothing to tell except that a bird pooped on his book bag, everyone was home. Now, when he had much bigger news, no one was around.

He ran upstairs and barged into Alicia’s room without even considering that she might be naked. Thankfully, she wasn’t.

“Eatz is giving me my own show.” It wasn’t exactly the way he had intended to tell her, but at the moment, it was the most practical.

“What are you talking about?”

“What I told you. That’s what the meeting with Sarah’s

uncle was for. That guy from the bat-mitzvah, remember? That's Ezra, the head of Eatz network. He wants to give me my own show."

"Oh my God! Dex, that's awesome!" Alicia jumped off her bed and hugged him so hard he nearly passed out. Then she ripped out a sheet of paper from the notebook lying on her desk. "Can I be the first to have your autograph?" she asked, handing him a pen.

He knew she was trying to make him feel good, but he was too preoccupied to play along.

"Maybe later." Dex started to leave the room, but turned around before he reached the door. "Can I see that letter again?"

Alicia opened her drawer and took out the notice from the bank.

Dex stared at it for a while. "Leesh, let's not say anything about this to mom and dad. Not Geema either. There's no sense making them worry." He knew he sounded like he had an actual plan in mind, but he didn't.

"Worry? You're going to be a TV star; you'll be able to pay for anything."

"Not exactly. This is more about the future than right now."

"Dex, that makes no sense."

"Whatever. I'm just telling you. I may not make much for a while." He waved the paper in the air. "Way past when this needs to be fixed." He put the letter back in Alicia's drawer.

"So no matter what happens we lose the restaurant."

"No. I'm sure we'll be able to work this whole thing out sooner than later," he said, trying to convince himself that it was still possible.

Chapter 15

They gave him one week. Ezra called and said the sponsors wanted Dex's show to air before the official start of the holiday season. That actually meant the day before yesterday, but Ezra was willing to give Dex one week to rehearse at home before filming in the studio. Marla had tried to convince Ezra that one week wasn't enough time, but he insisted that Dex was a natural and that his charm and skill would outweigh any little problems he might have.

"I'm not worried about the little problems, like spilling flour on the counter, or even dropping an egg shell into a batter," Dex explained to his mother. "It's the big ones, like setting the kitchen on fire, that scare me." He added whipped cream to the top of the strawberry shortcake sundae he made for them to share.

"You have nothing to worry about," Marla guaranteed. She took a big spoonful of ice cream. "You're an amazing chef."

"You're my mother. You have to say stuff like that. It's your job."

Marla opened the refrigerator and started rifling through the bins. "Having faith in you is not my job, it's my joy." She sounded wistful.

"What's wrong, Mom?"

"Do we have any sprinkles?" she sighed.

Dex laughed and got them from the cabinet. This was the first time in weeks she was eating something you wouldn't find in a rabbit cage.

"Listen Dex, I know a week doesn't sound like much time,"

she conceded, as she sprinkled the sundae, “but Ezra is a stranger and he believes in you and your talent. And he’d know better than anyone what people will watch. That has to count for something.”

“I guess,” Dex accepted, trying to be less negative. “It’s just that...”

“What?”

“It’s one thing to feel like a dork in gym class, but it would be a lot worse to prove it on national television.”

“That’s not going to happen,” Marla promised. “Call your friends and have them come over. What you need is an audience.”

#

Dex stood behind the kitchen counter assembling a line of ingredients and utensils. His rehearsal had to be authentic and he knew cooking shows always had that kind of stuff prepared in advance. That was the secret behind a meal made on TV being ready to serve in a half hour. Dex knew that with all the chopping and measuring he needed to do, he would have to add on at least another half hour.

The only thing he decided to save for his audience was the chopping. He knew people liked to watch a chef dice onions, grate ginger, and smash garlic. Maybe it was the speed and precision, or maybe they were waiting to see a professional make a mistake. He had to admit when Geema forced him to watch figure-skating, he counted on someone doing a butt-flop.

But that wasn’t going to happen to him. There would be no flopping of any kind. He had gone over the recipe a dozen times and he was more than ready to cook.

“Hey, Dexpert, looking good,” Alicia said from behind the

camera. She had started filming the night before as Marla set up seats in the family room for Dex's rehearsal. Earlier that morning, Marla booked a last minute commercial for glow-in-the-dark dishwashing gloves and Vince had gotten called to work when his assistant at the bakery came down with the flu. Neither would be at the rehearsal, but Alicia had promised to film everything so they wouldn't feel left out.

In Dex's opinion, Alicia was staying a little too true to her word. He complained she was shooting too much footage, but she said that was what editing was for.

"You're my work in progress," Alicia reminded him. "So deal."

Dex was so engrossed in his own thoughts about which bowls to use, and if sea salt would add more flavor than table salt, that he never heard the doorbell ring. He was taken aback when Kyle, Liza, Jordy, and Sarah walked into the family room, following behind Geema. Everyone said their hellos and then, as Marla had instructed them the day before, they all took seats in front of the kitchen counter like a real studio audience.

"How's it going?" Liza asked on the sly.

"I guess okay," Dex answered, then glanced over at Sarah. "What's she doing here?"

"You like her. I invited her." Liza smirked and gave Dex a little pinch on the cheek. "You can thank me later, doughboy."

"I will," Dex groaned, with a nervous smile. He walked behind the counter and took a few deep breaths hoping to quiet what felt like an octopus clawing at his gut. *Just start*, he murmured to himself. *Pick up a spoon, an onion, grate some garlic; do anything but stare at Sarah or fart*. Was this really show biz?

"Go ahead, Dex," Geema nudged, "You can start now."

Maybe she didn't realize he was trying. That was a good sign. It was much better for him if they thought he was waiting for them to be ready. He gave himself permission to stop obsessing, then began tying on a blue apron that read, *DINE WITH DEX*, a gift his parents had given him in honor of his new show.

The only thing missing was that big 'I-love-to-cook-on-TV' smile. He immediately planted one on his face and reminded himself it had to stay there even when he was chopping onions.

"Hey everyone! Thanks for coming!" Dex began before he could stop himself with yet another worrying thought. "So first off, it's really important to season your pasta water." He poured a handful of salt into a large pot. "Or you'll be stuck with nothing but a boring, wet noodle."

He got a chuckle from his audience and began to feel more comfortable. He moved over to another pot. "Classic marinara is a must-have in an Italian kitchen!" Dex exclaimed. "If it's not there you feel like part of your family is missing at the table."

Dex barely noticed as Alicia stood on a chair and held the camera above the cooking area.

"Looking good," he said, covering the pot after the addition of several garlic cloves. "Let's move onto our ground beef, pork, and chicken." Dex added the pre-measured herbs and spices.

"Now I don't know about you," he said, blending the mixture with gloved hands, "but I always like to rub my balls with some oil and garlic."

He heard Geema gasp and Jordy burst out laughing.

“Meatballs!” he shouted, realizing his little misstep. After a moment of hyperventilation, he continued. “Let’s go back to the sauce,” he said, regaining composure. “Now when you make tomato sauce, be sure to use the right utensils. I’ve got my own favorite wooden spoon, right here. My Poppy gave it to me.”

Dex lowered the spoon toward the pot, but a surge of hot steam burned his fingers.

“OW!” he yelped, letting go.

The spoon plopped into the boiling pot, and red hot tomato sauce splattered all over the counter and his apron. Dex did a pained dance as some of the burning sauce hit his head, and he smacked himself a few times to get it off. Jordy couldn’t contain his laughter and Liza punched him on the arm.

“Yo Chickee, don’t be bangin’ on my ‘ceps,” Jordy scolded, patting his wounded arm. Liza grumbled and turned away.

“I can’t do this!” Dex pounded his fists on the counter and started to walk away.

Alicia put down the camera and stopped him. “Remember?” she whispered in his ear, “failure is not an option.”

“Dex, stop worrying,” Geema advised. “No matter what happens, keep going. You’re doing great.”

Alicia was right. He had no choice. If they were going to save Poppy’s Kitchen, Dex had to be the best chef he could be. He pasted on the same smile he had mustered before and went back to the counter.

“Our pasta has been swimming long enough to be al dente, which literally means to the teeth, or a bit firm,” Dex offered, while he searched for something he didn't seem able to find. He scratched his head and opened a nearby cabinet.

"Ah, there you are!" he said, clutching the colander like a long lost friend. There was nothing entertaining about desperation and he was worried. He took a deep breath. *Just keep moving* was his favorite new phrase.

"Now we're going to put our spaghetti," he explained, as he began to pour out the water, "into this calendar. I mean... um...colander!"

Dex panicked. Another mistake, but this time he tried to stay focused on the task. Meatballs and spaghetti had been one of the first dishes he had ever made. He expected everything to go smoothly, only now the pasta was sticking to the pot. He was so nervous he hadn't filled the pot with enough water. A common problem for amateurs, but not so much for chefs who had their own TV shows. He carefully attempted to coax the spaghetti into the colander when his hand hit the side of the sink, sending all but a little of the pasta down the drain.

"Whoops," Dex chuckled, holding up the empty colander. "Dinner for one!" he exclaimed, before he had the chance to brood.

His audience nodded their approval giving Dex the confidence to continue.

"So, now that our sauce has cooled down, let's put the whole dish together." He took the pan of meatballs and emptied it flawlessly onto a platter, leaving a small well in the center.

"We've got our delicious meatballs," he sighed in relief, "and our perfectly portioned pasta." He felt relaxed as he arranged the meatball platter.

“And, to top off our dish, Poppy’s old-fashioned marinara sau--”

As Dex lifted the bowl of sauce, his foot slipped on a clump of pasta that had fallen on the floor. Everyone ducked as the sauce went flying forward, but there was no escaping its messy path.

“Yo D-Sizzle, what up wit da tomato rain?” Jordy complained, licking the sauce on his arm. “It’s fly, but you best use ‘dem noodles.”

Liza and Sarah were laughing all their way to the paper towels and Geema was applauding despite the mess on her lap. The only one Dex didn’t hear from was Kyle who was busy smacking his lips as the sauce trickled down his head into his mouth.

Chapter 16

“Come in,” Ezra responded to the faint taps on his door.

Dex entered hesitantly. Ezra was sitting in a big black leather chair behind an enormous glass desk, his face buried in a computer screen the size of a television.

“Have a seat,” Ezra said without lifting his head up. “How are you feeling, kid?” he went on, still staring at the screen.

“I’m okay. I guess.” Dex sat down on the far end of a row of four seats lined up in front of Ezra’s desk.

“Okay,” Ezra repeated, now peering over the screen.

Dex suddenly felt at a loss for words. Not the best state to be in after just watching the audience for his show being ushered into the studio on his way up to Ezra’s office.

“The woman at the front desk downstairs said you wanted to see me,” Dex added, pleased to be making intelligible conversation.

“Yes, I did. Do you know how important today is?” Ezra jumped out of his seat as if a bee had landed in his lap. “It’s your first show!” He patted Dex on the back a little too enthusiastically.

Dex lurched forward and nearly fell onto Ezra’s desk. “I know,” he replied, wriggling back into his chair.

“Your family here?”

“They’re in the reception area.”

“Lisa, one of my assistants, is working on getting you a dressing room.”

“I don’t really need one,” Dex declared. “I can get dressed at home.”

“Of course,” Ezra chuckled, “but it’ll come in handy to have a place to call your own around here. Trust me.”

Trust him. This whole situation was about trusting Ezra. If anyone had asked Dex a few weeks ago if he could imagine himself on his own cooking show, he would still be laughing. This definitely was not his idea, and right now the biggest plus was that Hunter, Sarah’s now *ex*-boyfriend, didn’t have his own wrestling show to use to get her back.

“You nervous?” Ezra asked.

Dex shrugged.

“Are you at least *this* nervous?” Ezra inquired, showing some middle-of-the-road amount with his hands.

Why did Ezra sound like he wanted Dex to be nervous? Nervous was not a good thing. Nervous made singers squeak and quarterbacks drop the ball. Nervous made actors forget lines and gymnasts fall off the balance beam. Nervous made him look like a dork in front of the girl he needed to impress. Would Ezra be pleased to know the extent of Dex’s talent; he could make pasta disappear and tomato sauce fly?! Bet he’d be thrilled to find out Vince had to call in a professional crew to clean up after that disastrous rehearsal.

“Yeah,” Dex obliged. “I’m at least *that* nervous.”

“Good. It’s always best when you are,” Ezra guaranteed. “Once the adrenaline kicks in, that’s when you really shine.” Ezra looked Dex in the eye as if he could read his mind. “When you’re as talented as you are, even your mistakes are magnetic.”

There was a strong knock at the door. A guy wearing headphones and a frown walked in and told Ezra about a sound problem on the main stage. Ezra shook his head and slapped his left hand over his mouth, shutting himself up before saying something regretful.

"Dex, you'll have to excuse me," Ezra said between pursed lips. "Seems like nothing can get done around here without me."

"Sure, no problem," Dex replied, walking out with both men.

"You're a good kid, Dex," Ezra said pointing at him. "I'm going to take you far. Just make sure you stay nervous." He smiled and disappeared down the hall.

Before he stepped into the elevator, Dex caught a glimpse of Preston LeTray trying to catch up with Ezra. He was scrunching his face like he had just sucked a whole lemon and Dex wondered why Preston was always angry. Maybe he needed to eat prunes. Geema said they always made her feel happier with the world.

#

"Where were you all this time?" Marla scolded the moment Dex stepped off the elevator.

"Talking to Ezra, just like I told you," Dex darted back. "Where'd you think I'd be?"

"I don't know," Marla admitted, "I guess I'm nervous. Your father had to leave."

"Why?"

"The night manager's wife broke her wrist, and apparently,

after only a couple of months on the job, your father is the only one who knows how to run the store," Marla squawked.

"Maybe Dad'll be discovered," Dex mused.

"Discovered? What are you talking about?"

Dex shrugged. "You know-Sarah's uncle had to go back to China because his daughter had twins early. I took his place and now I'm a TV chef."

"Somehow I don't foresee that happening," Marla contended.

"Where's Geema?" Dex asked, looking around the reception area.

"Ladies' room. She's taking those pills that make her..."

"Yeah, okay, Mom. TMI."

"These things are facts of life, Dex."

"Good. Can I please not have to think about how much my grandmother needs to pee before I make Lobster Mac 'N Cheese?" Dex pleaded.

A young, bouncy woman with short purple hair and a pierced nose walked over. She was wearing a low-cut top that offered a clear view of the tattoo of a gingerbread house that lived on her chest.

"Dex?" she asked as if she already knew.

Dex nodded.

"I'm Casey, the assistant producer of your show. I sent you the email."

"You're the producer," Marla interrupted with a muted snicker and widened eyes.

"Assistant," Casey corrected. "Nice to meet you, Mrs. Rossi."

"Likewise," said Marla shaking the young woman's hand.

"Yeah, I know who you are," Dex exclaimed, scolding his mother with his furrowed brow.

"Oh, okay. Good," Casey chuckled directing her focus on Dex. "Well, come follow me so you can see what your life is going to look like in about an hour and a half."

Marla shifted her gaze from Casey's tattoo to Dex's worried face. "You're going to do great, honey," Marla promised. "You'll see. You're a natural."

A crash of thunder outside interrupted her and Dex was confused at seeing her eyes get teary.

"Did you hear that, Dex?"

"Duh, Korea heard that."

She turned her head toward the sky, and threw a kiss up into the air, "That was Poppy. He's going to be with you."

"Thanks. I knew he would be."

Dex kissed his mother on the cheek and then met up with Casey, who was at the elevator texting something on her neon lime iPhone.

"Dex," Marla called down the hall, "Have fun."

#

The studio kitchen was intense. Dex had seen it on the virtual tour Casey had emailed him, when she had sent the script and overview of the show, but seeing it in person made him tingle. He stared at the stainless-steel double wall oven and got as excited as he knew some guys got about driving a Ferrari. But, how many of those guys could say with certainty what they wanted to do with their lives? Dex knew he was a chef. That had to count for something.

"So these are going to make your life a whole lot easier!" Casey explained, pointing to groups of utensils positioned in ceramic holders along the granite counters.

Dex chuckled. "I know! My father used to sell them."

He remembered how psyched Vince would be when he came back from conventions with new 'toys' for Dex to check out. Maybe after he saved Poppy's Kitchen from foreclosure, Dex mused, he could help his father open his own business again. Or maybe, he should be paying attention to Casey so he wouldn't make an idiot of himself on television.

Dex picked up a round disk that had a nub-like handle. "Know what this is for?" he asked Casey.

"Um, a Play-Doh pancake mold?"

"Close," he teased, "a hamburger press."

"Oh, that's so cool. I'm strictly a behind-the-scenes person, so I don't know much about this stuff," Casey admitted. "I can barely toast a bun let alone make a burger."

As Dex had expected, all the ingredients he'd asked for were measured out in ramekins, little cups. The vegetables were washed and the other items could be easily unwrapped. There was nothing that looked out of the ordinary, and as Casey finished explaining procedures and ended the tour, Dex felt surprisingly at home.

“Come on,” Casey instructed, “I’ll take you to make-up.”

Make-up? Like lipstick and the stuff Alicia would spend hours putting on her eyes?

“Don’t worry,” Casey said, “You’re not going to look like a runway model. They just use some powder to keep your skin tone looking even and bright on camera.”

Dex was relieved. He had enough problems without having to be labeled at school as the skinny kid wearing mascara. As Casey led him behind the back wall of the kitchen, Dex could see the audience. Not as many people as he thought, but then again this was a television show, not a P!nk concert.

The make-up room was at the end of a short corridor and reminded Dex of a mini version of Liza’s fathers’ salon. The walls were mostly white, except for the pale blue one that supported the huge mirror that ran the length and width of the room.

“Want to sit?” Casey asked, pointing to one of the four oversized, gray chairs positioned in front of the mirror.

Dex shook his head. Even though his legs felt as steady as licorice sticks, he was too excited to sit. “Nah, that’s okay.”

“Okay then. I’ll be right back,” Casey said walking out.

Dex eyed the portable coffee bar on the opposite corner of the room. It was worth a look. He walked past an elderly woman having her silver hair teased by a middle-aged woman with puffy platinum blonde hair and pounds of make-up.

"You want a hot *chawklit*, hon?" asked the blonde into the mirror, seeing Dex rifle through the assorted packages. "It's got those teeny *mawshmellows*. Really yummy."

"Oh, no that's okay." Dex said, putting back a package of instant chicken noodle soup. "I'm just waiting."

"Who are you waiting for? Does your mom work here?"

"No. I do," Dex said, letting this new reality sink in. "I'm supposed to get make-up."

"Oooohh! *Yaw* the kid. The kid with the show!" The blonde turned directly to Dex. "*Sawrry*. I had no *ideeyah*! What's *ya name*?"

"Dex. Dex Rossi."

"*Roight. Roight*. Ezra sent me an email," she remembered. "Just give me a minute to finish."

The blonde had the woman done and out of the room in seconds.

"Come sit here, Dex," she directed, plopping him into a seat behind a mirror with lights all around it.

"*Boy* the way, I'm Flo."

Dex watched as Flo picked up a tray of powders and creams, and a case of cotton swabs, brushes, and pads.

"*Yew* have great skin. Nice tones," Flo said applying a light coating of cream on Dex's cheeks. Then she dipped a brush in stuff that looked like very light cocoa and made big, sweeping circles over his nose, chin and forehead as if she were dusting a lamp.

Casey came back just as Flo was brushing Dex's face with something like corn starch, but she called it finishing *powdah.*

"*Yaw awl* done," Flo said, lightly holding up Dex's chin to admire her work.

"Thanks Flo," Casey said. "We're outta here."

She ushered Dex out the door as he was waving goodbye to Flo. "Don't worry, you look wondaful!" she reassured, giving him a brief once-over.

"Yeah, like it's Halloween and I'm going as my sister," Dex complained. "Are you supposed to feel this stuff on your skin?" Dex wanted to rub the coating off, but thought better of it.

Casey giggled, "Virgin skin has to get used to being dressed."

Dex hoped Casey didn't see him blush. Hearing the word 'virgin' regarding any part of him was embarrassing.

"Where is Flo from?" Dex asked, anxious to change the subject.

"Queens or Brooklyn," Casey answered. "When I first started working here, I could have used an interpreter to understand her." She patted his arm, "You get used to it. After a while, you can get used to almost anything."

Dex continued following Casey until they got to a path that forked into two different hallways. One was the color of sunflowers, the other, dollar bills.

"Your room is to the left, down the yellow-brick road," Casey said with a straight face.

“Huh?”

“That’s what Ezra calls it,” Casey explained. “All the newer Eatz network people get their start on this side. Once they ‘make it,’ they get moved over to the green side.”

“Wow- that sounds kind of weird,” Dex mumbled.

“Yup! Welcome to television.”

Dex followed Casey to a white door that had a blank, dry erase board affixed to the front.

“Sometimes you’ll get notes left for you here, but most of the time someone will be in touch with you.” Casey opened the door to a space the size of his bathroom. If he didn’t want claustrophobia he would have to ‘make it’ as an Eatz star pretty soon.

“Well, I have to get going,” Casey said, frowning at her watch. “A big, doofy guy, but please don’t tell him I said that, named Arby, is going to take you down to the stage area a few minutes before you go on. He’s nice, but not the brightest bulb on the Christmas tree.”

“What do you mean?” Dex replied.

“He’s been known to fill sugar canisters with salt,” Casey sighed.

“So he makes mistakes.”

“He’s the nephew of the vice president of the network. We don’t call them mistakes.” Casey’s phone buzzed and flashed bright colors. “Gotta run. I’ll catch you after the show.”

Dex watched her disappear down the path before officially

checking out the dressing room he was sure he didn't need. It's not like he had to wear anything special besides an apron, which, from the looks of it, was about all that would fit on the hook taped to the wall next to the narrow mirror. Except for the Nitro coaster at Great Adventure, checking out this room was the shortest three minutes of his life. Dex had seen closets bigger than this. Maybe he would ask Ezra if there was anyone else who could use the space.

Before he had the chance to make himself feel worse there was a knock on the door. Arby was a tall, chunky guy around Casey's age, wearing jeans. He didn't display any signs of stupidity. Until he spoke. "Hey, you're a kid."

Since Dex already knew that, he began to understand Casey's concerns.

"Nice to meet you," Dex lied. "I'm Dex Rossi."

"Yeah. I have it in a text message from someone. Can't remember who." Arby scratched his head. "I didn't think you were a kid. Maybe the message said you were, but I'm not sure."

"You know," Dex said, "I am a kid, but it doesn't really matter." He walked out the door to join Arby. "So, what's next, Arby?"

"Next?" Arby cocked his head to the side.

"You're taking me to the studio kitchen," Dex prompted. "Right?" Dex started walking down the path.

"Ooooh, right," Arby nodded as he followed Dex. "How'd you know my name?"

"Everyone knows your name around here," Dex cajoled.

“Guess so. I’m in charge of a lot,” Arby boasted. “So, your parents have a show or something?”

Dex thought about health class and the segment they did on smoking marijuana. He couldn’t swear to it, but Arby acted just like the example of someone ‘high’ they explained during the power point presentation.

“I’m starting my own show today,” Dex explained.

“Wow! You’re a little dude for that,” Arby said, sounding impressed. “How’d you get the gig?”

“To make a long story short, I kind of know someone.”

“Me too, little dude. Me too. We got something in common.”

Dex groaned knowing that for as long as he and Arby would be working together, Dex was going to have to get used to being called ‘little dude.’ The thought would have really depressed him if he didn’t have more immediate concerns.

“Do you know what time I go on?” Dex asked.

“Um. Well. Um. I could find out,” Arby offered.

“Don’t worry about it,” Dex grunted. “I’ll ask when we get there.”

Just before they reached the studio kitchen, a woman in a red sweater stopped Arby with her hand to his arm. She put a smile on for Dex, pointed him in the right direction, and then shuffled Arby into her office.

Dex finally arrived at stage left where Courtney, another twenty-something assistant, was waiting for him.

"You're on in ten," Courtney said, handing him an apron. "How are you doing?"

Dex shrugged. "Is my make-up okay? I can't feel it anymore."

#

An announcer boomed over the studio speakers:

Everyone get ready! It's time to Dine with Dex! There was huge applause and Dex could feel his heart begin to race.

And now, your chef of the hour, the youngest Eatz Network chef of all time, a little man who's big on taste, Dex Rossi!

There was more applause as a giant sign that read, *DINE WITH DEX* descended from the ceiling. Music started playing and Dex caught a glimpse of Marla, Geema, Alicia, Liza, Kyle, and Jordy, sitting in the front row applauding. Liza even did a few woop-woops.

The energy was at its peak when Courtney gave Dex a nudge into the kitchen. He scanned the audience, but the lighting made it impossible to make out faces. That was probably a good thing because he was terrified. All that kept running through his head was Arby calling him 'little dude' and tomato sauce flying through the air landing on everyone like pigeon poop.

Dex moved stiffly as he turned to the wall behind him. There was a large projection screen set up to display visual effects during the show. Above the screen was a contraption called the *DEX-O-METER* that resembled an old-fashioned elevator floor counter.

"Hey everyone, thanks for tuning in. I'm Dex, and my motto is: If you can eat it, you can cook it! And if it can eat you, run!"

The audience laughed. Dex began to feel his heart slow down to just below warp speed.

"Today I'm going to show you how to turn a trip to the kitchen into a mouth-watering vacation, with some Dex-cellent tropical treats."

The *DEX-O-METER* sprang into action, making a loud ding as its arrow pointed to the number one. Dex turned around to face the screen and made a finger-gunpoint gesture to indicate the appearance of a new food image. He could feel himself gaining confidence and even decided to have fun.

"First up, a drink that you won't need an ID to enjoy, and no, it's not a Shirley Temple.

It's an alcohol-free Mango Pina Colada swirling with fresh mangoes and rich pineapple ice cream. Then we're going to keep the waves crashing with my tropical take on an old favorite."

He motioned to the screen and again it switched to a new image. "My Lobster Mac 'n Cheese is sure to please bringing together a casserole classic, a creamy blend of Gruyere, cheddar, and muenster cheese and delicious Lobster."

"And don't worry about dessert," he exclaimed, flailing his pointer finger once more to switch the screen image, "because we have Chocolate Macadamia Nut Cookies, made with my favorite sweetener, Dex-trose. The perfect end to our Dex-otic kitchen getaway."

The audience laughed as the *DEX-O-METER* clicked

another couple of notches giving Dex the chance to end his opening on a high note.

"Now let's get cookin'!"

Chapter 17

"No, no, no! Stop thinking small." Preston LeTray threw the latest copy of *Spotlight on Bergen County* across his office. Yvette was a total ignoramus if she thought a local magazine would be enough publicity to overshadow that little jerk. He let out a full, long groan and turned to a chart on the laptop sitting on the table.

Yvette started to say something, but then shriveled into her seat like a puppy getting yelled at for peeing on the carpet.

"Have you seen his ratings? I have. Here." Preston twisted the laptop so she could see it.

"Isn't it bad enough I have to see his dumb three-foot smile on that billboard on Route 78 every time I'm on my way to work? That's where MY face used to be."

"I'm sorry, Pressykins," Yvette said, as she retrieved the errant magazine. "If you don't want to do an interview with *Spotlight*, that's fine. It was just an idea."

"We have to think bigger. Much, much bigger," Preston insisted, extending and pulsing his arms outright. "It's been a month since *Dine with Dex* started, and that little snot nose has been on the cover of every magazine that doesn't have a centerfold."

"I didn't see him on *National Geographic*," Yvette maintained with a faint smile.

"This isn't a joke!"

"Of course not, Pressy." Yvette stood behind Preston and started to massage his neck.

“Remember how we crushed *Fran’s Fixin’s*?” Preston recalled.

“Made her into crumbs,” Yvette whispered, as she kneaded his shoulders.

“And if we play our cards right we can get ahead of *Merri-Made Meals* within a couple of weeks.”

“Of course we can Pressy. That woman’s voice sounds like glass in a blender.”

“I need a guarantee. I need a plan so that this little jerk can’t get in my way. This is my network!”

“Just so you know, I found out the kid is going to be on *Jimmy Fallon*.”

“Isn’t that way past his bed time?” Preston sneered.

“Maybe, but the audience went wild over him on *Jimmy Kimmel*, and Whoopi had a blast with him on *The View*. It was actually kinda cute.”

“Yvette!” Preston bellowed.

“Right.” Yvette said, massaging his temples. “Pressy, don’t you worry.” She kissed his forehead. “No one’s going to get in your way with Yvette at your side.”

#

Alicia ran down the hall clutching her camera tightly. She was afraid it would be knocked on the floor by the hoards of students leaving the gym. Today she would be taking footage for her film as she walked through the school. Dex had told her to meet him in front of the cafeteria, but he didn’t warn her about the pep rally. She was navigating her way toward an empty corner of the white-brick hallway when an older man with curly gray hair stopped her.

“Excuse me young lady. Can I help you?”

“No, I’m fine,” Alicia answered.

“Let me rephrase that,” the man said, taking a less friendly tone. “You’re not one of our students, and you’re not a teacher. Do you have a visitor’s pass?”

Groups of kids stared at Alicia as if she were being arrested and walked to the other side of the hall.

“A pass? No, but I called,” Alicia explained. “You must be the new assistant principal.”

“Yes,” he said dismissively, “So what are you doing here with a camera?”

“I’m Alicia Rossi.”

“Oh! Dex’s sister. The film student!” the man cried. “Of course, I should have known. Here, let me help you,” he said, taking her camera case and slinging it over his shoulder. “I’m Jack Cassel.” He shook her hand. “And please, call me Jack.”

“Thank you so much...Jack,” she said, uncomfortable speaking to him as a peer. “Sorry for the misunderstanding.”

“Oh, no problem.” He was already walking down the left corridor. “Where are you headed?”

“My brother is waiting for me by the cafeteria.”

“Okay then. Follow me.”

"I'm not sure how much you know, but I'm doing a film project on Dex."

"Yes. I heard. Fascinating." Jack adjusted his glasses. "Privacy is certainly an issue. With his popularity on the rise, we sent home a letter to students and their families asking them to treat Dex with respect as they would any celebrity," Jack explained. "I'm afraid it did nothing. And today's likely to be especially nuts since he was on yesterday's cover of *Seventeen*. For the past couple of weeks now, reporters and photographers have been trying to sneak in to get to Dex." Jack sounded exhausted. "It's not the kid's fault at all, but I can't say it hasn't been a bit...difficult."

"Really? Wow! Would you mind if I got that on tape? Just a short interview?" Alicia asked.

"I suppose that would be fine," Jack said, handing her back the camera. He smoothed over his thick, silver hair with his hands. "My wife and I were on the news once when we had a flood in our basement. You should have seen the pictures they got of that." He wiped his face and the corners of his mouth. "This'll be cake."

After the interview, Jack spent several minutes trying to coax Alicia to be the new videographer for the school. "You really have a knack for this." Jack was fishing for something in his pocket as he spoke.

"Thanks so much Jack, I really appreciate the offer, but I'm in school full-time. As tempting as it may be, I'm not ready to accept that kind of position."

"I applaud your dedication. Your parents must be very proud of you." He had apparently found what he was looking for and he handed it over with a smile.

Alicia glanced at the offering. It was a William Alexander

Middle School pen imprinted with his name and extension number.

"Please feel free if you need a recommendation or anything. I can--"

Just then a hall monitor approached, saying something about a fight in the girls' locker room. Jack mumbled an apology. Alicia thanked him again and he wished her luck before disappearing around the corner.

#

"Dex!" Alicia called, spotting her brother in the crowded hall retrieving a bottled water from a vending machine.

"Leesh!" Dex tried to peer over a group of tall students to see her, but it was impossible. Finally there was a break in the crowd and he found his way over to her.

"Where are Liza and Kyle?" she asked, dusting the lint off her camera lens.

"Don't worry. They're coming." Dex took a sip of his water. "Kyle forgot his Tums in his locker."

"Oh good. That'll save me from having to edit out at least twenty burps." Alicia pressed a few buttons and was ready to record.

"You can hope." Dex took another sip of water and noticed a guy from the basketball team walking toward him.

Alicia started filming. Instinct told her this moment would be worth the battery time.

"Hey," the guy said, giving Dex a small jab to the arm. "I know this'll sound a little lame, but can I have your autograph?"

"*You* want my autograph?" Dex sounded confused. "Why?"

Kyle and Liza came up from behind him, "Because," Kyle said, "in case you haven't noticed, you're kind of a TV star."

"Yeah," said the basketball guy, "It's for my sister. She totally digs your show," he said, taking a black pen from over his ear and giving it to Dex along with a sheet of paper.

Dex shot Liza a quick look and tried not to laugh. Nobody he knew ever said 'dig' except the guy with long hair and three nose rings at the health food store on Main Street.

"What do you want me to write to your sister?"

"Um...how about, 'To my cool friend, Alex.'"

Dex signed the paper and gave it back to the guy, who tucked it neatly inside a folder and started to walk away. Dex laughed as he heard a voice yell, "Hey Alex, did he sign it?" and the guy answered, "Shut up, dude!"

"Cool," Alicia said, "I got to tape my little brother signing an autograph!"

"There's going to be a lot of those going on," Liza promised. "Everyone in school is tweeting about the class trip to see your show. See...," she said, showing him the tweets on her phone.

Dex was taken aback.

"And guess what else?" Liza gushed, scrolling down further on her phone. "Sarah tweeted this just this morning:"

SO DONE WITH HUNTER - AGAIN </3 #HEARTBROKEN

"I already knew," Dex admitted.

"That's impossible. She just posted it."

"She told me."

Before Liza could get more details, a dorky girl with braces, glasses, and pigtails held in yellow scrunchies interrupted them.

"Hi *Deck-th*!" she said with a pronounced lisp. "I think your show *ith thooper*, really *thooper*, but you haven't made anything for people with food *allergie-th*!" She spoke so quickly it was hard to make out what she was saying. "I'm *lacto-th* intolerant and if I eat *nut-th*, my *fay-th burth-t* with *pimple-th...*"

The girl stopped at her locker, still jabbering about something else wrong with her face, but Dex was too busy thinking about Sarah's tweet to hear her.

"Why'd they break up?" Dex asked. "Did Sarah say?"

"I thought you already knew."

"She told me at her bat-mitzvah. But, she didn't tell me why. And then I saw them together again!"

"Oh. Well, she didn't tweet it, but I heard from a very reliable source that she caught Hunter hooking up with Jade Carravaccio."

A girl with an unusually large chest walked by. "Speak of the devil," Kyle said.

Dex wasn't speaking. His eyes were locked on Jade's ample chest.

Liza reached up and clapped her hands in front of his face, practically up against his eyes.

"Hey!" Dex jumped back. "What's that for?"

"You need to pay attention to me. Sarah, remember? Hunter? Break-up?"

"Yeah!" Dex said. "I remember. Hunter's a jerk."

"Need a Snapple," Kyle said, turning away.

Just then a short boy with freckles holding a frying pan in his hand walked up to the group.

"Can you sign this, to my good friend, Max?" The boy held out a Sharpie. "Max is my sister Maxine. It's for her."

"Here you go," Dex said, pretty certain the kid's sister was in his English class and her name was Miranda. No point in embarrassing these guys. It must be strange asking another guy for his autograph.

"Hey, Dex," said a very thin girl in an over-sized purple sweatshirt that hung close to her knees, "can you sign this?" She held out her sleeve. "To Brittany, with love Dex," she giggled.

Dex looked at her quizzically, "You want me to sign your shirt?"

The girl nodded until her glasses slid down her nose and fell onto the floor.

Alicia started to record as the girl retrieved her glasses and put them back on. There was time before lunch was over and she decided to use every minute to tell Dex's story as completely as possible. There would be plenty of tape left for individual interviews later.

“Here you go,” Dex said, letting go of the newly signed sweatshirt sleeve.

A line was forming.

“Um, me next, waste-case,” yelled a kid wearing a wrestling team shirt, pushing away a kid in a suit who was clearly next in line.

“Guys, no problem,” Dex explained. “I have a few minutes before I have to go to class.” He took out his own marker, never noticing Sarah coming over to them.

“Hey, what’s going on?” Sarah asked Liza, watching Alicia filming.

“Oh. Hi. Alicia is doing a documentary about Dex for her film school.”

“Really? That’s kind of cool.”

A few girls bumped into Sarah as they tried to get to Dex.

“These girls are crazy,” Sarah mocked. “You’d think Dex was Zac Efron or something.”

“In this school, he’s the closest thing we’ve got,” Liza said.

Kyle was standing next to Dex, helping him keep the autograph line moving when he suddenly felt someone staring at them. “Tracey Waters is looking at us,” he whispered. “Man she’s hot. Uh-oh-I wonder if she found out that Liza hit her with my corndog.”

Tracey stopped mid-hall flanked by Tye and Aimee, her ladies-in-waiting. They were all dressed in form-fitting lilac shirts and tight jeans, wearing enough make-up to look like a coven of Barbie dolls.

Tracey left the girls to begin a well-choreographed sashay down the hall, her eyes fixed on Dex. She began flirting the moment she caught his attention.

"So Dex, I've heard about this little show of yours. Very attractive. All of a sudden I'm feeling totally like, interested. You are too, right?"

Dex was about to respond, but Tracey interrupted him.

"I knew it. You don't have to say anything. We don't have to be like normal boring people. You're my new all, baby," she whispered, leaning in to kiss him.

Dex was too shocked to stop her and their lips met.

"Yo Dex!" Liza barked.

But Dex and Tracey remained lip-locked. Tracey's arms were wrapped around Dex so tight he couldn't move.

"I think he's busy," Kyle groaned. "I'm busy hating him."

Liza maneuvered Kyle so he was standing right beside the couple. As Kyle continued to gawk, Liza gave him a firm smack on the back, making him burp loudly.

"Oh-my-God. I'm gonna puke!" Tracey screeched, pushing Dex away. She clopped back to her crew on her high heels holding one hand over her mouth. She looked left then right, clapped her hands once and they all walked away.

Liza, Sarah, and Kyle stared at Dex, who was too stunned to respond to anyone.

"Amazing...I've got to return a book," Sarah snarled, then darted away.

Alicia checked the time and immediately stopped filming. "I'm going to be late for class. See you guys later," she said, hurrying down the now empty hall.

Kyle gave Dex a medium-sized whack on the back.

"Thanks Kyle. I couldn't move."

The bell rang and Dex, Kyle, and Liza started walking to class.

"Crap! I left my history book in my locker," Kyle blurted, stopping in his tracks.

"Again?" Liza mocked.

"Tell me about it," Kyle groaned. "I'll catch up with you guys later." He turned around and walked back the other way.

"Where'd Sarah go?" Dex asked.

"The library. I think. Why?" Liza answered.

"No reason."

"Dex, you're not her boyfriend."

"I know. But she's free now."

"She's not even that nice to you."

"I know."

"You like her anyway."

"Yeah."

“Men are pathetic.”

Liza shook her head and went into her social studies class, knowing exactly where Dex was going.

The whole time Dex was on his way to the library he thought about what he would say to Sarah. He could tell her how sorry he was that Hunter turned out to be a creep. That would be easy enough, easier than telling her he wanted her to be *his* girlfriend. On the other hand, he could avoid talking about Hunter altogether and just tell her how weird it was to have everyone asking him for his autograph.

The doors of the library were right in front of him, and Dex still hadn’t made up his mind. Nonetheless, he took a deep breath and walked in quietly past the reference desk and saw no one sitting at any of the tables. Maybe Sarah was upstairs? He could only hope she hadn’t left the library before he had the chance to see her.

He felt his pulse quicken as he searched through each row of study cubicles. Although the library was almost empty, he couldn’t find her anywhere. If she wasn’t there he would go to her house after school. Yeah, just show up uninvited without any reason to be there. That would go over real well. *Mom, what’s this dork doing here?* But was that really what she thought of him? He didn’t know.

He was about to give up when he saw Sarah shift in her seat in the last stall at the end of the last row. In the whole library, she couldn’t have picked a better place to hide.

“Hey. I saw you in the hallway before,” Dex said, then cleared his throat.

“So?”

“Do you think Tracey’s into me?” Dex asked.

What?!? It was obvious that he had officially lost his mind. Did he really just ask the girl he loved if another girl liked him? Any moron would know that was the stupidest thing on the planet he could’ve asked. At that point, why didn’t he just ask her how she was dealing with her broken heart?

“How should I know?” she snapped.

“You’re friends. I thought maybe she told you.”

Now there’s a plan. Say something idiotic and continue to open your mouth and make it worse. Was there a reason he wanted Sarah to hate him?

“Well, she didn’t,” Sarah barked. “Why? Do you like her?”

“I dunno.”

He would have been better off tripping over his book bag and breaking his legs before he ever set foot in the library. When would the stupid pills he must’ve taken wear off?

“I have to study,” Sarah said.

“Okay.”

Finally, a word that didn’t need editing. But how could he leave without knowing where he stood?

“Sarah?”

“What now!?”

“I was thinking.”

“Could have fooled me.”

Dex's heart was beating like mad. He had to just say it:

"Will you....go out with me?"

Chapter 18

Preston was sitting at his desk, his face buried in the latest copy of *Food & Wine* magazine, when Ezra blasted through the door without knocking.

"It's time for one of our little talks, Presto," Ezra snarled, grabbing the magazine out of Preston's hands and sitting on the corner of his desk.

Preston stiffened and clenched his fists. He considered taking a swing at Ezra's jaw, but stopped himself when he decided he had nothing to worry about. He was, as always, doing a great job. Buford told him just last week that aside from that one nasty scent card that made Preston faint, all the others had been fine. Ezra must have run out of bran flakes or something to put him in this foul mood. Preston unclenched his fists, reminding himself that until he had the power to control the network and send Ezra packing, it was best to make nice.

"I know," Preston said nodding, "the idea of having my face on the air fresheners was a bit much. I told production to forget it, so don't worry, it's all taken care of."

"I'm worried alright, but it's not about that," Ezra said, looking squarely at Preston. "Your fresheners are fine, at least for the time being, but, your ratings stink!"

"That's impossible," Preston argued. "We all know I'm the finest chef in the line-up." He stood up and crossed over to a small stainless refrigerator and took out a bottle of water.

"Not according to this!" Ezra growled, holding up the newest ratings sheet under Preston's nose.

"I'm sure things will pick up," Preston said, swatting the

paper away. "My new food line is about to hit the market, and the fresheners are steps away from distribution."

"That's fine, but it's also fluff." Ezra crossed his arms, "If you keep slipping, you won't have a show or any Eatz money for your projects."

"That's ridiculous!" Preston sat back down in his seat as if it were a throne.

"You know what would be a great idea?!" Ezra exclaimed, ignoring him.

"My own line of cookware?"

"No."

Ezra got up and reached into his jacket pocket. "Start watching *him*," he said, tossing a wallet-sized promo picture of Dex onto Preston's desk.

"The kid?" Preston questioned. "Whatever for?"

"*Dex*," Ezra asserted, "has something special. He's been at the top of the ratings since he started." Ezra went to the door. "Definitely watch him. With a little luck, maybe you can learn something."

Ezra walked out slamming the door behind him. Preston was seething.

"You little punk," Preston grimaced, pounding his fist on the picture of Dex. "I'll watch you alright. I'll be watching you at every turn. Then I'll finish you off before you even see it coming!" He slammed his fist down on the picture again sending the neighboring canister of gummy worms onto the floor.

Yvette bolted into the office.

"What's wrong, Pressykins?" She looked at the floor. "Uh-oh. What happened?" She got on her hands and knees to clean up.

"That little moron is trying to ruin me!" Preston shouted, watching as Yvette gathered the candy. "He's turned Ezra against me. But he's crazy if he thinks he's going to work his way into my shoes."

"That won't happen silly. He's way too small. They'd slip right off!"

Preston cringed. He had little patience for Yvette's stupidity, but for now she would be helpful. Soon enough he would be in control of the network, he promised himself, and she too would be history.

"I heard he's having a bunch of kids from his school come for a live lunch special in the studio," Yvette relayed, still on all fours collecting candy and dumping it into the trash.

Preston paced around her.

"Hmm. Live lunch for a bunch of hungry, judgmental children," Preston snickered. "This sounds promising. I'm sure the little dirtbag will need help."

Yvette stood up to throw out the last of the worms. "But you don't really want to help him?" she paused, "Right?"

Preston rolled his eyes at her. "Can you get a hold of the prep list and menu?"

"Pressykins," she whispered, now massaging his neck. "I can get you anything you need."

Chapter 19

The Eatz studio kitchen was busier than Dex had ever seen it. He was getting more nervous by the minute. He'd never met the members of the morning crew who were building the set today, and today wasn't like all his other shows. This time his whole class would be his audience, there to watch his every move. If he screwed up, there would be no way he could show his face in school ever again. He'd end up some pathetic meme on Tumblr, something to keep all the kids laughing at him for weeks or even months on end. *Dumb-ass Dex.* Suddenly, he contemplated saying he was coming down with something. Ezra would have to send everyone home. The problem was that no one would buy that story. He was stuck and that made him want to run.

Casey, his primary assistant, came up and tapped him on the shoulder. "Hey, what's up with you?"

Dex didn't realize he was wearing his feelings. "Nothing, Case. Just a lot going on."

"Eh, you're a pro now," Casey reassured. "You have nothing to worry about. C'mon over here."

There was a small area behind the set, away from all the activity. "Here's the rundown," Casey said. Dex wasn't paying any attention. His stomach was doing flip-flops as he watched new gadgets and cookware being laid out in his work space.

He nodded toward it. "What's all that for?"

"Oh, just some products Ezra wants you to use for a new line the network is promoting."

Dex shivered. Yeah, now was exactly the time he wanted

to start dealing with stuff he'd never used before. Didn't anyone understand how scary all this was? Sarah would be deciding whether or not she wanted to be his girlfriend, while he was making chicken salad!

"Today is going to be real easy," Casey promised. "Ezra wants you to act naturally so there's very little script." She handed him a sheet of notes. "Just say a word or two about why you like the cordless garlic and herb-chopper, and whatever other new stuff you use."

"What if I don't need to use the other stuff?" Dex asked.

"Fair enough, but find a reason to use them," she chuckled. "We like making our sponsors happy."

Dex nodded, but his face was blank.

"Are you good with this?" Casey asked.

"Yeah, sure."

"Great, because I have to speak with the new lighting guy. There's a burnt bulb right by the stove that's..." She stopped herself. "Why am I bothering you with all this?"

"You're not bothering me." Dex glanced at the notes.

"Why don't you go over those and I'll see you in a few." She patted his shoulder and walked down the hall.

"Yo, little dude," Arby said, joining Dex from out of nowhere. "Scared, huh?"

"Nah, I'm cool."

"You're talking to Arby. I can smell your fear." Arby inhaled deeply and stared at Dex.

"Well, I showered and I'm not scared, so I don't know what you're smelling," Dex said, dismissing him.

"If you say so little dude, but I know something that can help you."

"You do?"

Arby reached deep into the pocket of his baggy jeans and cupped something that looked like a skinny cigarette. "A little bit of this can make you relax."

Just as Dex was about to tell Arby he wasn't interested, Ezra came over clutching a long, yellow legal pad.

People still use those pads? Dex mused. *Geema would be thrilled to know she wasn't alone.*

"What you got there Big Guy?" Ezra asked, watching Arby cramming his hand into his bulging pocket.

Hhmm...'Big Guy'... Maybe that's why Arby always called him 'little dude.' Somehow that explanation made Dex feel better.

"He was showing me some spices he got at the new health food store," Dex said.

Ezra nodded as if he was interested, but when he retrieved a pen from over his ear and jotted something down on his pad, Dex wasn't sure he was even listening.

Arby looked relieved. "I better go check on, you know, messages and stuff," he said, quickly shuffling away like a dejected poodle, his black curly hair swaying from side to side.

"You do that," Ezra called out gruffly after him.

Arby turned back to Dex when Ezra's back was toward him

and mouthed 'thank you little dude.' Then he picked up his pace to get to the waiting elevator.

Ezra's tone made Dex feel uncomfortable. So, Arby was doofy and annoying, but he wasn't a bad guy.

Ezra was checking his notes for what seemed to Dex like the billionth time when he finally turned to ask his usual question before Dex went on set: "So kid, you nervous?"

Dex gave his now typical reply, "Yup, just enough." It was what Ezra wanted to hear and up until this point it had been true. There was no need for Dex to tell him this time was different. That this time he might lose his breakfast all over the granite counters.

"Good! Glad to hear it," Ezra said as Casey walked over to them with the lighting guy.

There was something wrong with the fixture above the grill, and Dex was happy when they all left him to check it out. It wasn't that he didn't get along with everyone, even though they could all be annoying at times, he was just too anxious for company. He needed to be alone, or at least not with people who were reminding him of how important this show was.

Dex let them walk ahead of him, and when he saw them a safe distance away, he went back to the set to see what was going on.

"Hal, higher," directed a bearded guy in jeans to the cameraman setting up for filming over the stove.

"Hello, Dex," Preston LeTray nodded. "You remember my assistant, Yvette?"

"Yeah. But, what are you guys doing here?"

“We’re here to help, of course.” Preston smoothed the wrinkles in his plastic gloves.

“Really? You came to help me?!”

“Dex, we’re one big family here at Eatz. One hand always washes the other.”

“Not that our hands get dirty much,” Yvette offered. “We always wear gloves.”

Preston gave her a look and she stopped talking.

“So, Dex, what can we do for you? I see you have several things on the menu. Perhaps, I can do something simple like mix the chicken salad, while you prep your dessert?”

“Um, sure, if you don’t mind. That would be awesome. Thanks!”

Dex went to the pantry to check the ingredients he needed. He still couldn’t believe Preston LeTray took time out of his day to help him. What a great guy. Just knowing he was there, having a hand in the preparations, made Dex feel more confident.

“The school buses are, uh, uh, they’re like here!” Arby announced, coming in from a side entrance. Dex watched from behind a movable wall as familiar faces began to fill out the audience.

“Hey, little dude, you want me to help out with something?” Arby asked. “I have some free time.”

“I think I’m good,” Dex answered. “But, thanks.”

“You sure? I saw on the notes you’re making um, uh, like

some chicken salad. I looooove chicken salad, dude. I even make chicken salad. I mean I buy the chicken cooked first, ya know. I don't like kill it myself or anything. But, uh, like then, I make it. You use mayo? Right? 'Cause it tastes friggin' disgusting with like sour cream and ketchup."

"Yeah, I use mayo, Arby. Because your combination is too gross to even think of. Actually, Preston LeTray showed up to help. He's prepping the chicken salad now, so I'm covered."

"Preston? Is helping? Someone must've put uh, uh, something like in his oatmeal this morning."

"Why would you say that?" Dex asked, offended.

"No harm little dude. Just not like Preston, to be uh, you know, nice and all."

"He seems pretty cool to me."

"Maybe I'll ask him if uh, he wants like, you know, help." Arby started walking away.

Dex gave him a nod then turned back to the pantry, confident Preston wouldn't let Arby anywhere near the food.

One last review of the shelves and Dex was ready to check out the audience. He could see Alicia on the top tier making her way through the crowd with her camera and recorder interviewing kids. Maybe it was his imagination, but he had never had this many people come to see his show.

"Yo, D'!" Jordy said, waving his arm high in the air with Liza beside him.

Why were they having trouble getting backstage? Dex had put them on his permanent guest list right after his first show. He asked Courtney, now the backstage coordinator, to tell the security guy, who was dressed in pants up to his man boobs, to let his friends pass through. When were all the hassles going to stop? He hadn't even begun to prepare and he was already exhausted.

"Whoa!" Liza cried as she met up with Dex. "This is so beyond cool."

"Yeah, there are more badge-meisters here checkin' my junk than at the Jay-Z concert, yo," Jordy agreed in awe. "Pretty wack."

"I guess. It's not always like this," Dex said, bringing them to a quieter area further back. "Where's Kyle?"

"Sick," Liza sighed.

"That bites," Dex groaned. He waited a second, then continued, "Have either of you seen Sarah?"

"No. She went on a different bus, but I'm sure she's here somewhere."

Dex wondered why Liza sounded annoyed.

"Why didn't she come in with you?" he pressed.

Liza hesitated. "She's probably with her new boyfriend."

"What?! Boyfriend?" Dex wailed.

"I knew I shouldn't have told you now." Liza gnawed at her bottom lip, "But I didn't want you to get an eyeful of them together while you were frying something and then go and burn yourself."

"Who's she with now?!" Dex probed, hoping to sound more surprised than hurt.

"Bryce Watson," Jordy chimed in, "a beef-bump playa' wit choke-you arms." Jordy flexed his right bicep.

"Wow. That's news," Dex said, trying to sound indifferent. "I have to talk to the stage manager for a minute. I'll be right back."

Dex left them by the path right near the back of the set.

"You think he'll be okay, Jordy?" Liza asked. "I will shoot myself if I make him screw up because I opened my mouth."

"Ain't yo' ship to dip, Cuz. That boy best be sayin' Sarahnara," Jordy said, waving his hand goodbye.

"You know, you're a lunatic," Liza said, "but, I guess I agree with you. She keeps hurting him."

"No pass on how she messin' with him, but that girl's skurred like a lil' kitty. She wanna get wit him."

"Probably," Liza agreed. "I feel bad, but I still think all this TV stuff is pretty cool. I miss Kyle."

"Yeah. But, his snot balloons was nasty big. Dat boy needin' mad Kleenex today."

"Jordy, I'm gonna puke. Try to be more understanding."

"Aight, chill. Don't go punchin' babies. Let's bag him some 'shment."

Liza stared at him utterly puzzled. "'Shment?!"

"Yeah. 'Shment. Nou-ri-shment. Food, duh!"

Liza shook her head in disbelief. "Wow, even for you. Wow."

Dex came back determined not to let them or anyone see his disappointment about Sarah. He had a show to do and he couldn't let anything or anyone ruin his performance.

"How you doing?" Liza asked Dex, as if he had just gotten a divorce.

"I'm fine. Really," Dex lied. "But, I have to go to make-up. Come with me."

"Make-up?! Yo, sssshhhh...," Jordy said, putting his hand by his mouth, "that ain't right!"

#

The lights in the audience dimmed and a large teleprompter set up away from the camera's view instructed silence. The kitchen lights turned from a soft gold to a bright white as members of the crew took their necessary places. The announcer's voice boomed:

Five. Four. Three. A stage hand motioned 'two'...'one.'

Courtney gave Dex a now familiar shove into the studio kitchen.

"Hey Guys!" he boomed. "It's a 'School Day' in the studio. I'll be teaching my class from William Alexander Middle School how to revamp retro faves to make the grade. Let's get cookin.'"

The theme music began to play and Dex started to busily compose his menu. Even with all the crazy twists and turns of the morning, Dex felt relaxed. He had started at Eatz only a short time ago, but he had taken to his role quickly. Nothing had ever thrown him like the shaky rehearsal he'd had at home. At the studio he had no one to please or disappoint but strangers, and somehow that made his job easier.

As Dex continued to chop, mix, and simmer, he was relieved Casey had been right and that none of the new products were difficult to use. The good news was that in a little while this show would be over and he would no longer have to obsess about how things would go. Instead, he could go back to obsessing about Sarah. As he was working minced scallions into biscuit dough, part of him wanted to search the audience for her. The other part told him he was crazy.

'Lose her!' Dex heard a crew member shout backstage. He nearly knocked the mixing bowl off the counter. How could anyone read his mind like that? Then the guy shouted again, but this time Dex heard him more clearly.

"Looser, Fred!" The director motioned for Dex to keep going. It wasn't easy since Dex could see that one of the wires connected to the *DEX-O-METER* was pulled dangerously taut. A skinny guy in a brown sweater crawled around Dex's legs like a stealthy cat, careful to remain unseen by the audience behind the long kitchen island. He tried tugging on several wires before he reached the ripping cable just as it was ready to snap.

When the repair was done, the guy gave Dex a thumbs-up and slithered away.

Dex continued shredding cheddar cheese like nothing had happened. "It's important to be quick and light-handed so all the ingredients marry but the biscuits stay flaky. That's why I sprinkle the cheese over the dough and work it in with just a couple of easy motions. The result is a delectable biscuit."

Why did he have to say 'marry?' Now he was thinking about Sarah again, still in shock that she had gone for Bryce

Watson. Another wrestler he couldn't compete with. He took his frustration out on a fat Vidalia onion and with his giant knife took seconds to dice it into amazing bits.

A few chops and blends later, Dex was done and plating his dishes. Aside from the food he had just prepared, there were larger batches of each dish he and a group of assistants had made earlier.

"And that's how easy it is," Dex said, putting a final sprinkling of parsley on top of a plate of bite-sized sandwiches. "You guys hungry?"

The entire audience applauded and shouted "Yeah!"

The cameras still rolling, the crew began distributing mini-plates of food to the audience. There were random shouts about how delicious everything was. Dex managed to keep his mind off Sarah long enough to feel proud of himself. It had been a challenging day, but he stood up to it. Not to mention it was cool getting so many compliments from the kids he went to school with every day. For the first time since he'd started his show, Dex finally believed he was a chef.

And then the unthinkable happened.

All the smiles and cheers turned to moans and groans, as people began to retch and grip their stomachs. Dex stared at his classmates like he was watching a train wreck and could do nothing to help. And it didn't stop there. An instant later, a kid screamed:

"I'M GONNA HURL!!!"

Within seconds, he and everyone else started puking up everything on Dex's menu, from his Simply Caesar Salad to his Rocky Road Brownies. The audience soon looked like the cast of a cheesy horror movie, but there was more than just cheese flying from every direction. Girls screeched and boys grunted, all the while skidding around the mess of barf lining the ground. Teachers were frantically shouting to gain control between bouts of puking, but it was useless. The exits were jammed with vomit-covered people trying to escape.

Ezra ran frantically from the side of the stage to push the now unmanned commercial button to take the show off the air. "What the hell happened?" He blared at Dex.

"I don't know." Dex was whiter than pale. "Everything was fine and then I..." He looked out again at the chaos. "I quit!" He shrieked as he ran out of the studio too quickly for anyone to catch up with him.

Liza and Jordy couldn't believe what was going on. They had been too busy helping Alicia with interviews to eat. Liza saw Dex running out through a stage exit door that led to the street, but he was too far away for her to get to him.

Chapter 20

"I couldn't believe it!" Kyle coughed. "They cut to a commercial right after Tracey puked on the main camera."

Dex cringed as he and Kyle walked past the empty cafeteria. He wasn't interested in going out with Tracey Waters, but she liked to talk. A lot. If she was angry at him for what happened he could bet no one was going to forgive him any time soon.

The thing is Dex still couldn't figure out what happened.

Kyle pulled a tissue out of his pocket. "Do you know you made history?"

"I know I made something." Dex frowned. "How?" he asked, certain he didn't want to know. *Biggest group barf in the world* was all he could think of.

"Yesterday, in just that one day after your show, there were the most recorded absences in the history of our school!" Kyle blew his nose. "My mom's friends with the attendance lady."

"That's great, Kyle. I'm so proud. Bet next they'll be throwing me a party. Or a parade."

"Parades are cool. As long as you don't have to play a tuba. Take my word for it. That's not fun."

"Kyle, I keep going over the whole day in my head. I can't think of anything I did wrong."

"I believe you. Maybe it was just some mutant strain of puke bugs in the mayonnaise. My mom always says it's a dangerous food especially when it's warm. Was it warm in the studio?"

“No, not unusually. And I know everything was being carefully watched and prepared,” Dex swore.

“Well,” Kyle speculated, “maybe someone with a stomach virus coughed all over everything.”

Dex braced himself as a short girl with a tiny nose and thin lips approached them. She put her hand over her mouth dramatically, and then pulled it off.

“HUUUUURPH!” she croaked out, her mouth in his face as she grabbed her stomach. She then stopped herself and began laughing loudly, darting away before Dex could respond. She was followed by a tall, nerdy guy who was holding his stomach and making loud retching noises as he walked past Dex.

Kyle looked at Dex sympathetically. “Sorry,” he whispered before going into his science class.

Dex felt completely alone. And what was worse, he was scared. He hadn’t meant to hurt anyone, but it happened. The only thing left was payback.

Tracey Waters didn’t look like she had spent yesterday barfing. Every hair fell just where it was supposed to and her make-up was the usual loud mess of perfection. She wasted no time trapping Dex in her scornful gaze and surprised him by shoving a bottle of Pepto-Bismol into his hand.

“Here. Sign this,” she sneered. “We are so over!” Tracey spun around and left without even trying to catch his eye.

A group of kids standing not far behind Dex heard her and laughed. They continued to talk as if he were invisible.

“What a loser,” Dex heard one long-haired girl say.

"I heard he trapped a bunch of pigeons," a boy with the start of a mustache offered. "Then he cooked them and shoved them on toast."

Dex could still hear them as they began to walk away.

"Yeah, I heard that too," said a kid in a denim jacket. "I think the pigeons crapped first, and he left it there like a sauce."

"That is beyond gross," the long-haired girl remarked as she scrunched her face.

"He ain't no cook," insisted a kid in a Jimi Hendrix t-shirt.

"That's for sure." The guy in the jacket put his arm around the girl.

They were finally out of Dex's earshot when a kid who looked like a linebacker started toward him.

Dex shuddered and tried walking faster, but the kid blocked him.

"Hey, Skeletor," the linebacker said right up in his face. "You got my little sister sick, you skinny twiglet. Guess who got to clean it up?" He pointed to himself. "I should snap you into twins." He gave Dex a push and walked away.

Dex was shaking as he pulled out his phone and dialed. "Please come get me. Please..."

Chapter 21

"Dig in." Geema put a big pan on the kitchen table then got a wedge of parmesan cheese from the refrigerator. She didn't smile once.

Dex knew it was his fault.

"Vince," Marla said, holding up her hands to show him she was wearing her dinner gloves. "I have an audition tomorrow for Happy Golfers' Hand ointment. Can you please do the honors?"

Vince nodded and cut out big squares of lasagna that he slid onto each plate. When everyone was served he cut up Marla's food into bite-sized pieces.

"There is no way, Dex," Vince continued the argument Dex had started. "Quitting the show was your decision but, you are not going to be home-schooled."

"You don't get it, Dad. They hate me. They all hate me."

"Even if that were true, and I'm sure it isn't, how would leaving change that?"

"It wouldn't. But at least I'd live."

"You're being dramatic," Vince said.

"I'm being honest. They're all bigger than I am. Even the girls. You aren't there to see what I'm going through!"

"Honey, I think what your dad is trying to say," Marla flashed Vince a look, "is that you're strong and you can handle this. Isn't that right, Vince?" She looked at him again.

"Of course," Vince speared a stray noodle on his plate. "You can't quit everything."

“I’m not saying I want to quit school. I just don’t want to be there,” Dex persisted. “If I’m not there they won’t be in my face every day.” He pushed the food around on his plate.

“You’re right,” Geema chimed in. “But, you have to look at yourself in the mirror, and the way you see yourself has a lot to do with *what* you face.”

Dex knew there was some important message he was supposed to get, but all he could think about was the linebacker hunting him down.

“I know I must have done something wrong, but I still can’t figure out what.”

“Obviously one of the ingredients you used was spoiled.” Vince had an unruly string of cheese dangling from the corner of his mouth. “Go over the menu again. What did you use?”

“Use *this*, please,” Marla jumped in and handed Vince a napkin as she made a wiping motion. Just then, the house phone rang. “That better not be another reporter!” Marla groaned, taking a deep breath before answering the call.

“I’ve gone over all the ingredients and I’m telling you Dad, they’re really careful about refrigeration. They even throw out anything they *think* could be turning bad.”

“Okay, who was handling the food, besides you?” Vince helped himself to another hunk of lasagna.

“I don’t know everyone’s name. They have a bunch of people who help.” Dex took a sip of water. “Kyle said maybe someone who had a stomach bug touched stuff.”

“He could be right.” Vince grated fresh parmesan cheese over his plate.

“Well, I doubt it. I mean Preston LeTray, his assistant, and this guy Arby all seemed fine.”

“Yeah, but you never know with stomach flu. Dex, I’m sure you didn’t do anything wrong, but whatever the reason, you still have to deal with it.”

“Jazz asked about you,” Alicia said, finally done texting a message that had kept her out of the conversation. “He didn’t watch the show, but he saw it on YouTube.” She put her phone in her pocket. “He said it got more hits than Surprised Kitty and Baby Panda Sneeze combined!”

“Thrilling. So now everything’s gone viral.”

Marla came back to the table, completely giddy. “I got the job!!!”

“What?!?” Vince shrieked.

“I’m the next hands for Skin-So-Smooth!” She was grinning from ear to ear. “I didn’t want to say anything. There were over three hundred other models called in.” She held up her hands triumphantly. “These beat out six hundred others somehow. Now I don’t have to go on that dumb Happy Golfers’audition!”

“That’s so great, Mom,” Alicia said, back to texting with Jazz.

“Yeah. It really is,” Dex agreed, still picking at his plate.

“I’m not making much, but your Dad and I get to go to Aruba, all expenses paid, for a whole week!”

Vince got up and kissed her.

“The shoot starts the day after Christmas.”

“That’s wonderful Marla,” Geema said, hugging her close.

“But you guys’ll miss New Year’s.” Alicia was suddenly upset.

“I know Leesh, and I *am* disappointed about that,” Marla admitted looking at Dex. “But, I have to do this. It’s my job.”

#

Dex sat on his bed with his laptop open to Facebook. His wall was covered with comments that hurt him to the core: LOSER! You make me AND everyone else BARF!!!; Screw DINE WITH DEX, I’m DONE WITH DEX; Heard you’re a pigeon killer! Guess you hate animals as much as your audience; Dex--look up at the sky. Maybe you can see Halley’s Vomit!; PUKE YOU... DEXcrement!

One after another, after another. The list seemed endless, and as much as Dex wanted to slam the computer against the wall, something in him made him keep reading.

A knock at the door forced him away from the screen.

“Hey,” Alicia said, carrying a video tape. “I need to show you something.”

“Great. Is it a documentary about what went wrong?”

“No, actually, it’s a clip about what’s going right.”

“There is no right anymore,” Dex moaned.

“You are going to have to stop obsessing at some point,” Alicia warned. “There’s too much at stake.”

“Whatever. So show me. Did ‘Class Puke’ reach a billion views or something?”

She pushed the tape into his dvd/vcr player and flopped next to him on his bed.

“These are the interviews I did at your show before they served lunch.”

“*Before*, being the operative word,” Dex added.

“Just listen!” Alicia insisted pressing ‘play.’

A heavy girl in a baggy pink shirt was speaking. “For someone really thin, he knows a lot about what tastes good. I’m really looking forward to lunch.”

“Or bringing up lunch as it turned out.” Dex forced a laugh.

“Sshhh... Listen,” Alicia insisted.

A dark-skinned guy with dark spiky hair said, “I took an International Cooking class because Dex makes cooking look cool. My girlfriend might love me more if my food could taste like his.”

“He’s an awesome chef,” said a girl who wasn’t Tracey but looked like her. “He could so be my boyfriend.”

“Thanks Dex,” whispered a dorky kid, “for showing us that kids can be successful doing the unexpected.”

Alicia changed the tape. “These are the interviews I did with Liza and Kyle at school a few days ago. I asked them why they think you’re a success and if they think fame has changed you.”

Dex let out a long sigh and sunk back in his pillow while

Alicia turned the player back on. Liza was on the screen.

"That's a good question. Why is Dex a success? Um...I don't know. He's still, you know, Dex. But when he's on TV, he's like, Dex on TV. He's got watch--ability. Yeah, that's it. And when you see him cook stuff, you want to eat it. I don't think he's changed really. I mean, more girls kiss him now, but that's about it."

Kyle appeared on screen next looking wide-eyed and stuck, like a deer in headlights. This time you could hear Alicia speak.

"What do you think has been the biggest reason for Dex's success?"

"His white chocolate chip cookies are awesome." Kyle sounded like a robot.

"And?" Alicia prodded.

"His almond crusted crab cakes are real good too."

Alicia turned off the tape. "See. They think you're great. We all do."

Dex rolled his eyes. "Things are different now."

"Yeah. You gave up your lunch stand and you quit the show." Alicia started for the door. "But just remember, some things haven't changed, Dex. We're gonna lose Poppy's Kitchen."

"I get it. But, who's going to buy my lunches or watch me cook when my food made my entire class puke?"

That was an obvious question, but try though he might, Dex could not find an obvious answer.

Chapter 22

Alicia parked in the lot of the small strip mall at the intersection of Route 306 and Willow Cove Road next to Caldor's, a defunct department store where her grandmother loved to shop when Alicia was little. It had been vacant for decades, but a fleet of bulldozers and construction materials occupied much of the open space. Jazz had texted her to meet him there because he wanted her opinion about something important. She wasn't sure what he wanted, but she was sure she didn't want to miss spending time with him.

Alicia grabbed her bag and got out of the car. It was a lot windier than she had expected. The cold ran through her as she folded up the collar of her light leather jacket. A quick glance at her phone told her she was only a few minutes late. Meanwhile, Jazz was nowhere to be found. She was thinking of getting coffee when she felt a gentle tap on her shoulder.

"Hey," Jazz said from behind her.

"Hi. Sorry I'm late." Alicia rubbed her hands together.

"No bother. I really appreciate your meeting me." He turned on his camera. "I was around the back with the foreman."

"Oh. Okay," she said watching as Jazz adjusted the lens. "The foreman?"

"Yes." Jazz was now aiming his camera at Alicia.

"Why?" Alicia stuck her tongue out at the camera and laughed.

"It's my uncle. I'm filming the development of the new shopping center being built on this site."

“Wow. That’s ambitious,” Alicia mused.

“Do you think it’s too much?”

“It’s just that it won’t be finished by the time the project is due.”

“Well, I was thinking maybe of playing it up from a different angle. Like what goes on in the process from the perspectives of the crew.” Jazz stood on a large flat rock and panned the site from one end to the other.

“That actually sounds kind of brilliant.” Alicia was impressed.

She was still shivering and thought about standing closer to Jazz, but he was still engrossed in filming and she didn’t want to distract him. Besides, they were still only friends and she didn’t want to give him any ideas he didn’t already have on his own. Her friend Lola called her a ‘sad grandma’ for not telling Jazz she liked him, but Alicia still wanted him to be the one to make the first move if there was going to be one.

Jazz readjusted the camera lens. “How’s Dex doing?”

“Uh,” she hesitated. Were they close enough that she could be honest? But Jazz did look genuinely concerned. “Not so well actually. But thanks for asking.”

Jazz stopped filming. “What’s going on?”

“‘He keeps asking to be home-schooled.”

“Whoa. That bad. Poor bloke. I mean, I guess it could work for some kids, but I had a friend whose parents did that; turned him into a total bludger.”

“A what?” Alicia asked, trying not to laugh at the odd term.

“Oh right, you don’t know that one,” Jazz laughed. “It’s a guy who just hangs around and soaks up the air. Doesn’t get out, has his mates come to his place, that kind of thing.” Alicia smiled and nodded, enjoying his explanation.

Suddenly, a crane lifted a large block of cement and Jazz went back to filming.

“I know,” Alicia continued. “It sucks to be twelve.”

“For sure,” Jazz agreed. “Especially when you’ve sent heaps of people into a technicolor yawn.”

This time, Alicia couldn’t resist and burst out laughing.

“Let me guess,” she said. “That’s Australian for hurling?”

“I suppose,” Jazz said. “That’s throwin’ up, right?” Alicia rolled her eyes and nodded. “Oh, then yeah.” Then Jazz started snickering. “Hurling? Heh. Haven’t heard that one before.”

Alicia moved comfortably closer to Jazz. “What are you shooting now?” she asked, noticing Jazz moving the camera in an entirely different direction.

“My uncle’s other project. A new office building next to the mall. It’s being modeled after the one over there.” He pointed across the street.

“Which one?” Alicia asked.

“Perfect,” Jazz said distracted. “I’m outta tape.”

“Oh, don’t worry, I haven’t used this yet.”

Alicia went into her bag and took out her camera. Just as she got hold of the tape, her foot hit a rock and the tape flew into the air. As she and Jazz both reached up to catch it they fell forward, trapping the tape between their bodies. They looked at the tape and then each other.

For a moment, Alicia wasn't sure what to do. Should she move away? Should she say something? She couldn't make up her mind so she closed her eyes. And that's when Jazz kissed her. His lips felt warm and soft pressed against hers and suddenly the cold no longer bothered her.

A construction worker nearby whistled and Alicia and Jazz both flinched out of their moment.

Jazz chuckled as the tape began to slip between them and he quickly pressed against her to keep it from falling. His hand grazed her thigh as he reached for the tape and he put it into the camera before either of them could speak about what had just happened.

"So like I was saying, my uncle is using that great old building over there as a model." Jazz said, already filming.

"Over where?" Alicia asked.

"There," he pointed and showed her through the camera lens. "The one with all the detailing around the roof and windows."

"You're kidding!" Alicia exclaimed. "That's my old building. A lot of my family lived there over the years. The restaurant is next door."

"Poppy's Kitchen? I didn't realize it was so close."

"We used to have dinner there every Sunday. That's how Dex learned to cook," Alicia sighed. "He used to help Poppy make everything. But now it all feels like a waste. It's hard to believe, but my brother has actually given up."

Jazz put his camera away in the soft case slung around his shoulder. "But, if there's no show, no lunch stand, and maybe no school, what's gonna happen to Poppy's Kitchen?"

#

Dex dumped a can of pasta and sauce into a bowl and put it in the microwave. He wasn't even sure how canned spaghetti had made its way into the pantry. He figured it was an old mistake from one of Geema's shopping trips that no one had ever bothered to return. Dex wasn't sure why he felt he had to eat it. Probably to get used to a new menu, since he had vowed never to cook again. It was the least he could do after the mess he'd made.

It had been a couple of days since he'd gone to school, and his parents told him that he had the rest of the week to figure out a way to move on. He was still intent on home-schooling as the healthiest option, but he was safe for now.

The doorbell rang and Dex left the beeping microwave to see who it was. He took a peek out the window and saw Sarah, looking way too hot to be anywhere near him. She was dressed in jeans and a tan leather jacket. Her hair was long and loose without any ponytail or clips forcing it to behave. Her lips were a light frosty pink and her whole face looked shimmery. He wondered how long he could make her stand there just so he could keep looking at her. But, he couldn't do that. He had to let her in. He took a quick whiff of his armpits, which he determined were passable, then ran his hands over his hair. He was as ready as he could be and hesitantly opened the door.

“Hi,” Sarah said, then gave him a once over. “Can I come in?”

“Sure,” he answered, leading her to the family room.

“Nice shirt,” Sarah chuckled, taking a seat.

Dex looked down. He’d forgotten he was wearing an old Power Rangers t-shirt that still fit him. “Yeah. My real stuff’s in the laundry.”

“I don’t mind.” Sarah smiled. “Nice memories.”

“Is...is everything okay, Sarah?”

“You tell me, Dex.”

“What do you mean?” He sat down on the couch, opposite her.

“You weren’t in International Cooking. And that Presto guy’s show was on during your time slot.”

“It’s better this way,” Dex insisted. “No one’s barfing.”

“So. That’s it. Some kids barfed and you’re life is over.”

“You don’t get it Sarah. Nobody laughs at you. You think barf is my only problem?”

“Huh?”

“Forget it.”

“Dex, you can’t just say something like that and then--”

“Alright. Fine,” Dex argued. “Look at me.”

She eyed him up and down. “Yeah, so...?” Sarah was puzzled.

“Notice anything?”

“You wear dorky t-shirts?”

“No. Something besides that.”

“What do you want me to see?”

Dex was frustrated and hesitant to answer her. “Someone,” he managed to squeak out. “Someone like Bryce.”

“What’s so great about Bryce? He’s a dumb-ass jock. We broke up.”

“I thought you, um, girls, like guys like him,” Dex said starting to perk up.

“Yeah. The way guys like girls like Jade Carravaccio. My boobs sure don’t look like hers.”

“But that’s not what all guys care about.”

“Exactly.”

“Huh?”

“Not everybody orders the same sandwich, Dex.”

Dex felt himself start to smile and for the first time in nearly a week, he let it happen.

“And one other thing,” Sarah added. “I’d never order chicken salad. I hate it. So at your show, I ate everything else, and I was fine. I told Jordy and he agreed. We don’t think your cooking had anything to do with everyone puking.”

Dex raised an eyebrow.

"And Dex?"

"Yeah?"

"One more thing." Sarah sat down next to him and put her hand on his shoulder. She leaned in and kissed him in a way that made him completely forget the Power Rangers between them.

Chapter 23

"Dexy, it's been a while since I've told you a good bedtime story," Geema said from the couch. "I think it's time. Why don't you get us some milk."

"Sure," Dex said, walking to the kitchen.

"And those leftover Cocoa Kiss cookies you baked that I hid."

"Hid?" Dex asked, stopping in his tracks.

"In a bag behind the olive oil," Geema admitted.

Dex chuckled and came back with a crowded tray.

"Come sit here," Geema motioned.

Dex put the food on the table and sat down next to her.

"'The thing is,' Poppy used to say, 'it's a lot easier to stop a fire when you know how to adjust the flame,'" Geema began. "Long before he had his own restaurant, Poppy worked part-time at Gross's delicatessen on the lower east side of Manhattan. The deli was a family-run business, and Poppy's job was usually to work behind the counter slicing meats and refilling the salads and condiments. His friend, Stuie, the owner's son, was also a counter guy."

"Every once in a while," Geema continued, "especially around the Jewish holidays when it got really busy, the boys were asked to help prepare the entrees, sandwiches, and side dishes in addition to their other responsibilities. One night, after closing, there was an emergency. Stuie's grandfather was in a fender bender on the West Side Highway and got a mild concussion. Stuie's father had to go to the hospital and then take care of the car."

"That day the deli had gotten tons of orders for whole turkeys, roasts, and salads. There was more to cook and prepare than anyone had anticipated, and the customers needed to get their orders before sundown, in time for the Jewish New Year. Stuie's father was in a bind and asked Poppy and Stuie to make sure the meats were taken out of the oven on time, and that the vegetables for the salads were chopped and sliced. His only other request was to make the chopped liver. The liver was already cooked and the onions were sautéed, but it still needed to be mixed with the rest of the ingredients."

"But Poppy had already made a date that night with me," Geema went on with pride, "'the most beautiful girl,' he told Stuie, 'he had ever seen.'" Geema blushed and continued. "Poppy waited until everyone left to ask Stuie if he minded handling the work on his own. Stuie said it was no problem, except for the chopped liver. Stuie's father had left him a recipe and ingredients and told him they should make a big batch for the next day."

"Aside from the smell of liver making him gag, Stuie had no clue what to do. He wanted to be a baseball player and was only working at the deli because his father insisted. Poppy told him not to worry and to leave the chopped liver to him. He had a key and would make it to work way before anyone got there in the morning."

"'But,' Poppy would say, 'plans are like planes. They take off when they're good and ready.' And that's what happened on our date. Hour after hour flew and by the time he got to my front door, he'd forgotten all about the chopped liver. It was almost dawn when Poppy jumped up out of a dream and realized his mistake."

"He got dressed quickly and ran to the deli. It was too late to start making anything. Poppy thought quickly, packed the ingredients in a carton, and brought them home. Then he went a few blocks away to a 24-hour diner he knew and bought out their chopped liver. He ran back to the deli praying no one was there yet. The place was empty. He kept one eye glued to the door as he added a couple of unexpected ingredients to give the recipe a touch of originality. He had just finished filling the containers when Stuie came in with his father."

"Stuie looked relieved and gave Poppy an enthusiastic smile. Poppy was so grateful to be done with the ordeal that he passed the credit for the work, including the chopped liver, to Stuie. His father took a bite and beamed. He said it was the most delicious liver he had ever tasted. Poppy said all he did was help and that Stuie was the one with the talent. Stuie's father thanked them both and gave the boys the rest of the day off."

"And it all would have been fine if Morty Becker, of Becker's Diner, hadn't sent his pregnant wife, who had an intense craving for hot pastrami piled high on seeded rye, to Gross's Deli for lunch. She took one look at the chopped liver and asked for a taste. As he was handing her a sample, Stuie's father was bragging about what a gifted chef his son was. Mrs. Becker took one bite and started screaming that the chopped liver was her husband's. Stuie's father yelled back that she was out of her mind, and so the feud began."

"Poppy decided to keep his mouth shut. Which he said lasted about five minutes. Even though he needed the money, he couldn't lie. He marched into the kitchen and told Stuie's father all about me and the chopped liver from Becker's. Poppy told him he felt guilty, so guilty he even offered to quit."

"At first, Stuie's father was angry and almost accepted his resignation. But after a few very tense minutes, he started laughing out of nowhere, saying he remembered what it was like to be out with a beautiful woman. Poppy figured he must have had a good memory since Stuie's mother wasn't exactly a stunner. Poppy had no clue what was so funny, but he laughed along with Stuie's father until his apology was accepted and his job was secured. But, there was one condition: Poppy couldn't say a word about what happened to anyone, including Stuie. The terms were unshakable. It was to remain their secret."

"In the days that followed, the expression 'there's no such thing as bad publicity' became enormously evident. Becker's claim that Gross's stole their recipe helped both restaurants become more popular than ever before as customers went back and forth to decide who made the better liver."

"It was years before Poppy shared the story with me," Geema said, "And, he kept his word and never told Stuie the truth. But, he did give him his recipe, and Stuie and your grandfather stayed best friends."

"You see Dex, in life, there are no such things as mistakes. Every experience teaches us some kind of important lesson."

"As a matter of fact, it was Stuie who finally convinced Poppy to open the restaurant. It took some prodding since Poppy was humble and anything but a businessman. But Stuie assured Poppy that given his talent, he would be very successful. By that time Stuie was a lawyer, and he helped Poppy set up the whole business."

"For many years, before he followed his daughter's family to Israel, Stuie and his wife were regulars at the restaurant. Each visit he would leave saying, 'Ralphie, you gotta patent that pesto of yours.' And Poppy would say, '*You* gotta patent that pesto of mine.'"

"It was a long-running joke since we all knew Poppy didn't

care about that kind of stuff and would never bother. He believed very simply in *an honest day's pay for an honest day's work.* That was part of your grandfather's charm; he had no idea how wonderful he was."

"That's a really cool story Geema." Dex took a long swig of milk. "What's a patent?"

"It's kind of like a legal stamp of approval that a product belongs to you."

#

Dex couldn't stop fidgeting. A temp worker filling in for Casey had let him into Ezra's office, but told him 'the boss' was in a meeting and Dex could be waiting a while. There were just so many times he could go over what he wanted to say. He knew he would apologize. Not just for making everyone sick, which both Sarah and Jordy questioned, but for running away. Ezra was entitled to an explanation, even if Dex didn't have one. The door opened and Dex sucked in a deep breath, ready to defend himself. But instead, as soon as Ezra spotted Dex, he gave him a warm smile, which left Dex confused.

"I know I should have spoken with you about everything," Dex apologized. "But, I freaked. I'm really sorry. I won't let anything like that happen again--ever." Dex looked at Ezra squarely in the eye. "I'd really like my job back."

"I see," Ezra said from the seat he took on the corner of his desk.

Dex could feel himself trembling. What if he'd blown it and Ezra was too upset with him to take him back? Even if he reopened his lunch stand he'd never be able to make enough money to save Poppy's Kitchen, and the *Gymbuff* would be totally out of the question unless he wanted to be an eighty-year-old with a six pack.

Ezra stood up and Dex braced himself for the worst.

"Do you know what happened to your ratings that day?" Ezra asked.

"I guess they were pretty bad." Dex sighed heavily. Now he was really worried. "It was probably the worst thing that could ever happen on a cooking show."

Ezra handed Dex the ratings sheet. "Kid, in this industry there's no such thing as bad publicity."

Dex looked at the report and gasped.

"Your ratings went right through the roof!" Ezra shrilled. "Your YouTube clip went viral. Your audience wants you back. You're the biggest thing since..."

"Surprised Kitty and Baby Panda Sneeze," Dex finished.

#

Even though he hadn't closed his lunch stand for long, his customers had been sending emails and even letters asking when he'd be back. He thought they were just being nice; like feeling sorry for a batter who struck out and lost the game.

But as more and more people emailed him, Dex became even more confused. His increased popularity was as tough for him to digest as his chicken salad had been for everyone at school. He couldn't imagine how a YouTube clip of an audience full of kids puking had enticed people to line up for what he had to offer. Could it be that Ezra and Poppy were right? Was there truly no such thing as bad publicity?

Chapter 24

"Dex!" Alicia bolted into the kitchen nearly knocking Dex over along with a bowl of rum raisin pancake batter.

"Geez, Leesh! What?" Dex snipped, making sure the bowl was stable.

"Sorry 'bout that," Alicia apologized. "I just had the most amazing conversation with my old boss in L.A."

"You're not leaving again are you?" Dex was a little surprised at how much that possibility worried him.

"No," Alicia dismissed. "Actually, it was about his celebrity friends who went on Saturday Night Live to make fun of themselves."

"Hilarious," Dex chided dryly.

"Think about it, Dex," Alicia suggested.

"Okay. I just did. So what?"

"You should do it."

"*I* should do it?"

"Yes. Jazz thinks so too."

"That makes no sense."

"It makes all kinds of sense," Alicia insisted. "Everyone would see how cool you are."

"But I'm not cool," Dex whined. "I'm embarrassed."

"Exactly why you should do it."

Dex thought for a moment. It's not like he had much to lose at this point. "If I were going to do something like that, how would I do it?"

"We'll re-open your lunch stand with a new sign."

"What kind of sign?"

"Depends on the menu. But something clever." Alicia's phone rang. "It's Lola. Jazz'll be here in a few minutes. Think about it. We'll help you."

Dex looked through the pantry and refrigerator trying to decide what he could make for his grand re-opening. He didn't want to go too bold, but he couldn't play it overly safe either. He was flipping the last of the pancakes when the doorbell rang.

Alicia came into the kitchen with Jazz, who quickly snatched a pancake from the almost full plate.

"So, what did you decide?" Alicia asked, also grabbing a pancake.

"To make extra pancakes when I'm hungry."

"Sorry mate," Jazz said. "Didn't mean to steal your meal."

"Just kidding," Dex said. "So, what do we do?"

Alicia smiled. "It's new sign time!"

#

It was nearly midnight when Jazz, Alicia, and Dex finally posted the risky grand-re-opening sign proudly on the front lawn. There it was in bold black and red marker on a large white sheet of heavy oak tag:

DEX THE FOOD DUDE - GRAND RE-OPENING!

TODAY'S GAGBAG SPECIAL: UP-CHUCK ROAST with CARROT HURLS

TODAY'S DESSERTS: 'TOSS-UR' COOKIES, STRAWBERRY-RHUBARF TARTS

Dex was determined to take it all in stride and get back to work. How else could he save Poppy's Kitchen? Success was the only answer. Besides, he was never going to be able to show his face in school again if he didn't turn things around.

#

It wasn't much past dawn when Dex peered out the kitchen window to see the line for his lunch stand beginning to form. He would prove to everyone that he was still a good chef who deserved to stay on TV, because his cooking really *was* that good.

With nearly no sleep, Dex pushed the wheelbarrow to the door excited and ready to open shop. He was just about to leave when one of the wheels got stuck crossing the saddle. He tried pushing it harder, but that did nothing except make him sweat. He got down on his knees to investigate, but he found nothing that explained the problem. The wheel just didn't want to move.

There was only one solution. Dex took a long look at all the neatly-packed food nestled inside the wagon and sighed heavily. He would have to lift the dumb thing. There was no way. That sucker had to weigh a buhjillion pounds. Jazz and Alicia met up for breakfast and Vince went to work extra early. Marla had a late shoot and was still sleeping. The only one left was Geema. And he worried that she'd hurt herself carrying empty laundry baskets.

Dex got out his phone and called Kyle. "Yeah, yeah, it's Kyle," his voicemail answered. "Leave a message at the burp. EHHHHHH."

Great. He was probably showering. There was no one else he could think of. It's not like he could call Sarah and ask her to come over and help him do what all her other boyfriends could do with one pinky. No. He'd have to man up and do it himself.

He walked over to the cart and tried lifting the front end. He got it a couple of inches off the ground, and some of the sandwiches tumbled to the back. So much for presentation. He could take everything out of the cart and start all over again, but that would take forever. Besides, if he didn't get out there soon, it would get too late and he'd lose customers.

He took the deepest breath he ever took in his life and used every ounce of strength he had to lift the back end of the cart and push it forward. It moved. Only an inch, but it moved. If he could do that another ten times, he might be able to get it over the saddle before noon. He was so frustrated, he kicked the cart. A move that was nothing short of a miracle. The cart went right over the saddle like it had done every day for months.

So maybe it wasn't exactly the most heroic effort, but he still got the job done by himself. It beat having to ask for help and being rescued. It made him wonder about Sarah. He hoped she had wanted their kiss to mean more than a moment of pity. There was no way of knowing yet. He could ask her, but that would be dumb. No sense in putting *that* cart before the horse.

It was a little after seven and the line already stretched halfway down the block. Dex braved the morning chill as he went down with the wheelbarrow to greet the first customers of the day. He had to admit, seeing Rhonda and other familiar faces made him feel better. There were also a bunch of new people. He was glad Kyle showed up. It was going to be a busy morning.

Chapter 25

Dex yawned over a bowl of garlic cloves. It was his first day back on the set of his show and he was a lot more tired than he wanted to be. His director would be calling for 'action,' in less than an hour. Wrong day to be making One-Pot Chicken Supreme, a dish loaded with cut-up chickens that had him chopping every vegetable the local farm had to offer.

The morning had been nuts with his lunch stand opening early and closing late. By the time he and Kyle had gotten everything back in the house, they had to run to catch the bus. Then when Dex got to school he had an algebra test and had to make Italian Wedding Soup in International Cooking. To make matters worse, Sarah had been absent.

There had to be some way to keep his eyes open that didn't involve coffee. That stuff always made him run to the bathroom.

"Dex, glad you're back, kid," Ezra said, coming in from the back entrance of the studio kitchen. "Here's a little something for you." He handed Dex a chocolate bar wrapped in dark purple foil with foreign words imprinted on the cover. "A friend of mine, maybe you've heard of him, Bobby Flay, picked this up when he was filming a special in Guadalajara. He said you should try it in your Dexican Cocoa Loco."

"Bobby Flay? THE Bobby Flay?"

"Only one I know, kid." Ezra put his finger to his lips. "But keep it quiet. Bobby still works for the *other* network."

"Oh, I won't say anything," Dex promised. "Bobby Flay tried *my* cocoa recipe?"

"Said it was outrageous," Ezra offered matter-of-factly. "You can eat this one if you want. Bobby gave me a whole case of them and I can tell you each variety has a fascinating flavor profile." Ezra gave him a tap on the shoulder. "Later, kid," he said and left.

The good news was Dex felt totally pumped. Bobby Flay thought *his* hot cocoa was amazing. That trumped Alicia getting him a latte when he was visiting her studio in L.A. Dex started chopping garlic like a machine without even remembering how tired he was.

#

Preston walked by the studio kitchen and nearly fainted when he saw Dex working at the counter. What was going on? Preston had taken over Dex's time slot after the live lunch horror, and he was planning to keep it that way. Things were going deliciously. Why was the little punk standing in Preston's spot smiling and using his favorite Ginsu knife?

Preston was so disillusioned he never noticed Ezra approaching him.

"In my office in five, Preston," Ezra directed, pointing to his watch. Then he ran backstage, calling for an audio check on a faulty mic next to the food processor.

Preston got off the elevator and walked down the hall to Ezra's office scratching his head. He couldn't imagine what the stodgy creep needed to discuss. Preston had already assured him that sales of his new products were underway and going slowly, but surely. The market was a little sluggish, but that certainly wasn't his fault. So what if it would take a little longer to get everything moving. No big deal.

Besides, it was undeniable that his ratings were noticeably improved when Dex was out of the picture. That meant that given the chance, people still wanted to watch him. Preston would make that nitwit Ezra sit tight while he worked his usual magic. And this time when he did, there'd be no room left for error.

Preston marched into Ezra's office ignoring the secretary's direction to have a seat in the waiting area. He helped himself to a chocolate-covered cherry sitting in a box on Ezra's desk and then took a seat.

"Ah, so here you are," Ezra remarked taking his seat. "And you've already insulted my new secretary and eaten my chocolate."

"Your secretary? Sorry, I hadn't noticed. I just assumed the chocolate was out for us to celebrate." Preston smiled as he remembered the one point he knew would be the all-important clincher. "I'm sure you noticed how well I did in the ratings last week."

"I'm afraid that's not quite the case, Preston." Ezra closed the box of chocolate. "Truth is we've hit the wall. Your products aren't selling. We're going to have to pull the plug on our investment."

"That's preposterous. Simply mad." Preston could feel the panic grip his throat. "We have a contract you know."

"It expired."

"Expired? That's amusing. I didn't realize." Preston began to wring his hands. "Well at least I have my show."

"Yeah, about that...Preston, I'm sorry. We're expanding 'Dine with Dex' to an hour. He's taking over your time slot."

"But my ratings went up!" Preston repeated, as if Ezra hadn't heard him before.

"Yeah, and the second Dex came back, his ratings were nearly twice as strong as yours were while he was away."

"He wasn't away, Ezra," Preston sneered. "He quit! He walked out on you, on all of us! He simply cannot handle the pressure of working here. He's already proven that."

"Ehh, that was a fluke. He was working in front of the kids from school. Would've made any kid nervous."

"Exactly my point. He's a kid." Preston softened his voice, summoning every ounce of sweetness he could muster. "Don't toy with me Ezra. We're men. You're talking about a kid here."

"A kid whose ratings went through the roof with that lunch fiasco." Ezra stood up and sat on the corner of his desk. "I couldn't have asked for a better outcome if I had planned it myself."

"Surely there must be something I can do to change your mind." Preston was repulsed to hear himself begging, and suddenly wanted to throw up.

"No, there's nothing." Ezra reopened the box of candy and popped a chocolate into his mouth. "Not unless Dex forgets how to cook altogether and his New Year's special is a total bust." He laughed. "But, I don't expect his goose to be cooked any way but gourmet, and neither should you. Heck even that kid's mistakes have turned to gold."

Preston sat motionless.

Ezra began to chuckle again, but stopped himself. "Preston,

it's been a good run, but I'm going to need you to clean out your office."

"But I have a show scheduled for today," Preston argued.

"Change of plans. Your last appearance will be the guest spot on Dex's New Year's special. It's airing live." Ezra handed Preston the schedule. "You'll have plenty of time to thank your fans and tell them you're moving on."

#

Preston was pacing back and forth fighting the impulse to throw everything that wasn't his personal property right out his office window. Yvette was at his computer frantically typing.

"Anything yet?" Preston demanded.

"Are you sitting down, Pressykins?!?"

Preston took a moment from his pacing to glare at her.

"Oh, right," she said watching him pick up speed as he resumed. "Well, I did some digging and found out a bit of interesting news about, uh, 'Poopy's Kitchen.'"

Preston glared at her again.

"You know," Yvette prodded, "that slop joint the kid talks about all the time."

"Of course I know. 'My Geema's restaurant,'" Preston whined mimicking Dex. "What about it?" Preston asked in his own voice.

"My friend Nan over at Meridian Bank told me, in the strictest confidence, that the old hag who owns the place can't afford to keep it. And the bank has the right to sell it."

“So?”

“So, she said if you bring her a check today, you could own the place by tonight!” Yvette wrapped her arms around Preston’s shoulders.

“You’re kidding!” He reached into his drawer and pulled out a silver pen.

Yvette dropped her arms and began kissing his neck.

“I guess Ezra is still playing it cheap and safe with the newbies or Dexy would’ve already paid that bill.” Preston smiled and took out his checkbook from his jacket pocket. “Yes, it’s such a shame that a handsome, well-informed businessman might just beat him to it.”

Chapter 26

Dex was on his laptop watching Guy Fieri and his son on YouTube making waffles in Times Square. Dex was thinking about adding waffle sandwiches to his menu. It would be a challenge to use them like bread, but he was pretty sure he could pull it off.

He didn't want to jinx it, but it seemed like the most important things in his life were improving. Somehow the rotten chicken salad seemed to have made everything better. The lunch stand was more popular than ever with new customers showing up every morning. Kids had stopped bothering him at school, and even though he and Sarah never talked about their kiss, they were finally Facebook friends.

To top things off, Ezra hadn't freaked out and was actually talking about building Dex's career. He mentioned the possibility of expanding his show, maybe even giving him a special. There were enough 'maybes' being tossed around to fill a salad, but the one sure thing was working meant money, and money meant saving Poppy's Kitchen.

Dex was replaying the kiss with Sarah in his mind when there was a knock on the door. "Come in," he mumbled.

"Dex?" Vince opened the door. "You okay? You sound bummed."

Dex wasn't about to tell his father he ruined his daydream about Sarah.

"No. I'm fine," Dex sighed. "Just tired."

"Oh, okay." Vince sounded relieved. "It's just the girls are out shopping and I was hoping you were up for some Super Mario."

"Sure," Dex said, thinking the distraction would be a good thing.

"And a pizza?" Vince grinned like he was the kid.

"Sounds great."

Dex put down the laptop and arranged the game.

"You know Dex, I'm really proud of you." Vince was already clicking his way through the first level.

"You are? Why? All I did was make a mistake."

"A mistake is a mistake, but you didn't let it own you." Vince beamed. "Things got tough, but you came through."

"Everyone helped," Dex admitted. "I'm not so sure I could have done it all by myself."

"Maybe, but it was still on you." Vince put the controller down. "I wanted to wait till everyone was here to tell you, but I can't."

"Tell me what?"

"I just got a call from Ezra. The ratings came in." Vince scrunched his face, sending a shot of terror through Dex that made him suddenly doubt his good fortune after all.

"Okay..?" Dex said cautiously.

"You're..." Vince started. "Well, you're NUMBER ONE!"

"Really!?" Dex pumped his fist into the air. "Number one?!"

"I know." Vince hugged Dex and kissed the top of his head. "It's amazing! And he wants you to host the New Year's Eve special. It's live at the studio!"

“That’s awesome!” Dex shouted, then stopped himself. “But wait, you and Mom won’t be home.”

“I know. But don’t worry. Geema and Alicia will be. And I asked the hotel to give us a room with the biggest TV they have so we won’t miss anything. And when Mom and I get back we can have a big party at Poppy’s Kitchen to celebrate.”

“The restaurant?” Dex’s stomach turned.

“Of course,” Vince insisted. “Geema’s been stubborn about keeping the renovation a surprise, but I’m sure it’ll be ready by then.”

#

“Things are getting complicated, Leesh.”

Dex watched as Alicia was trying to change the tape in her camera. “Can you start knocking from now on? You are still my little brother, famous or not.”

“Sorry, I just...I just can’t take lying to everyone anymore. Dad just told me he’s planning to have some party at the restaurant when they get back from Aruba. How are we going to have a party at our restaurant if the bank owns it?”

“You said we’d have enough to buy it back.” Alicia looked frustrated as the tape kept kinking up in the same place.

“We might. It’s not like I haven’t been trying.”

“I know,” Alicia whispered. “I’m sorry all I had to give you was what I got from the Rosenbaums.”

“No big deal. It all counts.” Dex grabbed the camera from her to fix the tape. “I think we should tell Geema we know the truth about the restaurant and we’re working on getting the money to buy it back.”

“We can’t!” Alicia protested. “That letter didn’t even say how much she owes.”

“So?”

“So, we don’t want to risk getting her hopes up. What if we don’t have enough?” Alicia asked. “We need to find Geema’s records. That’s the only way we’ll know for sure.”

Dex gave the tape a final tug to fix it and handed it back to Alicia. “And how do you figure on doing that?”

“Duh, when she goes out,” Alicia sneered.

“Double duh, there’s a reason we didn’t do that already. She never goes anywhere!” Dex shot back.

“True,” Alicia scowled. “Well, something is bound to come up.”

Chapter 27

Dex was lying on his bed staring out the window too preoccupied to read. Sometimes he had to wonder if he was missing out on being an ordinary kid. In most ways it was insanely amazing to be different. He didn't know anyone his age who had a business and a TV show, but there was another side to it that weighed heavily on his mind. What would happen if he couldn't buy back Poppy's Kitchen? It would be like losing his grandfather all over again, and the possibility plagued him more than he cared to admit.

Alicia was right. Failure was not an option. If Vince was proud of him for coming through once, Dex would have to do it again. Only this time, Vince wouldn't know about it. He was just about to start reading *Great Expectations* to prepare for his English test when Alicia burst into his room.

"Geema went to the dentist!"

"Yeay?!?!?! Dex applauded. "Teeth are good?" he added, shrugging.

"No Dex-factor—we have time to look through her room for the bank statements."

Dex didn't even bother to argue. He jumped up and followed Alicia into his grandmother's bedroom. The full size bed was covered by a new floral comforter that had matching curtains that hung from both her windows. There was a large white dresser with a mirror hung above it next to a desk with thin, very swirly legs. A small chair was tucked into the desk and the rest of the wall space was taken up by bookcases and white wooden shelves. Geema called it 'shabby chic,' to convince herself it wasn't cluttered, but it was kind of hard not to notice her inability to throw things out.

"I think she saved every card anyone ever gave her," Dex moaned, holding up a 'HAPPY 50th BIRTHDAY' card covered in now-faded flowers. "I'm not sure we'll have enough time to find anything, even if her appointment lasts a year."

"Well don't give up before we start," Alicia scolded.

"Fine." Dex opened the top drawer and saw a stack of bras and underwear. "Um...Leesh, this is just all kinds of wrong."

"What are you complaining about now?" Alicia asked, her head buried in a notebook titled *My Poetry.*

"Look. Actual granny-panties. Eeeew." Dex held up a pair of white lacy panties.

Alicia turned around. "Ooooh!" She snatched them away.

"Just so you know, there is no way I am going through my grandmother's drawers." He immediately blushed remembering Geema called underwear, 'drawers.' "Not for anything!" Dex went to the closet and slid the door open.

Alicia put down the notebook and went over to the dresser.

"Dex, did you know that Geema wrote poems?"

"Kinda. She said she used to write when she was in high school." He found a box at the bottom of the closet and took it out to open it. "It feels weird going through her stuff."

"Yeah, I know what you mean. I'm not loving this either," Alicia admitted as she searched between layers of clothes. "But, if we want to help her, what choice do we have?"

Dex put one box back and took out a curious light-blue circular container that had a zipper running around its center. He opened it cautiously, chuckled, then went into the closet.

"Did you find anything yet?" Alicia asked, busily going through more clothing. "Dex?" She turned to address his silence.

"Dex, where'd you go?" She went to peek out the door. When she returned she found Dex wearing a glamorous blonde beehive wig on his head.

"What do you think?" Dex laughed.

"I think you look like a dweeb," she said, struggling to stay focused. "Come on, we have to be serious about this." She went back to the dresser, took another look at Dex, and burst into a fit of laughter. "Thanks," she said. "I don't think I'll ever be able to look at you the same way again." She couldn't stop laughing.

"Why, you think I'm pretty?" Dex asked, trying to keep her going.

"Gorgeous," Alicia teased as Dex took off the wig.

They both went back to hunting when a loud squeak caught their attention.

"Was that the door?" Alicia turned to Dex, who was now wearing a short black wig that made him look like Rihanna.

"I think so." Dex snapped off the wig and quickly put it back in its case.

"Oh crap!" Alicia panicked. "What are we going to do now?"

They both stood frozen as they heard the front door slam.

Geema's voice bellowed through the house. "Leeshie? Dex? Where is everyone?"

"Go stall her," Alicia ordered. "NOW!"

"Stall her? How?!?"

"Uh, I don't know. You entertain people for a living." Alicia pushed him out the door. "Keep her entertained! I'll clean up. Go!"

"Hi Geema!" Dex called out from the top of the stairs. He flew down to greet her.

"Here. Let me do that for you," he said, helping her take off her coat. Then he pulled out a hanger from the closet in the entryway.

"What are you up to?" she asked suspiciously. "I want to say thank you, but you don't watch enough Cary Grant movies to be doing that move."

"Up to?" Dex tried to think quickly. "I was...doing homework."

"Homework. Okay. I won't keep you." Geema started for the steps.

"I thought you were going to the dentist," Dex said, guiding her into the family room.

"I did. I don't have enough teeth to be there that long." She sighed. "I'm beat. I think I'll go take a nap."

Dex put his arm around her and laid his head on her shoulder. "Why don't you stay down here on the couch? You can keep me company."

He sat down and practically pulled her down next to him.

“I thought you were doing homework,” Geema said, studying his face.

“I was. I’m done. It was on some love poem. Those are always short.”

“I suppose most of them are.”

A lightbulb went off in Dex’s head as he remembered what Alicia found in the bedroom. “Did you write poems?” Dex asked.

“A long time ago.”

“Remember any of them?”

“No.”

Dex fumbled for another idea. “How did you meet Poppy?”

“I thought I told you that story a hundred times, Dexy.”

#

Alicia was sorting through papers and books as she was cleaning up the piles she and Dex had made.

“Come on,” she muttered under her breath. “If I were bank statements, where would I be?” She looked in a *Better Homes and Garden* magazine. “In the garbage,” she answered herself, “because everyone except Geema uses the Internet.”

Alicia had to stop when she noticed a large laminated picture that looked like it came from a photo album wedged between two brightly-covered books facing outward on a shelf. It caught her attention and she allowed herself a moment to look at it.

“Wow!” Alicia let out, her eyes fixed on her grandparents’ wedding picture. She hadn’t seen it in years. Her grandmother was wearing a long, tapered white satin gown and a crown with a narrow veil, and she held an arm bouquet of roses. Her grandfather looked a little like Ashton Kutcher in a top hat and a tuxedo with a carnation pinned to his lapel. “Geema, you were so young and such a beautiful bride.” For a second, Alicia imagined being in a wedding gown standing next to Jazz. It was a daydream she didn’t let herself have too often, but her mind couldn’t help but wander.

“Okay, no more time for this!” Alicia shook her head as if to snap back to reality and quickly went through a batch of mail she found tucked into a red folder. She was nearly done when she heard a noise that sounded like keys being thrown on a table. Alicia closed her eyes tightly, as if that would keep her search a secret. “I give up,” she whispered. “I have no clue where Geema put the stupid papers.”

She went to place the photo album back on the shelf and a worn scrapbook fell to the floor. Alicia picked it up to put it back, but a bunch of papers that looked like old menus fell out and covered the rug. She began shoving them back into the book when she found several envelopes from Meridian Bank stuffed in between the pages in back.

“Yes!” Alicia let out a sigh of relief.

#

“You really want to hear this story again?” Geema griped.

“Yeah. I...uh...need to know it for class. You know, love stuff. It’s like due tomorrow.”

"You're acting strange," Geema noted. "But okay, sure. I'm too tired to argue."

Dex made himself comfortable on the couch.

"We met at my friend Bev's apartment. She had just gotten married and she and her husband Bill threw a big house-warming party. Turned out to be the building your Poppy grew up in. Your great grand-poppy Emilio was the super, known to all as the best repairman on the block. He trained Poppy to help him with some of the work, which came in handy the night of Bev's party.

Right in the middle of Perry Como singing, and Dino Antonucci frying eggplant, Bev's toilet started playing a song of its own. She called Emilio, but he was out of town visiting his sister. Bev hadn't met Poppy before, but he promised her he would be able to fix the problem. When my Ralphie walked through the door, he didn't look like he was there to fix a toilet. He looked like he was ready to go dancing. He was so handsome I couldn't help myself so I followed him. I stood by the bathroom door and watched him work. And he watched me watch him. So I met your Poppy over Bev's toilet bowl. That may not sound very romantic, but we all became good friends after that."

Geema yawned. "Dexy, I'm falling asleep." She got up and approached the stairs.

Dex stopped her. "Wait, before you go upstairs, I need you to look over the menu for my New Year's special."

"Now?" Geema moaned.

"Yeah, I have to let them know all my ideas by...what's today?"

"Friday."

"Yup, by today. I just have to get them from my room. Don't go anywhere, promise?"

"Okay," she sighed and flopped back on the couch.

Dex could see his grandmother nodding off, so he ran up to his room to make a call.

"Liza?" Dex asked into his cell phone, hearing a lot of background noise. "What's going on?"

"Oh Dex, you should be here to see this. Jordy is doing a sewing project for Home and Careers class and he wrapped his face all up in thread like he's Frankenstein's cousin or something."

"Sounds scary," Dex said.

"Yeah, he ain't goin' on *Project Runway* anytime soon."

Dex could hear Liza's voice trail off. "Your tongue is going to get stuck in the threads, fool! I'm telling you watch that needle, Jordy. You're going to mess up your lips and no one's ever gonna kiss you."

"Liza!" Dex yelled into the phone.

"Sorry Dex, I gotta go help him. I'm crazy mad because I was supposed to hang with Kyle."

"Listen, I need a favor that'll help you out too."

Dex bounced back into the family room waving a file of papers in his hand.

"So, Geema, here they are."

"What time is it?" Geema asked as she opened her eyes.

"Did you miss the bus?"

"No. It's not morning," Dex chuckled. "You just got back from the dentist."

"Don't laugh. I'm an old woman. I need my rest," she yawned, taking the file from him. "These are for your show?"

"Yeah. For the special." Dex got up and peered out the window.

"These recipes are fine." Geema laid the file down beside her. "Very creative, and you don't need a stitch of help from me." She stood up.

"Really? Don't you think you could come up with something better for the roast?"

"No, dear, I don't. Dexy, I love you, but right now, I'm too exhausted to think straight. We can talk about this again later if you want to."

Dex watched with dread as his grandmother headed up the stairs. There was nothing more he could do to stop her other than scream 'Fire!' and that seemed useless unless he went and started one himself. He prayed that Alicia had found the bank papers and that their plan hadn't been a complete bust.

#

This time Alicia was sure the noise she was hearing was footsteps. She glanced around the room, realizing she left a mess. One quick peek out the bedroom door revealed Geema coming up the top stairs. Alicia grabbed a pen and quickly stuffed the envelopes back into the book. "Here goes nothing," she mumbled as she casually stepped out of the room and closed the door behind her.

Geema was halfway down the hall. “Leeshie? Why were you in my bedroom?”

“Oh, I—I—I-- just needed to borrow a pen,” she explained, lifting it up to show her. “I’ve been in my room working on my film and my pen just exploded. I’m sorry, is that okay?”

“Don’t be silly sweetheart, of course it’s okay. We have no secrets around here.” She started walking toward her door, sending Alicia’s heart pounding away. “But, I definitely need a nap,” Geema continued. “Dex has had me...”

Alicia was about to have a panic attack when the doorbell rang.

“Oh, what now?!?” Geema snarled.

Alicia shrugged. “Do you need me to get it, Geema?” she asked, counting on a ‘no.’

“That’s alright, you keep working. It could be your dad’s friend from the bakery. I could have sworn I told him to come by tomorrow.” She sounded confused. “Anyway, I’m teaching him how to make Pfeffernusse. One mistake with those cookies and you have hockey pucks.”

Alicia cheered silently as she watched Geema clop back down the stairs. She dashed back into the bedroom and frantically began to clean up.

Geema opened the front door and perked up when she saw Liza and Jordy. “Hey kids!” she greeted. She was happy to see them, as she was in no mood to bake. “Come on in. Dex is... somewhere. I’ll get him.”

Liza looked exasperated. “Actually, we’re here to see you.”

“Me?” Geema yawned as they all sat down in the family room.

“Yeah. Dex can cook, but he can’t sew, and I am done trying to help this boy,” Liza scowled at Jordy. “Can you help him, Geema? Please!?! I have to go to Kyle’s to finish a biology lab.”

“Oh sure,” Geema agreed. “Go work. Some days are set aside to be crazy and for me, this is clearly one of them.”

“Thanks!” Liza said on her way out.

“What seems to be the problem, Jordy?” Geema asked, trying to shake off her exhaustion.

“I wouldn’t have no problem if I didn’t gotta thread no pillow.”

“Pillow?”

“Yeah. That HC class is mad foolish. Ms. Hamwell say I gotta thread a pillow outta clothes. We ain’t got HGTV at da crib. And Liza be givin’ me da evil eye wit’ how I sews my threads.”

Geema stared at Jordy blankly, uncertain of anything he had said. She took a moment to process. “Are you saying you wants me, I mean, *want* me, to help you sew a pillow?”

“Word, Grandmomma,” Jordy agreed as he dug into his book bag and pulled out a pair of boxer-briefs that could have fit an elephant.

“Oh my! What in the world are those?” Geema’s eyes were like saucers.

“These my pillowcase.” He untied a huge plastic bag.

“And these my stuffin.’”

Geema put the parts of the pillow together then took the needle and thread from Jordy’s sewing kit. He sat next to her and studied her hands as she showed him the stitch he needed to use.

“You got nice nubs, Grandmomma.”

“Pardon?”

“Yo’ fingahs. They know where it’s at.”

“Thank you. I think.” Geema handed the needle over to Jordy. “Here, now it’s your turn.”

He took the pillow and began to work hesitantly. He suddenly pricked himself and yelped in pain. “Hoover dam!” he shouted and threw the pillow down.

“It’s okay.” Geema assured him. “You’re good. Really good. You’re getting the hang of it.”

Jordy picked up the pillow and started to sew again.

“See, it’s not so hard when you just put your mind to it,” Geema reassured.

After a few stitches Jordy started to feel more comfortable. As he finished the first part of the top of the shorts, he started beat-boxing an accompaniment.

“You good, G-momma says, real good child. You get the hang of it, yeah, you get da hang. See it’s not so hard when you just put your mind to it. Bling Bling!” Jordy rapped.

Geema was impressed at how well Jordy was working and she found herself swaying to his beat.

“You wanna rap wit me?”

Geema giggled. “I can’t do that.”

“Why not?”

“I could start with one reason and add about a hundred before you can count to ten.”

“Dat be in ya head. Take it to da mic wit ya hand,” Jordy said to a beat, cupping his hand over his mouth like a megaphone. “You say I be good. You be good.”

Geema tried a few times, but couldn’t keep the beat.

“Nah Grandmomma, try again. You gotta say what you sayin’, but say it like da music be da...da sticky, holdin’ your words.”

“Okay. I’ll give it another go,” Geema rapped with gusto. “You good. Really good child. You gettin’ the hang of it. See it’s not so hard when you just put your mind to it. Um, what was after that? Oh right. Uh, ding, ding!” she yelled, motioning with her hand as if she were riding on a trolley.

“Whoa. Chill. Stay chill.” Jordy was almost finished sewing the whole top of the pillow.

“Chill. Right.” Geema shivered for effect. She looked at Jordy’s work. “You’ll be done in no time.”

“Here be a needle. Here be a thread. I sews what I sews. My stitches got cred.” Jordy rapped, finishing the last stitch on top. Before he moved on, he got Geema on her feet and taught her a private handshake that ended with her in a dip.

The two of them collapsed on the couch laughing harder than Geema even knew she could.

#

Alicia and Dex sat on Dex's bed carefully counting the money from the tomato cans.

"You have no idea how glad I am you got Liza and Jordy to show up. Too bad they missed seeing you as a blonde."

"Very funny," Dex said. "Keep counting."

"I'm telling you Dex, it was like in the movies. The doorbell rang just when she was about to go to her room. I still can't get over it."

"So? How are we doing?" Dex asked.

Alicia looked down at the desk and checked the paper where she jotted down the amount due. "According to this, we're still short."

"No way." Dex insisted.

"Way. The cans are empty and we counted everything."

"No, not everything." Dex jumped up. "Lunch today."

He dug into all his shirt pockets and pulled out a wad of bills. Then he checked his pants and a sweatshirt he had slung over his desk chair. There was cash in those too. He dropped everything he found onto the bed and wrung his hands as Alicia counted all of it.

"Well?" Dex asked like an expectant father in a delivery room.

Alicia leaped up from the bed and hugged him. "You did it Dex! You did it!"

Chapter 28

Preston walked into the bank wearing a long, charcoal trench coat with a matching hat and black-framed sunglasses. The only thing missing was a sign over his head saying 'In disguise' with an arrow pointing down at him. He scouted the long row of desks and side offices, but he wasn't sure where to go. He decided to ask one of the tellers.

"Where's Nan May?" Preston demanded, interrupting a transaction at the first teller's window.

"Excuse me, *sir*," the teller chided. "You'll have to get in line."

"That line?" Preston barked, pointing at several people waiting.

"That very one," the teller scowled. "And wait your turn."

Preston wanted to say his usual, 'Do you know who I am?' but he couldn't risk being recognized. This time, there was too much at stake. He skulked away and noticed an office door labeled 'Nan May, Banking Associate.' His eyes lit up behind his dark glasses.

Next to the door stood a woman with enough gray hair piled on top of her head to hide a flock of eagles. Preston waited behind her, rolling his eyes at her full-length, cheap, fake fur coat and recoiled at the smell of her overwhelming rose-scented perfume.

"Aaaaccchooo!" Preston sneezed, turning his head over his shoulder. He was terribly allergic to roses.

Everyone around blessed him, but by his fourth sneeze

they were done. The line had dwindled down to Preston and the gray-haired woman. He was about to complain about how long everything was taking when another sneeze caught him by surprise. This one escaped before he had the chance to turn his head, and a big wad of snot landed like a bull's eye right in the middle of the gray-haired woman's bun. Preston's first reaction was to find a tissue and wipe it off, but that would draw too much attention. *Why bother?* he decided. With all that hair, it could be hours before she would even notice and by that time he would be gone.

It was taking every ounce of control for Preston not to burst out laughing, but he didn't want to encourage any conversation between him and this woman, who had now become his walking tissue. He was relieved when a second representative opened her office door and called for the next customer. Before walking in, the gray-haired woman turned to Preston and wished him a speedy recovery from his cold. He smiled as politely as possible and heard Nan May call him into her office.

Preston took a seat and yawned.

"Are you a tired boy, Mr. Presto?" Nan said with a pasted smile not expecting an answer.

Preston cringed. It had been seconds and he already had no patience for this woman. For an instant, he even missed Yvette.

"It's such a pleasure to meet you," Nan said, batting her lengthy false eyelashes. "I'm such a big fan. Well, smaller now. I've lost five pounds on your diet." She batted her eyes again in an attempt to flirt that made Preston's stomach turn.

“Great. You look, uh, uh lovely,” he forced himself to say. “So, where are the papers? Where do I sign?”

“You really think so?” Nan gushed. “That’s so nice of you. Not many people-”

“The papers, Miss May,” Preston interrupted.

“Please, call me Nan. Or Sugar. The choice is yours,” she whispered.

“The papers?” he repeated.

“They’re almost ready.”

“Almost?”

“Yes. We’re a bit short-staffed today. Sorry,” she said, not being the slightest bit apologetic. “When’s the big day?”

“As soon as I sign the papers.”

“Yvette said you two are getting married.” Nan smiled. “You don’t strike me as the marrying type. Am I wrong?”

“Miss May--”

“Uh-uh-uh...” Nan shook her finger at him as if he were a naughty child.

“Nan. I am in a terrible hurry. Do you think we can speed things up...please?”

She looked at the time. “I can check and see if they’re ready. Don’t go anywhere.”

Nan left the room shaking her hips so hard Preston thought she might dent the walls. Had Yvette really taken to lying about becoming his wife? As soon as Poppy's Kitchen was his, he would never have to deal with either of these ridiculous women ever again. And who knew? Maybe in time Marla would realize what she gave up and dump Vince so she could marry him. Then they could happily ship her brat off to The Culinary Institute of New Zealand where he could learn how to make fern root taste exciting. That should take decades. With Dex out of the way he and Marla could finally be the couple they were meant to be and live the life he had always wanted.

"Here they are!" Nan said, holding the documents in her hand.

Preston snatched the papers from her and reviewed them. "Do I sign here?" he asked, pointing to a line.

"Yes, wherever I made a cute little 'X' for you."

"Right. How thoughtful." He couldn't have been more sarcastic if he'd tried.

"I aim to please."

"Indeed." Preston signed the papers and immediately rose to leave.

"The check?" Nan asked.

"Of course," Preston muttered, filling out the information."Okay then, thank you." He started for the door.

"Oh, Mr. Presto, you forgot to sign something."

"I did? What? Where?"

Nan took out a Presto's Pesto Meal, from the mini-fridge wedged under her desk: *Chicken Breasts and Pesto Peas.* "It would mean simply everything to me," Nan cooed, puckering her lips, "if you would sign my breasts."

Chapter 29

The Rossi kitchen smelled happy. Alicia was sautéing garlic and onions while Geema bathed a roasted chicken in an orange wine glaze. Dex was in charge of the *latkes,* the potato pancakes, which he was glad to see were sizzling to a golden brown. It was *Chanukah*, the Jewish festival of lights, a food-frenzy holiday that Geema said was all about miracles, especially if she could still fit into her clothes when it was over.

Dex's parents used to tell him how lucky he was that both Santa Claus and Chanukah Harry knew where he lived so they could both leave him presents. But, by the time he was four, Dex had figured out that it was Poppy, not Santa, wearing a red velvety costume and eating cookies by the chimney. And though he tried, the closest Vince could get to Chanukah Harry was to wear a blue robe and a chef's hat adorned by a Star of David. Despite the failed attempts it wasn't a huge disappointment to Dex. He didn't really care who was in charge of bringing him toys.

"Did you hear from Mom and Dad yet?" Dex asked, getting orange juice from the refrigerator.

"Just to say they're flight had been delayed," Geema said, flipping the *latkes*. "I'm not sure what time they'll get to Aruba, but I'm guessing it'll be awhile."

"Oh."

"Why, is there something wrong?"

"No. Nothing. Just wondering," Dex said, putting the juice back. "Hey Leesh, wanna invite Jazz for dinner next week? I can order a kangaroo roast from a website I found online."

"As yummy as a kanga-roast sounds, I'd rather invite him

for brisket and pasta primavera." Alicia stirred the vegetables a few more times and set the pan to simmer. She went over to Dex and grabbed his sleeve so hard his shirt nearly came off his head. "Geema, I need to show Dex something. We'll be right back."

"No problem...hon--" Geema turned to find herself talking to the air. "Kids," she sighed to herself, scooping the *latkes* onto a white platter lined with paper towels.

#

"Did you get the box?" Alicia asked, walking into Dex's room.

"The box?" Dex stared at her blankly. "What box?" He turned on the light in his closet.

"For the money, remember, the little matter of her *HUGE* present!" Alicia scowled, discovering she had sat down on a pair of Dex's dirty socks and quickly tossed them into the hamper.

"Right, the money. Are we doing that tonight?"

"No. I figured we'd wait until summer. Maybe by then Poppy's Kitchen will be a swim club." Alicia pounded her palm to her head. "Wake up Dex!"

"Sorry. I thought we were waiting for Mom and Dad to get back."

"Why? We decided not to tell them what happened. Anyway, there's no time to waste."

"The bank said New Year's." Dex looked in his closet.

"And you trust them?"

“You have a point.” Dex tried to find a box, but couldn’t. “I don’t have anything to fit all the money. Maybe you do.”

“The only empty box I might come up with would be too small and definitely not intended for gifts. I’m PMS’ing, just take my word for it.”

Dex took a deep breath and let the smell of the garlic floating in the air calm him down. “So, now what?” He was getting hungry.

“You know, I think mom bought a rolling duffel bag for the trip. Maybe she kept the box. I’ll go check.”

Dex went to his computer and brought up Facebook. His heart fluttered. He had a private message from Sarah.

HAPPY CHANUKAH PIZZA BAGEL! XO

It was signed ‘XO!’She signed a message to him, ‘XO.’ Maybe Geema was right; Chanukah *was* a holiday for miracles. Dex didn’t care if Alicia wanted to dump the money into a giant trash bag and tie it up with a ribbon. Everything was going to feel perfect for the rest of the night.

“Look!” Alicia came in with a huge box and a roll of blue and silver wrapping paper. “Count on mom not to throw anything out.”

They tossed the money into the box and used the entire roll of paper to wrap it. Alicia tried to lift it, but it was too bulky for her to hold on her own. Dex, feeling more confident since his wheelbarrow triumph, took the other end, and the two of them guided the gift down the stairs. They left it behind the couch out of Geema’s sight and went into the kitchen.

“Smells great in here,” Dex said, taking a seat at the table.

“Oh good,” Geema said, “I was just going to come get you before everything got cold.”

“Dex and I need to talk to you, Geema.”

Dex frowned as his stomach growled. No one ever seemed to care when he was hungry.

“About what? Oh no, did I leave my teeth in the bathroom sink again?” Geema sounded mortified.

“No, it’s nothing like that.” Alicia looked at Dex, made a face of disgust, then turned back to Geema. “We just want to give you a Chrisma-kah present.”

Dex and Alicia headed to the couch, both signaling with their hands for Geema to come with them.

“Present?” Geema called. “Why are you spending your money? I don’t need anything.”

“Too late,” Dex said as he and Alicia presented the wrapped box at their grandmother’s feet.

“What in the world have you done?” Geema questioned as she took her time to unwrap the box without putting a single rip in the paper.

Dex swiped a chocolate kiss from the candy dish and tossed one to Alicia.

“Holy sh---ekels!” Geema cried, seeing the stash of bills. “Where did you...how did you? Did you take a banker hostage?”

“Don’t worry. He’s well-fed,” Alicia kidded.

“We found out the truth,” Dex admitted.

“The truth?” Geema said, perplexed. “The truth about what?”

Dex and Alicia both went over to Geema and gave her a hug. She continued to look completely baffled. When the two finally let go, tears streamed down their faces. Alicia was still sobbing, and she gave Dex a signal that he could be the one to say it.

“Poppy’s Kitchen,” he whispered.

Geema’s expression changed from confused to flabberghasted.

“How?” she said, tears now welling up in her eyes.

“It doesn’t matter. Mom and Dad still don’t know. Leesh and I are hoping you can buy it back from the bank before they have the chance to find out.”

Geema reached out her arms and hugged them both again, this time all three of them holding onto each other through a steady stream of tears.

Dex and Alicia had gone to their rooms as soon as the dishes were done. Golda was glad to have some time alone to sit at the kitchen table with a cup of tea and digest both her dinner and the evening. Every few moments she’d stare down into the box of money in disbelief.

Ralphie, we have incredible grandchildren. Poppy’s Kitchen and all your hard work means everything to them. You would be so proud. I don’t know how they got this kind of cash, but I really hope it had nothing to do with your crazy cousin Carmine doing something illegal.

One thing was certain, she would pay them back every dime and then some as soon as the restaurant was up and running again. She took another sip of tea, put down the mug, and stared back into the box.

It was pretty early, but Dex wanted to sleep and dream. He turned off his light and left his door slightly open, hoping to catch a whiff of the holiday aroma still hovering in the air. He got into bed feeling grateful that everything was starting to work out. Geema had the money to buy Poppy's Kitchen back, and Sarah was practically ready to list him as her boyfriend on Facebook. The only thing left was buying the *Gymbuff* to prove to Sarah that he could look like the kind of guy she went out with.

"Dex?" Geema whispered, tapping lightly on his door. "Are you sleeping?"

"No. Come in." Dex sat up and turned on the lamp next to his bed.

Geema was carrying a basket of folded laundry. "This is your stuff. It's all ready to be put away."

"Thanks, Geema. You didn't have to do that."

"That's why I wanted to."

"What's that?" Dex asked, pointing to an old book that was nearly falling apart, lying on top of the clothes.

"I'm glad you asked. It's something I want you to see."

She sat down next to him and carefully opened the book. Dex looked at the first few pages. There were a bunch of cards and letters, and some old photos pasted to the pages, but he couldn't recognize anyone.

"Who is *that*?" he asked, pointing to a scrawny, little man who was in almost every picture.

"You don't recognize him?"

"No. Should I?" Dex asked, wondering if it was a great uncle he didn't remember.

"I should think you would. It's your Poppy."

"Whaaaa?! No way!" Dex was stunned. "This guy looks like a pretzel stick."

"I know. Can you imagine that in just a few short years," she said turning a few pages, "he looked like--this?"

Geema pointed to a good-looking, well-built man who Dex could clearly tell was his grandfather, smiling in front of a refrigerator.

"Awesome!"

"It is amazing what a little time can change. For everyone."

"Yeah," Dex agreed. "It's pretty cool. So, why are you telling me all this?"

Geema put the book down and gave Dex a little kiss on the forehead. "During intense questioning, Alicia failed to produce the hostage you took to get all that money."

Dex raised his eyebrows.

"She told me what you gave up to help me."

"Oh." Dex bit his bottom lip.

"It takes a very big man to put others first. I'm so proud

of you." Geema stood up. "And one day, when you're all old and wrinkly like I am, you'll look at *your* scrapbook and see how well you filled your Poppy's shoes."

Chapter 30

"You're still here?!" Dex exclaimed, dropping a heavy wad of dough onto a baking sheet as his grandmother lumbered into the kitchen still in her robe.

"I live here," Geema teased, getting a glass from the cabinet.

"When are you going?"

"As soon as I get married again." She took a carton of orange juice out of the refrigerator.

"GEEMA!" Dex exclaimed.

"Dexy, calm down. I was tossing and turning most of the night and I just woke up," Geema explained. She took a sip of juice and sat down at the table.

"I'm sorry. I just want to know we have Poppy's kitchen back.

"We will, Dexy. We will. I'm going to get dressed first, okay?"

"Okay," Dex muttered with a frown.

"What are you doing here?" Alicia mumbled half asleep as she shuffled into the kitchen still in her pajamas.

"I've been getting a lot of that this morning," Geema complained. "Good thing I'm tough."

"She's going to get dressed now," Dex answered.

"Oh, good." Alicia said, leaving the kitchen then walking back in. "I think I wanted water." She took a bottle out of the fridge and left again.

“Do that when you’re old and everyone thinks you’ve lost your mind.”

“Who said she hasn’t?” Dex chuckled.

Geema smiled. “It’s all going to be fine. You’ll see.”

#

“Dexy?” Geema called from the back door. “I’m going.”

Dex appeared like a bolt of lightning. “Do you have your phone?”

Geema felt around the inside of her purse and pulled it out. “Check.”

“Is it charged?” Dex asked.

“Looks like three bars,” she said, holding the phone a full arms length away from her. “Should be enough.”

“Yeah. That should be fine,” Dex agreed.

Geema opened the door.

“Call me as soon as you’re done,” Dex insisted.

“Okay, okay! Whoa...” Geema said nearly tripping over a big ball of fur as it went scurrying into the house. “What the heck was that? Where did it go?”

“Oh my God! It’s Ardith!” Dex screeched running after the animal. “Ardith!”

“Who’s Ardith?” Geema called.

“Our raccoon,” Dex answered chasing the animal as it darted across the kitchen knocking over the garbage pail.

“We don’t have a raccoon,” Geema called out to Dex.

“We do now,” Dex shouted back from the other room.

“We don’t even have a cat. Your father is allergic to everything.”

Geema picked up the trash and tied the bag tightly. Then she shoved the pail into the corner and tiptoed out of the room into the hall. “Dex?” Geema called with a tone of uncertainty.

“I’m here.” Dex was crawling along the floor as the animal shrieked at him and rolled over the couch like a sloppy gymnast. “Ardith!” Dex shouted as the raccoon scampered through the room and then leapt onto the top of the large wall unit.

“I don’t like this one bit. I’m not even sure what’s up there.” Geema gnawed at her bottom lip. “She better not--”

Ardith clenched a couple of fake flowers between her teeth and chewed them until she seemed to figure out they were flavorless. Scorned, she spit them out and either in defiance or disgust, knocked over the large vase and the rest of the silk arrangement. She let out what sounded almost like a giggle when it crashed onto the wood floor. Then she leapt off the unit in a bold Superman move and headed up the stairs chirping away like a confident rock star.

Dex ran after her with Geema closely behind. Dex combed the hallway, but Ardith was playing Hide ‘n Seek and there was no trace of her anywhere. He stopped at Alicia’s door and started pounding on it.

“Leesh, get up! Ardith is back!”

“You know what,” Geema said, “go get the broom.”

"The broom? I told you I'll clean later," Dex banged on Alicia's door again.

"Not to clean. To prod her out."

"Hear that Leesh? Open the door or Geema's going to use the broom on you."

"I meant on the raccoon," Geema explained.

"Oh," Dex blushed. "But, I don't want to hurt Ardith." Dex started to open Alicia's door.

"Prodding is not hurting. It's suggesting," Geema explained. "And I suggest you don't open your sister's door or you might end up hurting."

"Fine. But, I don't understand how Leesh can sleep through everything."

Dex and Geema started scanning all the rooms searching for Ardith who seemed to have quietly vanished.

"Are you getting the broom or do I have to go back downstairs?"

"I don't want to scare her."

"Dex, you haven't seen this animal in a while and you don't know where she's been. She could have rabies."

"Rabies?!"

"Yes." Geema nodded. "That's the part they left out of *Bambi*."

"Bambi didn't have rabies and neither does Ardith."

"And how do you know this?"

“I just do. You don’t understand. Ardith is the closest thing to a pet I ever had. She used to hang around all the time,” Dex explained. “She was the one who kept me company when I first started my business. But after the last storm, she disappeared. I thought she got hurt or something.”

“Well, if it’s any consolation, for the few seconds I saw her she looked fine, but we can’t let her just roam around the house,” Geema said.

“I know.”

“What’s going on?” Alicia asked, coming out of the bathroom. “You’re *still* here, Geema?”

“That’s why you didn’t hear me knocking,” Dex said. “You weren’t even in your room.”

“Good one, Sherlock. So, is anyone going to tell me what’s going on?”

“Ardith is back. So back that she ran into the house when Geema was about to leave.”

“Oh wow! So she’s okay!”

“Yeah, but Geema says she has rabies like Bambi.”

“Bambi didn’t have rabies,” Alicia insisted.

“That’s what I said. And neither does Ardith.”

Geema put one arm around Dex’s neck and the other around Alicia’s. “Let’s forget about Bambi for now and tell me why on earth you named this critter Ardith.”

“My old babysitter. Remember?” Dex asked. “The one with the real dark eyes who wore lots of make-up...Her name was Ardith.”

“And your mother used to say she looked like a raccoon. I remember her,” Geema nodded. “Okay, one mystery tackled. Now how are we going to tackle Ardith?”

“Geema, you can’t. You have to leave,” Dex panicked. “If you don’t the bank will close before you get there.”

“I am not leaving this house with a wild animal running around.” Geema took off her coat and threw it over the railing.

“Well, we don’t want to hurt her,” Alicia said.

“Yes, we know,” Geema agreed. “But we also can’t make up the guest room for her until she’s ready to leave.”

“Dex, maybe we can Google what to do,” Alicia suggested.

They all went into Dex’s room and huddled around his laptop.

“Well, she’s not afraid of loud noises so the pot and the spoon won’t work,” Dex said, reading from a web site.

“If she wanted food she would have gotten into the garbage outside,” Alicia added.

“Maybe she’s pregnant and looking for a warm delivery room,” Geema mused. “That happened to my friend, Kay. But it was a gopher in her attic. What a mess.”

“Ardith is not pregnant,” Alicia insisted.

“How do you know?” Geema argued. “She’s cute. I’m sure a lot of raccoons have been interested.”

Dex stared out his window from his bed. “Looks like the rain is letting up.”

"Eheheheheh," Ardith squeaked, darting past Dex's room. He sprang up and ran after her, but she was already back downstairs playing with the box of tissues on the end table.

"Geema, you should go." Alicia checked the time. "Dex and I are fine. We can take care of this." She flew down the steps.

"No. Absolutely not," Geema argued from the top of the staircase. "I'm going to call animal control. That critter has done enough damage."

"Wait," Dex urged the moment he heard Geema's plans. "I think I know how to get her out."

They all followed Dex into the kitchen. He took out a jar of peanut butter and a leftover hamburger.

"You better hope she's pregnant," Geema remarked.

"I just remembered that she used to shove her nose into the empty jars of peanut butter I threw out. And I have to get rid of the burger anyway." Dex made the concoction and put it on a paper plate near the door.

Then he took the jar of peanut butter and brought it into the family room. Ardith looked at him quizzically as she nosed a lamp off the table onto the couch.

"Good save, Ardy!" Dex held out the jar as the animal seemed to contemplate his agenda. "Come on girl, follow me."

Ardith wiggled behind Dex as he made his way into the kitchen. "Leesh, put the plate outside," he instructed.

Alicia moved quickly and Ardith tumbled out of the house to collect her prize. Geema slammed the door shut.

“Well, that takes care of her for the moment, but since she was comfortable enough to visit, we have a problem,” Geema sighed.

“Go!” Dex cried. “We’ll worry about this later.”

Chapter 31

Golda could not imagine this day getting any crazier as she walked through the doors of the bank. After a restless night's sleep, a cocky raccoon, a thunderous downpour, and a profane exchange for a parking space, she was looking forward to life getting back to normal. She knew everything would fall into place as soon as she had the restaurant back. There'd be no better way to start off the New Year.

Of course, that was assuming she'd even be home in time to watch the ball drop. Why were the lines so long? Was there a sale on money no one had told her about? She didn't feel like being patient, but she had no choice. Golda took a deep breath and was immediately sorry she had.

There was a lady in front of her wearing a long fake fur, whose hair was piled up high in a poofy, gray bun, and she smelled like roses and tuna fish. It was a combination that was making Golda feel light-headed and queasy. She tried to position herself a little further away, but all the lines were jam-packed making any relief difficult.

With fainting and vomiting out of the question, Golda needed to find a less drastic yet equally effective diversion from the stench. She was just about to join Madonna in a chorus of 'Santa Baby' that was playing through a series of wall speakers when Nan May tapped her on the shoulder and ushered her into her office.

"Happy Holidays, Mrs. Marino," Nan said, smiling broadly and blinking to the music. "What can I do for you today?"

"I think this will cover it," Golda said, opening a suitcase full of money on Nan's desk.

“Is this for deposit?” Nan asked.

“Of course not. I’m here to take back my restaurant. This should be enough to pay off everything.” She looked at the suitcase and realized how odd it looked. “Legally, of course,” she insisted.

“Oh dear!” Nan exclaimed.

“What do you mean, ‘oh dear,’?” Geema replied.

“I’m very, um, very, um, very sorry,” Nan stammered, “but I’m afraid that won’t be possible.”

“Why?” Golda demanded. “All the money is there. You can count it!”

“I believe you,” Nan blinked. “But, there was another buyer.”

“The notice said we had until New Year’s.” Golda closed the suitcase.

“Yes, but the fine print explains that the bank has the right to accept another offer.” Nan showed her the papers.

“Well, I don’t think that print is very fine at all. As a matter of fact, I think it’s just-- awful!”

Golda trudged through the late afternoon rain in a daze. This was all her fault. Maybe she should have told Marla. Maybe someone could have helped. It had been foolish of her to believe that no one else would buy the property and that she’d have time to work something out. And now the reality was setting in. She had lost Poppy’s Kitchen. How was she going to tell Dex it slipped right through her fingers and now belonged to a new owner? He’d worked so hard to earn all that money.

Golda let out a long, heavy sigh. The thought of breaking

their hearts filled her with unspeakable despair. She got into her car, but held the keys in her hand. She didn't want to go home. Not now. Maybe not ever. But, she had no choice. Dex had the Eatz special in a few hours and she had promised to go. There was no need to say anything until after New Years, after she had some time to figure out what to do next.

Chapter 32

Dex was trying to stay focused, but he couldn't understand what was taking Geema so long. He shook a huge sprinkle of confectioner's sugar and sifted a hint of cocoa all over the top of his Dextraordinary Eggplant, a stuffed French toast using eggplant as the bread for a peanut butter and jelly sandwich. The presentation worked, until he realized in his anxiety that he had garnished it too soon. He shoved the whole platter back into the oven and looked at the time.

"Geema back yet?" Alicia asked clomping into the kitchen in her high-heeled boots.

Dex wasn't thrilled that he had to raise his head up to talk to her, but he had to admit she looked pretty.

"No, not yet," Dex answered. "Did you do something different? You look really good."

"Geez, you sure know how to give a compliment," Alicia muttered.

"Oh come on, you know what I mean."

"Whatev," Alicia said, tapping his arm. "Thanks I guess. I'm headed to Lola's party. Call me when Geema gets back!"

Before she walked out the back door, she whipped her head down between her legs, and then jerked it up quickly. She did this a few times before spraying her hair with a small can of stuff she took out of her pocketbook. Seeming satisfied as she looked into a small compact mirror that she also pulled out of her bag, she left.

Dex wasn't sure how she wasn't too dizzy to walk much less drive after all that. Girls were definitely weird. Especially the cute ones.

Through the living room windows Dex could tell it was almost sundown. Ardith the raccoon was long gone, as was her messy trail of mischief since Dex and Alicia spent nearly an hour repositioning all she had knocked over during her brief but busy stay. Dex tried Geema's cell phone, but there was no answer. The bank had to be closed by now. It was New Year's Eve. Where was Geema? How long could it take to buy back what was yours in the first place?

Dex put out some snacks and drinks and was grateful when the doorbell rang. He needed to take his mind off the restaurant. Liza, Jordy, and Kyle hung up their coats on the wall hooks in the entryway and headed into the family room.

"Smells good in here," Liza sniffed.

"Yeah, I cut one." Jordy inhaled deeply.

"You know," Liza said, "I think in a past life you were a pig."

"Past life?" Kyle joked.

Jordy hit him on the arm. "Hey dude, you're supposed to be on my side."

"She's cuter," Kyle said, winking at Liza, as he walked over to the food.

Dex went back to the door to take a look outside.

"Sarah's on her way," Liza said, rolling her eyes. "Dex, you are more transparent than Saran Wrap."

"How do you know? Did she call you?"

"Of course she called," Liza said. "Don't you know? Since you started liking her, she and I have become besties."

"That's cool. I guess," Dex said as he got *Twister* out of the hall closet. He tossed the game on an end table. "I'll be right back."

Dex went into the kitchen and tried calling Geema again. There was still no answer.

"Hi guys!" Sarah said, making a sudden entrance. "I knocked, and I rang, but no one answered. The door was open so---"

Dex bolted to the door as soon as he heard Sarah's voice. "I left it open so you could come right in," Dex admitted as he helped her off with her coat. He noticed the way her long, shiny, hair hung loose around her shoulders and wondered if she would be angry at him if he kissed her right then and there. Something made him decide she would be, so he kissed her on the cheek instead. He hung up her coat and then awkwardly took her hand.

Dork. Don't do that now, in front of everyone. Besides, your palms are sweaty.

Dex dropped Sarah's hand more abruptly than he had intended. "Um, I have to go to the kitchen." *Yeesh.* "Um," he continued, turning away, "to finish making the eggplant."

As Dex walked away, Sarah started laughing hysterically at Jordy squeezing garlic-cheese dip through the spaces between his front teeth. If she thought that was more funny than disgusting, maybe Dex didn't have to worry so much about his own dorkdom. He took the eggplant out of the oven hoping that once the food was served, Sarah would forget his sweaty palms.

Dex was putting the pan on the counter when Geema flew in through the back door and nearly knocked him over.

"Sorry, hon," Geema apologized. "I didn't mean to scare you. It's cold out there."

"Where have you been?"

"Been?" Geema echoed.

"I was worried. I called your cell a bunch of times and you didn't answer." Dex could feel his cheeks getting fiery. "Well, how did it go?"

"How did what go?"

"The bank, Geema." Dex rolled his eyes. "Did you buy back Poppy's Kitchen?"

"Oh, the bank," Geema said, putting a shopping bag down on the table. "I got there too late. It was closed."

"That makes no sense," Dex argued. "You had plenty of time."

"Sense or no sense," Geema almost raised her voice, "the bank was closed. Plain and simple. But, I did have time to buy you these." She pulled a big bag of Dex's favorite salt and vinegar potato chips out of a small package of groceries.

"Thanks," Dex mumbled. "Geema--"

"Dexy, I'm tired. If I don't take a nap, I won't be awake enough to go to your show later." She left the room before Dex could offer one more word of protest.

Dex wasn't sure why his grandmother was in such a cranky mood. She was always the optimistic one who would say 'Bumps in the road are just a way to make the ride more interesting.' Why weren't things interesting this time? Sure, he could imagine she was disappointed when she got to the bank and it was closed, but there was nothing anyone could do about it until the holiday was over. Maybe she really *was* tired. He grabbed the eggplant and went inside.

Kyle, Liza, and Jordy were on the *Twister* mat and Sarah had just spun 'Right hand green.'

"Okay, next one is, 'Right foot red.'"

This left Dex underneath Kyle whose arms were now wrapped around Liza's arm and Jordy's leg. Liza was between Jordy's legs and had an arm around Kyle's leg.

"'Left hand yellow.'" They all started laughing because that left Jordy's butt right under Liza's nose.

"Yo Liza, I'm illin' a little after dat bean dip," Jordy laughed.

"Stop trying to cheat!" Liza said, holding her breath.

The doorbell rang.

Dex got up to get the door and everyone fell over. "Ahh, sorry guys. I ordered pizza."

The doorbell rang again just as Dex opened the door. A limo driver in a black suit and cap was standing at the doorway. Without a word, the driver signaled with a gloved hand to usher Dex out the door and into an Eatz company limo parked in front of his house.

"Already? I'm sorry. I must've messed up the time," Dex said to the silent driver. "I'll be right back."

The driver let out an impatient huff that made Dex uncomfortable.

"Hey guys, my driver's here and in a rush. Please tell Geema I had to leave." Dex headed to the door. "Oh, and save me some Doritos. I'll see you later."

Sarah stopped him at the door with a glossy smile. "This is for good luck."

She kissed him softly, but longer than the first time, then turned and went back to *Twister*.

As he walked out, Dex licked his lips. Chocolate mint, his new favorite flavor.

#

Dex was in a daze. Was Sarah finally his girlfriend? It was hard to know for sure, but that kiss made it seem like it might be possible. As he followed the driver down the front lawn, he glanced back at the house hoping to hold onto the moment as long as he could. He licked his lips again. Maybe he would make chocolate mint cookies tonight. It wasn't on his menu, but he was feeling inspired.

The driver opened the limo door, but Dex was too engrossed in his thoughts to move until he was practically pushed inside the car. Maybe he should have asked Sarah to come with him. No. He couldn't do that. It was still too soon. And he had given the one guest pass Casey emailed him to Geema. The good news was he would be home by midnight, just in time to start the New Year with his hopefully new girlfriend. No matter how he looked at it, this was going to be a long night.

Dex looked out the window. Why weren't they moving?

Were they out of gas? Dex turned his head over his other shoulder and jumped.

"Mr. LeTray? What a cool surprise!" Dex tried to do a 'high five,' but Preston ignored him. "Nobody told me we were rehearsing."

"We're not," Preston said snidely. "I'm actually going to be directing."

"Really? Directing? That's awesome . Directing our show, while we're doing it? How?"

"Not how, who."

"Who?"

"You."

"Me? You're directing me? Why?" Dex was puzzled.

"I'm correcting a mistake," Preston leered.

"What mistake?" Dex asked.

"The one Ezra made when he fired me instead of you."

"He fired you?" Dex's eyes widened. "I had no idea."

"Of course you didn't. You were too busy sucking up to see anything, Dexy."

"That's not true," Dex protested.

"You're not the first snake in the grass I've had to finish."

"Finish?" Dex gulped.

The limo driver giggled and Dex realized it was LeTray's assistant, Yvette Bidet.

"Pressy," she said, "the kid thinks you're going to--!" She made a deep, loud clicking noise while moving her flat hand against her throat in a slicing motion.

"It's not like the thought hasn't crossed my mind, but I'm a reasonable man."

"That's good to know," Dex said, completely unconvinced. "I'm still not sure what you want."

"To begin, how about gratitude." Preston said, rolling the 'r' in a way that would have made Dex laugh if he hadn't been terrified.

"I thanked you for helping me."

"Not enough."

"Why?"

"Because, I made your success. I ended up pushing you right to the top when I helped season your chicken salad."

"It was you!" Dex gasped.

"So, what of it? It did nothing but help you. It's history now." Preston snapped his fingers and waved his hand in the air as if he could make the past disappear. "However, I did make a recent purchase that I am certain will interest you."

"Okay," Dex said, anxious to end the conversation. "What?"

"A certain...restaurant was in dire need of an owner who could pay the bills on time."

Dex gave Preston an icy stare. “You couldn’t have. We’re buying it back.”

“No dear, uninformed Dexy. According to this, seems you’re too late.” Preston shoved an official-looking document under Dex’s nose.

“I don’t believe you.” Dex felt the tears welling up in his eyes.

“Your choice, but this is the deed to the property,” Preston insisted. “Timing is everything.”

“Is that why you came here? To tell me you’re destroying my family?”

“Well, I admit that has been fun, but I’m more practical than that.”

“So what do you want? For me to beg you to give us our restaurant back?”

“Absolutely,” Preston gloated. “And one more thing, Dexy. Listen very, very carefully. You stole my show. I want it back. I’ll sell you the restaurant if you do as I say without a word to anyone. Because I promise you, one slip, any slip, and Poppy’s Kitchen becomes Poppy’s Parking Lot!”

Yvette laughed until she saw Preston glare at her in the rear view mirror.

“What do you want me to do?” Dex muttered.

#

Dex got out of the limo and watched Yvette drive off as a different limo pulled up alongside him. “You ready to go, Mr.

Rossi?" the driver asked as he opened his window.

"I forgot my Eatz I.D. I'll be right out." Dex replied, the life draining from his voice.

Chapter 33

"So you can't say a word to anyone," Dex told his friends who were now piled on the couch. He put his Eatz I.D. tag around his neck and walked towards the front door. "But, I don't know what to do." He was too angry to be sad and too sad to think.

"What do you *want* to do?" Kyle asked through a puff of cotton candy.

"Don't ask," Dex scowled.

"You can't let that thug boss you around," Liza argued.

"Liza's right, Dex." Sarah crossed her arms. "He's *so* not a *mensch*."

"Say what?"Jordy asked.

"A *mensch*," Sarah repeated. "It's Yiddish for a decent, good person."

"Cool. A *mensch*." Jordy nodded. "I dig that."

"If I were you," Kyle warned, "I'd play along. This Preston dude sounds pretty serious. And come on, you've seen him with a Ginsu knife. He could turn you into a sushi roll before anyone would notice you were missing!"

"Yeah man," Jordy agreed. "And yo grandmomma's gonna wig out if Pop's place gits 'dozed down to da gee-round."

"Guys, promise me you won't say anything to her," Dex pleaded.

"Don't worry, we won't," Liza promised as everyone nodded in agreement.

“Good, ‘cause Geema went to the bank today thinking she was going to buy back the restaurant, but they were closed when she got there. Holiday hours. If I do what Preston wants, he’ll give me back the restaurant and she’ll never have to know what really happened.”

“Dex, is there anything we can do to help?” Sarah asked.

“No,” Dex sighed. “Just don’t hate me for doing what I have to do.”

#

Alicia stood by the M&Ms waiting for Jazz. Lola’s party was not working out exactly the way she had imagined. In her version of New Year’s Eve, Jazz had already finished what he needed to do for his film project and had gone to the party *with* her. The six-foot hero was stuffed with anything *but* ham and cheese, and everyone wanted to talk to them because they were the best-looking, most exciting couple there. And, while she was dreaming, he had given her the most original, exquisite promise ring she had ever seen.

So far, none of that was happening. Lola’s house was too small to fit all these people and every time someone went for a handful of pretzels from a snack table awkwardly placed by the loveseat, their Christmas tree would start leaning over like it was about to fall on top of the buffet table. Alicia had already pulled a Mickey Mouse ornament out of the hummus dip.

Most of the guys were milling about guzzling beer. Others were at the tables taking plates of food that smelled like gym clothes. There was one group on the couch watching some special about Amish students waiting to see the ball drop in Times Square for the first time. What was she doing here? If Jazz didn’t call soon, she would have to find an excuse to leave.

To make matters worse, Lola, her stunning, modelesque friend, parked herself in front of Alicia as she found new ways to make out with her boyfriend.

"Hey Alicia," Lola said, coming up for a moment of air. "I can't wait to see your brother's show later. What's he making anyway?"

"Not a clue." Alicia nearly retched watching Lola lick the bridge of her boyfriend's nose.

"That sounds soooo amazing," Lola gushed as her boyfriend kissed her eyebrows in return. "Can't wait."

"Me either," Alicia said, excusing herself before heading toward the door.

Where is he? Alicia jumped as her phone rang. *Finally*. She answered the phone with a desperate, "Where are you?!?"

"Oh, Liza," she corrected herself. "Sorry. I thought you were Jazz. He's late. Did Dex leave for the studio yet?" Alicia listened intently. "What?!" Her phone beeped signaling an incoming call. "Liza, it's Jazz. I have to talk to him. Tell everyone to stay put. I'm on my way."

Alicia answered Jazz's call. "Hey, where are you?!?" She couldn't hear him and stepped outside. "You found...what?" She was straining to hear him through the bad phone connection. "You're breaking up. Just meet me at my house."

#

Liza was in the family room crushing their finished pizza boxes into small squares and then pushing them into a too-small plastic garbage bag as if she were stuffing a sausage.

"Yo, I'm a dude. I can make that happen," Jordy said, watching Liza struggle with the trash.

"Did I ask for your *manly* help?" she snapped.

"Don't be be-otchin' at my door, sista." Jordy threw a mini marshmallow up in the air and caught it with his tongue. "I'm doin' sweets. I ain't gunnin' for a clash."

"Sorry," Liza apologized. "I'm not looking to start up with you either." She walked the bag over to Jordy. "You can help."

The two of them got everything to fit and tied the bag up neatly.

"I got 'dis." Jordy carried the bag to the pail outside.

"Alicia should be here any minute," Liza said walking over to the window.

"Hope so," Sarah said turning on the TV, "'cause it's getting late."

"When does Dex's show start anyway?" Kyle asked as he popped a couple of his Tums. "Feels like Geema left for the studio hours ago."

"It just feels long," Liza explained. "Always does when you're waiting on something."

Jordy walked in with his arm around Alicia. Liza looked puzzled and rolled her eyes at him.

"Wha'? Don't be buggin' yo' peepas, girl," Jordy argued. "It's glacial out there."

Alicia was still shivering as she took off her coat and slung it over the couch. "Thanks for trying to keep the wind away from me Jordy. You are a true gentleman."

Jordy gave Liza a small, triumphant *'hmph'* and sat down on the rug.

"Honestly, I don't understand any of this," Alicia admitted. "What does Preston LeTray have against Dex?" She took a handful of almonds.

"D-sizzle got dat spacewaster thrown off da island, yo," Jordy offered.

"Huh?" Alicia asked.

"They tossed him like greens and canned his beans," he clarified.

Alicia still looked baffled.

"Dex's show is so good they fired Preston!" Liza explained. "But Dex can't just cave to that sleaze. He better think of something."

"I don't know," Kyle said, munching on a carrot stick. "Presto's scary. I'd be afraid noooooot--to listen to him," he explained as he burped.

The doorbell rang and Alicia sprinted to get it.

"Hi. I'm sorry I'm late," Jazz said as Alicia answered the door. "I got here as soon as I could."

Kyle, Sarah, and Liza were lined up behind the couch, their elbows resting on the top with their faces in their hands. Jordy was sprawled across the couch beneath them.

The TV was on and Alicia recognized the Amish kids

standing in Times Square. They were on at Lola's party too. Why was everyone watching them?

"Hi Jazz," the group said almost in unison.

"Hey." Jazz pulled a video tape out of his pocket. "Leesh, set up the VCR. I have to show you all something."

Alicia's heart quickened. This was the first time Jazz had called her by her nickname. She flipped on the recorder, watched the screen turn blue, and made a mental note to revisit this feeling later, after they were done saving her family from potential ruin.

"Remember when you came to the construction site and I ran out of tape?" Jazz asked.

"Of course I do." Alicia blushed, remembering their first kiss.

"You gave me a tape of yours."

"Yeah, I remember. So?"

"You thought it was blank. It wasn't!" he exclaimed. "And I made a copy onto a DVD."

Kyle, Liza, and Sarah suddenly looked up and gave Jazz their full attention. Jazz pulled out the disc from his inner coat pocket and put it on the coffee table. He handed the tape to Alicia.

"What is this?" Alicia asked.

"You'll see," Jazz promised. "I'm not exactly sure of what I taped over, but what's there is incredible. Truly incredible!"

Alicia anxiously put the tape in the VCR. There was nothing but static.

"Give it a minute to get past this part." Jazz sat down next to Jordy who was now upright and watching intently.

The tape began in a very clean, white kitchen with a middle-age man standing in front of a counter full of ingredients that suggested he was making some kind of sauce.

"Hey," Liza said. "Isn't that guy Poppy? I mean he looks young there, but it still looks like him."

"Yeah," Alicia confirmed. "It's Poppy at the restaurant years ago. This is so cool. I don't remember ever seeing this tape and I was pretty sure I'd seen all of them."

As the tape continued a phone rang and Poppy excused himself to someone as he left to answer it.

"It gets way more interesting," Jazz promised.

In the next frame, Alicia's warm, fuzzy feeling started to fade. There he was, Preston LeTray, the creep who was terrorizing her little brother, standing alone, hovering over ingredients in Poppy's Kitchen.

"What's he doing there?" Kyle asked.

"Not sure yet," Alicia answered, "but, I don't like the look in his eyes. Something isn't right."

"Here it comes!" Jazz prompted.

The others stared at the TV set, transfixed by the unfolding video clip.

Preston looks to his right, then to his left, and then behind him. He looks down at a sheet of paper with the bolded words: POPPY'S PESTO.

Preston starts hunting for something, his eyes rolling over shelves and counters. He settles on a piece of paper towel and plucks it from a roll hanging on the wall. He gives another look around and quickly grabs a pen from his pocket. He recites each ingredient as he writes it down. When he finishes he kisses the sheet of paper towel and says, "Someday, this will make me famous." He shoves the towel into his pants and exits the screen.

"Then it goes back to the construction site," Jazz said, ejecting the tape. "I'm just glad I didn't rewind or we would have missed all this."

"Dat fool hijacked Poppy's recipe, yo!" Jordy squeaked.

"Sure does seem that way doesn't it!" Alicia scowled. "No wonder Preston waited until Poppy was gone to put out Presto's Bestos. He knew Poppy would catch on."

"How did they even know each other?" Sarah asked.

"That's a good question," Alicia admitted. "I think he was friends with my mom when they were younger."

"Some friend," Liza squawked.

"This bloke's been at his anger a very long time." Jazz handed Alicia the tape. "And that was way before his beef with Dex. Begs why."

Alicia sighed, turning the player off.

The TV switched back on and was now showing a commercial for Presto's Pesto.

"Naturally." Alicia shook her head and took another handful of almonds.

As soon as the commercial ended, Dex's New Year's Eve special began.

Chapter 34

Dex was sweating even though his hands felt ice cold. There was no graceful way to ruin his career, no matter how nany times he tried to play out different scenarios in his head. Vith each disastrous flip of his spatula, Dex was slowly but surely nding his reign as the only kid ever to have a show on the Eatz ietwork. But, he decided it was a sacrifice he needed to make or Poppy's Kitchen and to spare his family from yet another loss. 'hrough it all Dex hoped Poppy was watching and proud of him.

The second cameraman was focused on Preston in his lean, crisp white apron triumphantly plating a sumptuous large oast drizzled with glistening, brown gravy surrounded by new otatoes and spears of broccoli. The instant Preston placed own the pewter tray holding the savory entree, the video screen perator displayed a close-up of it on the giant screen above both hefs that read:

KING PRESTO'S CROWN ROAST

Dex had to remind himself to smile, something he was ertain he had forgotten considering this whole show was a sham. e pasted on a lifeless grin to keep up the pretense that he was in we of Preston and no match for his kitchen mastery. Dex couldn't elp feeling annoyed as the audience applauded Preston's dish, ıd he felt like a phony going through the motions of a chef when was purposely not acting like one.

A pot of smoky barbecue sauce was simmering, and Dex ade sure to let it splatter on his already stained apron as he oured it into a bowl. True to his word to Preston, Dex was a ılking culinary mess. He had let an assortment of items explode ıto his apron: a plastic ketchup bottle, a jar of duck sauce, a ntainer of grape juice, a bowl of honey, and a can of black beans.

He had promised to be covered in mistakes right through dessert, which from the way he was feeling, could not come soon enough.

"To continue with our holiday feast—OWW!" Dex yelped, bumping his elbow on purpose into the bubbling sauce pot causing more splatters.

"Hey Dex," Preston chuckled, "looks like you've been hitting the sauce."

The audience broke out into wild laughter, sending shivers down Dex's spine.

"Preston, this crown roast of yours looks fit for royalty."

"It does. Doesn't it!"

The audience applauded in approval.

"Now let me go to the oven," Dex began, "to check on my Chipotle Chicken Chunks." Dex went to the oven.

"Let me help you," Preston insisted. "This is how it's done." He plated Dex's heap of chunks onto a plain white platter.

"Thanks so much, Preston."

"Good thing he didn't make chicken salad," Preston snickered. "Right everyone?"

There were small hisses from the audience as the digital screen switched to display an unappealing image of Dex's chicken dish. The caption at the bottom of the screen read:

MMM MMM CHUNKS!

Dex again opened the oven door, which he had deliberately

set too high, letting out a huge waft of smoke. He grabbed a nearby plastic cutting board still holding chopped broccoli to wave away the offending air.

The audience gasped as the little green florets went flying all over the kitchen.

"Dex, your broccoli was on that!" Preston chided. "And even *you* can't cook vegetables on the fly."

As planned, the audience was rapidly falling into Preston's trap.

Dex hoped Geema wasn't getting too freaked out. Maybe she would blame his performance on exhaustion or nerves. She was his grandmother; she had to make excuses for a catastrophe like this.

During a segment on new kitchen gadgets, like the all-purpose collapsible plastic colander and the automatic cucumber peeler, Dex had the chance to slip into his dressing room, which for once he was actually glad to have. There was a text from Marla:

Do u have the runs? Take Pepto-Bismol...u look uncomfortable...

Awkward. His mother thought he was screwing up because he had diarrhea. Dex texted her back:

Not sick. Just tired-- I guess.

He didn't realize she was still there, but another text appeared right away:

then y all the probs? u've been cooking since ur 4 and never messed up this way...ur dad thinks the pressure is getting 2 u...I think somethin's wrong...so what is it?

Dex chuckled at Marla's 'texting-mom' style, but wasn't sure what to write back. All he knew was he couldn't text her the truth.

Nothing's wrong. I'm tired. Have fun. Talk later. He reluctantly pressed 'send.' Yeah, that would have to do for now.

There was a knock at the door, and Dex hoped against hope it was news of a blazing fire raging in the studio kitchen, forcing everyone to leave immediately. He opened the door to no such luck.

"Hey little dude, they need you back on set," Arby relayed, drinking a bottle of Mountain Dew. "Want some?"

"Uh, no thanks." Dex put his phone back in his pocket. There was a new text from Marla, but he didn't want to write back another lie.

"Can I ask you something, little dude?"

"Uh, sure."

"Okay, like, you cook and all that, and like, you're good at it. So, why are you like *so* not good at it tonight?"

Dex sighed. If even Arby, who often forgot the second slice of bread on his sandwiches, had noticed the continuous kitchen disasters, Dex knew he was doing a great job of trashing his career. But, it had to be.

"I dunno," Dex lied. "Some days are like that."

"Um, like this is none of my business, but like, I don't think so. That Preston d-bag is all in your face."

Had he underestimated Arby's ability to reason?

"I wish I could tell you Arby," Dex admitted. "But, I can't."

"Try me, little dude. I'm like good at, you know, like, keeping my mouth shut about stuff." Arby took another swig of his Dew. "Who knows? You saved my butt. Maybe I can help you."

Chapter 35

"Oh, not again. I can't watch this anymore!" Liza cried, blocking the TV with her hand.

There was Dex at the kitchen counter on set, looking stoic in his filthy apron mixing a bowl of mashed potatoes that looked more like thin, lumpy cream-of-wheat.

"Poor bloke," Jazz said. "This is a travesty."

"D-sizzle gonna fizzle." Jordy threw a jelly bean in the air and caught it in his mouth.

"This is so wrong," Kyle said, sipping eggnog.

"My poor brother," Alicia sighed.

They watched as Dex moved over to the range and stirred a pan of minced garlic into charred dust. Preston was standing at the nearby counter chopping parsley and smiling as if Dex wasn't there.

"We have to help him," Sarah said. "What're we going to do?"

"Wait a minute," Kyle shrieked. "What about your Uncle Ezra!?! He could probably do something."

"Doubtful. He's on a safari in Africa. He won't be back until next week."

Alicia was only half-listening to the conversation. She was much more interested in the footage of Preston's *REGAL RUMMY RELISH* that was now flashing on the studio screen. Then the footage shifted back to the chefs preparing their next course.

Alicia jumped up. "I have an idea! Jazz, grab the DVD.

Guys, I have the Eatz network app on my phone. We can watch in the car."

In seconds they were all out the door and piled into Alicia's back seat. Jazz tied his sneaker and slid into the passenger's side.

Alicia was freaking out as she kept turning the key in the ignition with no response. "It won't start!"

"It's old," Jordy said. "Old don't like cold."

"Well right now I don't care if my car would be happier tanning in Florida." Alicia tried turning the ignition again. "I just need it to start."

"Why don't we take my car?" Jazz suggested.

"There are six of us and your car is a Beetle," Alicia complained.

"Well none of you are all that big," Jazz reasoned. "I think we should try it before it gets too late."

Jazz jumped out and was ready to go before everyone had even gotten out of Alicia's car. Alicia sat up front and watched in the mirror as everyone else piled into the minuscule back seat.

"Yo, it's like we playin' *Twister* all over again," Jordy said, stretching his arm over Liza's head.

"Sorry 'bout that, but at least it runs." Jazz pulled out of the driveway with a start that made everyone moan. "Yeah, not used to all the weight. Hold tight. It's going to be bumpy at best."

Alicia took out her phone and found the live feed for Dex's special. "Can you go any faster Jazz? It looks like they're already up to dessert!"

“This isn’t the Batmobile, love!” Jazz fed the car a little more gas.

“ERRRRRRRRRP!” Kyle released. “Oops. That one’s gonna stink.”

“Nah uh, Kyle! You upchuck another windy and I’m’a chuck you out da car!” Jordy warned.

“Oh man, Kyle. And here I was thinking about kissing you at midnight,” Liza admitted.

“Really?” Kyle’s eyes bugged out.

“Well, you are cute and all,” Liza offered.

“I am?” Kyle asked in disbelief.

“Yo, get a room,” Jordy whined. “I’m gonna hurl.”

Jazz was stuck in traffic at a light in front of a cable company. A small group of irate employees were carrying signs claiming their boss was the spawn of Satan and chanted that customers should switch to the leading competitor. When the light changed and he could finally move again, a group of rubberneckers forced him to inch his way out of the lane.

“What’s taking so long?” Alicia groaned.

“Not the best night to be in a rush to get anywhere.” Jazz gave her hand a sympathetic squeeze.

“Anyone else feeling that bean dip?” Sarah moaned.

“Noooooo, don’t tell me you’re...” Liza cried shoving closer to Kyle.

Sarah laughed. "Just kidding. It would be nice to be there already."

"At your service young lady." Jazz pulled into the crowded parking lot of the Eatz building and tried unsuccessfully to find a spot. "What now, love?" Jazz asked looking at Alicia.

He called her 'love' at least twice and so far she had no time to live in it. Another thing on her 'to do' list for later.

"Um...maybe street parking?" Alicia offered.

Jazz drove around the block, but there were no free spaces.

"Take the rear," Jordy said.

"Pardon?" Jazz asked confused.

"Go around the back of the building," Liza translated, shifting in her seat.

"OW!" Kyle shrieked. "Liza, watch it, please!"

"Ha, she got you in da almond joys!" Jordy laughed.

Jazz drove around the back and found a spot near the dumpsters. "Good call, Liza," he praised.

Alicia turned to the back seat. "Does everyone know what to do?"

They nodded and nearly fell out of the car when the doors cramming them in were finally opened. Sarah, Kyle, Liza, and Jordy went running ahead into the building. Jazz pulled Alicia back before they got to the door.

"I know it's not great timing, but I don't want to forget," he started. "This isn't exactly the way I figured on spending tonight, but..." Jazz reached into his pants pocket and pulled out a small black box. "I wanted to end this year and start the next one with you."

Alicia's hands trembled as she took the box and opened it. It was an open gold heart with a diamond chip hanging on a gold chain.

"Oh wow, Jazz..."

Just as their lips met, they heard Dex's studio audience applaud from inside.

#

"What are all of you doing here?" said a very tall, lanky security guard. A small TV built into the side of the front desk was tuned to Dex's special.

"We're here to catch the end of the show and surprise my brother," Alicia said, pointing to the TV. "I'm Dex's sister, Alicia Rossi."

"I wouldn't brag about that right now," the security guard warned, his voice deep and raspy. He looked back up at the TV screen to see Dex dropping more cookie batter on the counter than on the baking sheets. "Poor kid's just choked. Been going on all night."

They all hovered around the TV to watch.

Dex carries a pan over to the counter and gets a kitchen lighter from a drawer. "One quick flick of my mini-torch," he says, flicking the control, "and this will be..." He hesitates, still flicking the switch. Nothing happens. "Hmm. It's, uh, broken," he concludes.

*In a flash, Preston walks over and grabs the lighter from Dex. "Did you mean to do **this**?" Preston corrects him, dramatically flicking the lighter on, then sets the pan ablaze instantly. The audience applauds Preston's success.*

"So," Alicia cut in, distracting the guard once again, "now you see why we have to get to my brother. Please let us get into the studio. I told Dex we'd get him home in time to watch the ball drop."

"Oh, I think he's already dropped the ball, honey. I hope one of you's his Fairy Godmother." He led them to a door near the elevator. "Go through here and up the stairs."

"Thanks!" Alicia turned and led the way.

"Wait, guys. Not there!" Kyle interrupted halfway up the stairs. "That's the door to the audience."

"We'll have to sneak down from the audience then," Liza whispered.

"We'll get caught," Sarah argued.

"Yo. Yo!" Jordy was standing at the bottom of another set of stairs off to the side, pointing to a door behind him labeled:

CLOSED SET: STAFF ONLY

Jazz was standing beside Jordy at the door to the closed set.

"Leesh, I think you should stay here and watch the door with Liza and Jordy," he whispered.

"Are you sure?" Alicia wasn't convinced. "I think I should come with you too."

"Yo, me too," Jordy insisted.

"Hey, and me," Liza added.

"Too many feet, too much noise," Jazz explained. "Jordy if *you* get caught, no one will understand what you're saying. That'll give us more time."

"So," Liza said. "Let Jordy watch the door."

"Liza, you're Jordy's backup. And, Leesh, I'll be too distracted if you're with me."

Alicia blushed. "If you say so."

Jazz looked to his left and right. "Sarah, you know what to do?"

Sarah nodded as she clutched the DVD tightly.

"Kyle, you're my cover," Jazz said slowly opening the door. "And, if anyone has to run or gets lost, go upstairs to the audience pavilion."

Liza shrugged, confused.

"It says it here." Jazz pointed to a building directory hanging on the wall in between the stairwell and the elevator.

Jazz, Sarah, and Kyle snuck their way behind a series of multi-colored wires and equipment and scanned the area to find the controls for the giant video screen. Jazz saw two cameramen stationed above the kitchen and now understood how they got direct shots of what was cooking in the pots and pans. They inched their way over a little bit more and saw the operator, a big, hairy guy in a plaid shirt sitting in a small chair on wheels. With his eyes slightly closed, he looked like a bear ready for a long winter's nap.

The area was too tight for them to make the switch while the guy was sitting right behind the control panel. Sarah was petite and fast, so Jazz decided she should make the swap as soon as the guy got up to do something besides doze and catch himself falling off his seat. There was nothing they could do but wait.

Alicia peered through the set door to see the progress Jazz and the others were making; Liza and Jordy kept watch of the main entrance through the glass pane of the door nearest the security desk. They felt pretty sure no one else was expected to come in when they saw the guard take off his shoes and start clipping his toe nails.

"Any biz on the up?" Jordy asked.

"No, nothing's happening yet," Alicia whispered. "Oh. Wait. The guy just adjusted his headset. I'm not sure what that means."

The operator frowned and got up from the control panel as if looking for something. He took a few steps away and Sarah quickly made her move. She tiptoed over to the panel desk and slid under it. The slot for the disc was only within an arm's reach away. The operator was talking to a cameraman and Sarah slowly pushed the 'open' button on the player. Just as she went to put in the DVD, Kyle let out a loud burp.

"What the hell was that?!" the cameraman responded as he eyed the operator.

"A burp. But it wasn't me!" the operator swore.

"I know. Yours woulda sounded like a beast mating. It

was her," the cameraman said, pointing to Sarah who was skulking away.

"Get her out of here!" The operator hollered at a short, bony, gray-haired man in a tight hoodie who wore a badge and looked like the resident rapper at a senior center.

"Hey, little miss," the guard called out.

He saw Sarah heading for the exit and grabbed her hand. "What do you think you're doing?"

"Whatever I want. Ezra Langer is my uncle," she demanded, trying to break free.

"Mine too princess. But he's out of the country so you're shrimp out of luck."

Sarah still couldn't get loose. She moved her hands behind her back and fumbled with the DVD, then quickly tossed it behind her, praying it would land somewhere the others could retrieve it.

Jazz and Kyle watched the DVD soar through the air. Picturing the running backs he'd seen playing football, Jazz tried to angle himself to catch it and hopped as high as he could without blowing their cover. But there was no way. Catching it would mean waving like a moving target at the entire crew from behind the barrier of unused cameras and speakers keeping him and Kyle safely hidden.

Sarah's jaw dropped in horror as the disc fell through a long vertical slat in the floor. Her head slung forward until she felt herself being pushed toward the side door. She looked up to get her bearings and spotted Alicia through the crack in the door.

"Run!" Sarah cried.

Alicia and Liza started for the stairs. Jordy started to run too, but then went back to the door and opened it. "Yo, Sarah, punt the dude. Like now." He let the door go and ran.

Sarah gave the guard a hard kick to his shin, making him buckle and drop his hold on her.

"Come back here you darn brat!" he cried rubbing his bruised leg.

Sarah ran through the doors and followed the sound of footsteps trekking up the stairs. She was relieved to see Alicia, Liza, and Jordy safely standing under a canopy by a set of double doors marked by a sign reading:

AUDIENCE: QUIET! LIVE SHOW IN PROGRESS

#

Kyle and Jazz watched the operator go back to the controls.

"Jazz, I am so sorry, man." Kyle took out a roll of Tums and popped two in his mouth. "I didn't even feel it coming."

"Well mate, that's why it's always good to have backup," Jazz whispered.

Kyle finally let himself smile. "A backup?!" he yelled in a whisper. "Where is it?"

Jazz went into his coat pocket then began to panic. "What? Where'd it go?" he grunted, throwing his fist down in frustration. He began to edge his way back to the exit, signaling Kyle to follow behind.

As soon as they walked out, Jazz headed for the steps.

"Where do you think it went?" Kyle asked.

"Not sure. Gads, I feel like such a dill."

"You feel like a pickle?"

"Idiot, mate, idiot."

"I told you I was sorry!" Kyle pleaded.

"No, I feel like an idiot--that's what a dill is."

Kyle cocked his head to the side, now completely bewildered.

"Oh crikey, just shut up and stay with me," Jazz huffed as he began to rush back toward the lobby.

Jazz kept a watchful eye on the floor as he and Kyle ran through the doors and into the lobby. No one was at the front desk to chase them away, but since the small TV was still on, they knew someone would be back soon. Jazz scanned the entire floor but spotted only a straw wrapper in one corner and a half-tarnished penny near the front doors.

"This makes no sense!" Jazz yelped as he turned all his pockets inside out. "None at all. I had the backup right in my left pocket."

"Wait, which pocket?" Kyle probed.

"Right in my left one. I left it right there!"

Between Jazz's accent and his own confusion, Kyle was stumped. He decided not to ask another question only to get an answer he was sure he'd misunderstand. It was better to be one dill shy of getting into a bigger pickle.

Jazz checked over both his shoulders to see if anyone was around before he started helping Kyle rummage through papers and supplies on the counter. They still hadn't come up with anything when they heard footsteps.

"Oh man, not again!" Kyle whispered, this time clenching his mouth tightly to avoid another unwanted outburst.

"Follow me," Jazz ordered.

They started back toward the stairwell when they saw a pudgy man they didn't recognize come out of a narrow door behind a potted plant near the desk.

"Hey!" the man shouted.

Jazz turned around slowly.

"Um," the man began, "uh...like...who are you? And who's the little dude?" the young man went on.

For a moment Kyle felt grateful there was someone with them who seemed just as confused as he was.

"I'm Jazz. The little dude is Kyle," Jazz explained. He then had a realization and continued. "And you must be Arby. Dex told us about you. We're friends."

"Cool."

"We're actually looking for something..."

Arby pulled the DVD out of a deep pocket. "This?"

"YES!" Kyle cheered.

"Oh, cool. Good. Cuz, I like found it on the floor and I was like, what am I gonna do with this? And like, I didn't think it would be cool to give it to anyone."

Jazz exchanged a quick glance with Kyle. Dex hadn't been

exaggerating at all about Arby's conversational skills. Jazz looked up at the clock and felt another twinge of panic. The show was minutes away from the end.

"I watched it," Arby admitted.

"Fine with us," Jazz said. "We want everyone to know the truth."

"Me too," Arby agreed. "Like that Presto dude is a whopping poser. You know. I was thinking. You could like, play this," Arby rubbed the disc, "on the big, flat screen. It's way better than the food pics."

"That's the plan. Want to come with us?" Jazz asked. "We could probably use your help."

"Would, dude. But, Frank, the security guard, ate like, Presto's microwave tacos, and like now I have to hang at the desk, 'til, he's like...you know...done evacuating the building, if ya know what I mean."

"Got it," Jazz said, stifling a laugh.

"Sucks. The dude at the controls is kinda like, slow," Arby said, scratching the top of his head. Dandruff began falling steadily to the floor beside him, making Kyle's stomach turn as he pretended to be listening intently. Jazz was staring at the floor, hoping Arby would take the hint. He didn't.

"And ya know, come to think of it, like even if you used my name, like it probably wouldn't help, but I mean you can def try if you want."

"Got it," Jazz reiterated. "Thanks for the DVD." He started to walk away and ran back. "Thanks for your help, Arby. Happy

New Year."

"Sure." Arby turned to the TV and started guzzling his bottle of Mountain Dew.

Jazz and Kyle ran back and cautiously entered through the doors. Despite all the excitement, the operator still looked ready to use the control board as a pillow.

"Alright. You know what to do, right?" Jazz asked Kyle.

Kyle nodded. "Not use Arby's name."

"He's a friendly bloke, but that's a given." Jazz rolled his eyes. "Seriously, are you ready?"

"Yup," Kyle nodded.

"Okay. Let's try this one more time."

Jazz clutched the DVD as Kyle inched his way over to the control panel. This time he didn't want to take any chances. On Jazz's cue, Kyle tried to let out a burp, but nothing would come out. He tried a few more times. Still nothing. He held his nose and tried gulping air. When that didn't work, Kyle jabbed himself in the stomach a few times. He looked at Jazz and shrugged.

With no burps streaming on demand, it was time to get creative. Kyle eyed an unused camera stand and strategically knocked it over, making it land on the operator's empty seat. The noise was startling and caught the cameramen's attention, but the frazzled crew members couldn't stop shooting to come over. Kyle reached down and pressed the 'open' button on the giant screen video player and at the same time Jazz pushed the disc across the floor like a hockey puck and stood up. The operator came running over as fast as his stocky frame would allow.

“Who *are* you kids?!?” the operator barked. “Did my ex-wife send you to punish me or something?” The operator continued to stare Jazz down.

“Me? I’m with Dex. I’m the new intern,” Jazz invented on the spot.

Kyle tried to work quickly as Jazz kept the operator’s attention focused on him.

“I didn’t get any memos about a new intern. Unless they got rid of Arby.” The operator shook his head then took a few steps backwards, nearly tripping over Kyle as he tried to get to the controls.

“What the...! You kids are killin’ me tonight,” the operator yelled. “Give me back the friggin’disc. NOW!”

“Okay, okay.” Kyle nearly broke down in tears handing it over.

“I should call security and have you both kicked out on your butts,” the operator threatened. “But it’s almost New Year’s. I wanna go home already and I’m feeling generous. So-- get outta here, and just let me do my job!”

The operator grabbed the DVD and put it in the player.

Kyle and Jazz quickly exited and ran up to the audience pavilion. Before they went in, Jazz patted Kyle on the back. “I’m sorry, mate. I know you really tried.”

“Don’t be sorry.” Kyle handed Jazz a DVD labeled:

DINE WITH DEX NEW YEAR’S SPECIAL

“Get out of town! That means he just put on the--”

“Yup, he sure did!” Kyle interrupted.

“Good going, man,” Jazz praised him. “You really did it!” He gave Kyle a high five, and then the two quietly walked upstairs to meet up with the others.

Chapter 36

"Frank, please tell me I didn't miss the show," Geema said to the security guard she'd met several months ago when Dex began working. "It's been such a crazy night," she went on. "Road closings, unbelievable traffic, and then a detour to the hospital so my driver could film his wife delivering their baby a month early! Have you ever tried to get any kind of car service on a holiday?"

"Can't say I have, Miss Golda," the guard answered, taking a swig of antacid. "But, if you want to talk crazy, I had Presto's tacos for dinner. Every part of me hurts south of the border."

Geema tried to cover her disgust with a pained nod as he went on.

"If you hurry you can catch the end of the show. That's a whole 'nother kind of crazy. Your boy's been having quite a night."

#

"Whoa! Preston, that's an awesome-looking cake," Dex said as if Preston had reinvented baking.

"It is, isn't it," Preston beamed.

Dex unrolled a sheet of phyllo dough and let it tear. "This is really hard to do. Preston, how'd you do all that so fast?"

"I'm a true professional," Preston boasted. "Careless errors are for amateurs."

Preston rolled his eyes at Dex and continued mixing a bowl of chocolate glaze.

"While Dex is struggling to finish his baklava before next year, I'm going to put the finishing touches on my extraordinary Napoleon cake."

Dex looked down at the torn pile of phyllo dough in front of him wanting to laugh. This was such a joke since *baklava* became one of his specialties when he was six-years-old. Next to a *cannoli*, it was Poppy's favorite pastry and he would always complain that the Greeks got to claim the recipe first.

But, he did what he had to do and dutifully measured out too much honey and chopped a cup of walnuts until they created a powder. Everything exactly wrong. If he could just get through this segment without screaming out the truth he'd be okay, and this charade would finally be over.

Dex could see Preston reveling in all his sugary glory. It was unfair and Dex knew it. He had seen several assistants prepare almost every ingredient at Preston's station prior to the show. The only thing left for Preston to do was some chopping and set-up in front of the camera.

It was a process. When Preston was done, he would put his dish aside on a shelf out of view and pull out a beautiful pre-made version. Dex wasn't sure why Preston would even consider doing this during a special. It was kind of like lip-syncing; going through the motions, when someone else had done the work. Dex didn't rely on anyone else. He made all his own dishes. Maybe that's why Ezra fired Preston. Maybe in real life, Preston was a fake and not really a chef at all.

Dex was at the counter separating eggs to make a second dessert, his French Dreamy Cloud Cake, which required fluffy baked meringue and a rich vanilla custard. He was thrilled this was the last dish of the evening, even though he had already accepted what he assumed people were thinking of him. As he beat the eggs, he kept thinking about why he had made this decision in the first place. It was all for his family. No matter what, he would take pride in carrying on what had taken decades for his grandparents to accomplish.

The family restaurant was called Poppy's Kitchen, but Dex knew that his grandmother had been at the heart of everything there from the first meal served to the last. It was a legacy that he would do anything to preserve, even embarrass himself, which at the moment he was doing very well.

"Uh-oh," he repeated, almost like a broken record at this point. "Dropped a piece of shell in this." Dex scrambled to grab more eggs.

Preston was standing at the end of the long counter near the refrigerator sliding chopped chocolate and bananas into a blender filled with coffee. When he was done he whizzed the mixture on 'high.'

"This smells obscenely delicious," Preston exclaimed as he poured the thick drink into glass mugs and topped them with whipped cream and powdered cocoa.

"Now we're going to finish our New Year's dessert table with my Chunky Monkey Cappuccino." Preston signaled the operator to push the button behind him to flash a close-up on the screen. The inviting coffee image appeared and Preston turned to Dex.

"Oh, yes...and Dex's..." Preston paused. "What are you making again?" Preston turned lightly tapping his elbow against a plate that sent an errant banana peel onto the floor.

"I'm making meringue," Dex said, dropping an egg yolk into the bowl.

“No you’re not, you’re making a mess,” Preston chuckled. “You can’t put in egg yolks and expect meringue. Right everyone?”

“RIGHT!” the audience yelled.

“It’s just about ten, only a short time away from the New Year,” Preston said from behind the long counter. “I want to thank you all for watching. Dex would thank you too, but he has to do something with the eggs he ruined when he botched his meringue.”

“They’ll make for a great New Year’s Day omelet though,” Dex noted as he held the bowl full of egg and walked toward the refrigerator.

Preston grabbed the bowl out of Dex’s hands. “I’ll take that. There’s no room left on your apron for another spill.”

“Thanks,” Dex said, looking at the mess on his apron. “I guess you’re right. Again.”

“So true.” Preston smiled and pointed to the screen. “Here’s a look at everything we’ve made tonight.”

Seeing Preston’s signal, the operator pushed the button, but the screen stayed blank.

“And from me to you, have a delicious New Yea---” Preston said as his foot hit the banana peel that had fallen earlier, sending him onto the floor face first into the bowl of beaten eggs he was still clutching in his hands.

The audience gasped as Preston rose with egg covering his face.

“Don’t worry, I’m alright.” Preston got to his feet and faced the audience, but no one acknowledged him. Their eyes were glued to the screen and an ominous hush fell over the set.

It took a moment, but with some careful listening Preston thought he recognized at least one voice coming from the screen. It was his, but he sounded younger and less polished. The other belonged to an older man, but he couldn't place him.

Preston wiped the egg from his eyes, but they burned, keeping him from looking at the screen. The other voice was becoming more familiar now. How could he have forgotten? It was Marla's father. But, none of this made any sense. Why would their conversation have been taped, and why would it interest an audience? All he remembered from that night was being distraught because Marla had broken their engagement and ruined his life.

But then it hit him. That was also the night he swore that someday he'd be redeemed. That was the night he...No. It couldn't be. There couldn't be a tape of...

Preston flashed an egg-hazed look at Dex, who was too engrossed in watching what was on the screen to notice. Should he dare look?

Preston reluctantly followed the gaze of the audience and focused on the screen as the DVD revealed every moment of his stealing Poppy Marino's precious pesto recipe. He shuddered in horror as each move framed him as the guilty criminal who had built an empire on a well-crafted lie.

The tape ended and the screen went blank. The audience started to boo and shout:

"Preston's a phony!" yelled a deep voice.

"Preston cheated us all!" screamed an older woman.

“I’m still not skinny you fraud,” shouted a hefty lady.

“You’re the worst-o!” one man began, and the chant caught on.

“YOU’RE THE WORST-O! YOU’RE THE WORST-O! YOU’RE THE WORST-O!” the audience was drawing close to a riot.

As Preston heard the enraged shouts, the room began to spin and the air became too thin to breathe. He stripped off his apron, ran to an exit and disappeared into a small crowd of New Year’s Eve partiers outside.

“I can’t believe you did this,” Dex said, turning to Preston only to find him gone.

The audience continued to jeer, but Dex knew he still had a job to do.

“Okay, everyone. It’s all okay! Listen, please.” Dex’s voice helped quiet the chaos. “Thank you my friends. Thank you. Let me tell you the whole story. Let me explain what really happened tonight.”

#

A few minutes later Dex was sitting in his dressing room appreciating the silent calm. He was glad his assistants had rushed him off stage and past hoards of fans who were toting everything from gum wrappers to food processors for him to autograph. He wasn’t in the mood to talk. He certainly wasn’t in the mood to be a celebrity. The only saving grace was the possibility that this YouTube clip might surpass his Barf-a-thon. But probably not.

A knock at the door jarred his thoughts back to reality.

“Come in,” Dex said reluctantly from his chair.

Geema came in and looked at his face through the mirror on the wall.

“You look kind of pale. This must have been quite a night,” Geema said.

“What do you mean, ‘must have been?’”

“Long story, Dexy. I didn’t get here until Preston got egg on his face and ran out of here like a bat out of hell.”

Dex sighed heavily. “That’s actually the best news I’ve heard all night. Glad you missed most of it.”

“Are you okay?” Geema asked, patting his head.

“I guess. Just happy it’s over.”

“It is. And we’ll all be fine, even if Preston owns the restaurant.”

Dex gasped. “How’d you find out?!”

“The bank didn’t close early. I lied.” Geema got a tissue from her bag and dabbed at a few stray tears. “I didn’t want to upset you before the show.”

“I don’t understand any of this,” Dex confided. “Where did that DVD even come from?”

“It was a copy of a tape that told only half the story,” Geema said. “Jazz found it by accident. One day Alicia gave him a tape to use when he ran out while shooting his movie. She thought it was blank, but it wasn’t. Alicia, Jazz, and your friends came down here tonight to make the switch and show you and everyone else what a fake Preston is.”

“They came down here?”

“They sure did. Who else would have gone through the trouble of sneaking around the entire back stage for you?” Geema threw the tissue in the trash. “That’s what you call loyalty. I sent them home. Told them we’d be back by midnight to celebrate, as promised.”

“Geema, how did Preston even know Poppy?”

“There was never any reason to tell you. Your mother was engaged to Preston a long time ago. But I guess, even then, she could tell what kind of person he really is. So she gave him back his ring and told him she wouldn’t marry him.”

“And that’s why he stole Poppy’s recipe?”

“Have you ever heard saying, ‘All is fair in love and war?’”

“Yeah. Kinda. Why? Do you believe that?”

“No, I think it’s a load of bull, but your grandfather always accused me of being the unromantic type.”

“So, that’s why Preston hates us? Because Mom didn’t marry him?”

“Honey, I don’t have the answer. The important thing is we know we always have each other. That’s as rich as anyone can get and there isn’t a Preston on the planet who could ever take that from us.”

Chapter 37

Preston was clearing out his desk. He didn't care. No one could prove anything and in a few weeks this would be old news and he would have a new job at another network. It was just a silly sauce, not the Mona Lisa. He would certainly hold onto the restaurant, and with a few sweet words he could keep Yvette on at least for a little while. He might even have to hire her awful friend Nan from the bank until he could get more grounded. It would be slow to start, but in time, it would become the empire he always knew he deserved. If he played his cards right, Marla would finally realize they were meant to be together. It was all going to fall into place. It would just take patience.

Without even a knock, Arby and two men in dark coats bolted into his office.

"Et tu, Arby?" Preston said, eyeing one man holding a pair of handcuffs.

"Yeah, um, like, I know that one," Arby boasted. "Shakespeare...Listen mean dude. My uncle told me to like, well, you know, to call security to kick you out before Ezra comes back."

"Care to celebrate the New Year, gentlemen?" Preston asked, extending a bottle of champagne from his desk.

"No sir," the men said.

"But these dudes are cops." Arby explained. "Little dude told me all about the visit you paid him in a company car. And all about the chicken salad. Not cool. You did like, um, you know, a whole mess of wrong."

"Preston LeTray. You are under arrest," said the man with

the handcuffs.

"This is an outrage," Preston shouted. "You have no proof of anything."

Arby held up a plastic bag filled with empty vials of medicine. "Found these in a dumpster when I was looking for my Mountain Dew bottle. Can you believe, I like forgot to like, you know, rip off the coupon? Lucky thing there was a garbage workers' strike."

"So what?" Preston argued.

"I started thinking--" Arby continued.

"That must have been a day worth remembering," Preston mocked.

"Once on *Fear Factor* they said this stuff," Arby held up the bag, "makes you puke and with all those barfing kids I like, um, well, you know, something was rotten in the state of Denmark."

"Wonderful. So you know Shakespeare. This means nothing," Preston insisted.

"Ever watch *CSI*? I love that show. They collect all kinds of, you know, evidence. So, I did that. Got everything I could. Even spoke to Ms. Bidet. Man is she angry at you! Said you promised to marry her then flirted with her friend at the bank."

"Never! I never said or did any such thing," Preston barked. "Lies. All lies."

"Well, she, you know, said she was done covering for you. And then she handed over all kinds of like, papers and stuff."

Preston looked horrified.

"It took a real long time for everything to be collected, analyzed, and processed, including your fingerprints," Arby explained, "but they, um, finally, got it all done."

The man with handcuffs spoke. "Preston LeTray, you have the right to remain silent. Anything you say can and will be used against you in a court of law..."

#

Dex felt good to finally be home in his room. No more of Preston's threats hanging over his head, no more audiences to calm down and win over. He knew everyone was waiting for him downstairs, but before he started the New Year he wanted to ditch the smell of the evening's menu still permeating his clothes.

He went to his closet to get a pair of jeans and found himself staring at the *Gymbuff* model in the ad, whose chest and pecs were still worlds beyond his own. Would *he* have done anything differently if *he* had been in Dex's shoes? Would *he* have agreed to ruin *his* career if he believed it was the only way he could help his family? Maybe *he* wouldn't have had to make that choice. Maybe *he* looked too strong to mess with. It was hard to know. The truth wasn't all that clear.

A lot of things had gotten strange, but the only thing he really wanted to think about was how he was going to kiss Sarah at midnight. He wasn't paying attention when he took his shirt off and banged his elbow right into the framed picture of Poppy and Geema, the photo at the restaurant that had been safely hanging on his wall for the past two years since Poppy died.

Now it had fallen face up on the floor with a big crack going right through the glass.

Haven't I screwed up enough for one night?!?

Dex bent down to pick it up and noticed his eyes were teary. What was up with that? Yeah, he loved that picture, but he also wanted to kiss Sarah. Now was not the time to star in his own Hallmark commercial. *Get a grip.*

He picked up the frame cautiously and thought maybe Geema still had that crazy glue in her room for manicuring her nails. Maybe that would work. It was worth a shot. As he held the frame, a large, flat envelope fell out from behind the photo and into his other hand.

The envelope was only slightly faded, but Dex opened it carefully. His heart began to beat faster, giving him the feeling this could be important. Inside the envelope were two sheets of paper. First was a hand-written note with little splatters of green sauce decorating the secret recipe underneath:

Ralphie, thanks for finally filling out the papers I sent you for the patent. The official document should arrive in a few weeks, but it could take months. Not that you'll do anything with it. But, maybe now I'll leave you alone. Hey, I moved to Israel, I ***have*** *to leave you alone. Meanwhile, I am enjoying the recipe you sent, paisan. I made a copy and sent back the original for you to keep with your records. But, what happened to the tape you said you made? Regards to the family. Let's try to keep in touch. Stuie.*

The other paper was a letter of authenticity granting Ralph Marino an official patent for his Poppy's Pesto.

If we have the patent, Dex was remembering his conversation with Geema, then, *Preston wasn't just a thief to his family, his friends, and his fans anymore. He was a thief to everyone—a proven criminal! With a sauce recipe that had made millions of dollars Poppy's family should have gotten.*

Dex flew down the stairs and heard everyone counting down.

"4, 3, 2, 1. HAPPY NEW YEAR!" the group cheered.

The news could wait, at least for a minute.

Dex walked over to Sarah, took her face in his hands, and planted the happiest kiss of his life right on her lips.

She looked a little surprised when he backed away.

"I have incredible news," Dex said bursting into a huge grin. "Presto's Pesto is ours, and we can prove it!"

"What?" Geema asked.

Dex handed her the papers. For the first time in ages, Geema was speechless.

Epilogue

"It's hard to believe tomorrow we're actually re-opening Poppy's Kitchen!" Dex beamed and turned his head.

"Why'd you do that?" Alicia asked, turning her camera away.

"Do what?"

"That stupid thing with your head."

Marla, Vince, and Jazz entered through the front door of the restaurant hauling packages followed by a delivery crew bringing in new chairs. Vince showed them how to arrange the seats and then he, Marla, and Jazz went into the pantry to put things away.

"I didn't do anything stupid with my head," Dex insisted. "You did something dumb with the camera."

"Dex, this is the final scene of my documentary. I have been filming you for months. I know if you're doing something dumb with your head!"

"And I know when you're shooting weird."

"Kids, stop arguing." Geema said, coming into the dining room from the kitchen. "I'm trying to rehearse my speech."

"Geema, I don't need you to rehearse. I want everyone to sound natural," Alicia explained, resting her camera on a table.

"Actually, you should record me now," she reasoned, "so I won't forget what I want to say."

"But it's just a simple question about Dex."

“Dear, if I’m on film, it isn’t simple. I have something to say, and I should be allowed to say it.”

“You tell her G’momma,” Jordy said as he, Sarah, Kyle, and Liza placed small bouquets of little white and red flowers with slender stems into sleek crystal vases.

“You can say whatever you want, Geema, just act natural,” Alicia said, holding up a centerpiece and inspecting it.

“Ya hear G’momma, it’s all good. Just don’t be bogus for the frame,” Jordy explained.

“Thank you,” Geema said. “Exactly whose side are you on?”

“Ours,” Jordy said. “We all have a together thing.”

Geema patted Jordy on the head. “You say a lot more than anyone thinks.”

Alicia picked up the camera and went back to filming.

Geema went over to the bar and took a glass and a bottle of champagne. “Leesh, please record me now, while it’s on my mind.”

Alicia turned the camera toward her grandmother. “Okay, sure,” she sighed, “start whenever you want. I can edit out mistakes.”

“EHHHHHHHHRP!” sounded Kyle as he put down a platter of fresh mozzarella and sun-dried tomatoes.

“Like that,” Alicia noted as she hit ‘record.’

“Nights like these tell the real story about family and friends,” Geema said, holding up a glass of champagne.

“Geema, it isn’t even noon yet,” Alicia corrected.

“You’re a director, improvise,” Geema suggested. “A few months ago, I would have never dreamed of eating chicken salad again--”

“I don’t think we should bring that up again,” Alicia squawked.

“But, it’s true. Did you want to eat chicken salad after that show?”

“No, but I never liked it in the first place.”

“Me either,” Sarah chimed in never taking her eyes off the floral centerpieces she was arranging.

“Can you let me finish?” Geema groaned.

“Sure. Go ahead.”

“So you can think lousy chicken salad is a bad thing. Or, you can realize that it’s no different than life.”

“Chicken salad and life.” Alicia pursed her lips and made a vibrating sound. “Okay, how so?”

“After every curve ball life throws our way, things always get set straighter with the next pitch.”

“I actually like that,” Alicia said. “I can make it work. Meanwhile, what do you think is next for Dex?”

“Maybe a bar-mitzvah. It’s a little late for him, but we’ve had a lot going on.” Geema excused herself and went to the ladies’ room.

"How's it going?" Dex asked Sarah as he inspected the centerpieces. "These look great!"

"They do look pretty good," Sarah agreed. "It must be weird for you to have the restaurant back. Good weird, but still weird."

"Yeah, it is. I miss Poppy. I know he would be proud...of all of us. Sarah, thank you for everything. Especially for reminding me how important it is to have faith. You know, and when to step up to the plate..."

"And that is a **wrap**!" Alicia said from behind the camera.

"I didn't know you taped that."

"I know! It was a perfect candid!"

"So, we're done?" Dex asked.

"Yup!"

"Hey everyone!" Ezra shouted, coming through the door with a crew delivering champagne.

Marla, Vince, and Jazz came in following the noise.

"Champagne?" Geema said, coming back into the dining room. "I didn't order any more champagne."

"I did," Ezra admitted. "I just got a call from DreamWorks. Dex, how would you like to star in a movie?"

THE END

Get free *Dexipes* from Dex's kitchen and learn more about Persnickety Press books at

www.persnickety-press.com